THE HEAVY BEAR

Other Titles by Tim Bowling

THE HEAVY BEAR

Tim Bowling

This is a work of fiction. All characters, organizations, places and events portrayed are either products of the author's imagination or are used fictitiously.

Buckrider Books is an imprint of Wolsak and Wynn Publishers.

Cover image: Photo by REPORTERS ASSOCIES/Gamma-Rapho/Getty Images
Cover and interior design: Peter Cocking
Typesetter: Mary Bowness
Author photograph: Jacqueline Baker
Typeset in Lyon Text
Printed by Ball Media, Brantford, Canada

The publisher gratefully acknowledges the support of the Canada Council for the Arts, the Ontario Arts Council and the Canada Book Fund.

Buckrider Books
280 James Street North
Hamilton, ON
Canada L8R 2L3

Library and Archives Canada Cataloguing in Publication

Bowling, Tim, 1964-, author
    The heavy bear / Tim Bowling.

ISBN 978-1-928088-32-5 (softcover)

    I. Title.

PS8553.O9044H43 2017   C813'.54   C2017-900984-2

6 5 4 3 2 1   22 21 20 19 18 17

Who would be a father?

– D. H. LAWRENCE, *Sea and Sardinia*

———————

— Prologue —

I SENSED SOMEONE standing beside my bed and flung the sheets back. But no menacing figure, knife in hand, loomed over me. At first I saw only the empty darkness. Then the walls and the dresser emerged from the murk, and I was peering through an undersea camera at the ruins of the *Titanic*, the forgotten contours of some vaguely familiar life. I sat bolt upright. The bottom half of a body still hung in the window, as if frozen in ice. I tried to cry out, but the silence, much heavier than any I'd ever known, drowned the words in my throat.

The body slid out into the greater darkness. A low growl accompanied the departure, immediately followed by a powerful, mysterious odour – rank, wild. The kind of smell I hadn't experienced since my youth on the Fraser River over a Christ's lifetime ago.

A hatful of moonlight splashed on the hardwood floor, the wild smell faded and I was just a middle-aged father and husband again. I pushed the little button to illuminate my watch-face. One o'clock. Someone – or something – had been in my bedroom in the middle of the night. Why? To steal? I dismissed the idea at once. I didn't know why, but the intrusion felt more personal than any random act of thievery.

Careful not to disturb my wife, I quickly rose, dressed and, with my pulse still pounding, followed the figure through the open ground-floor window.

All around me the air flowed like fragranced bathwater. The scent of the neighbour's freshly cut grass filled my nostrils, while the cathedral beams of our block's towering Dutch elms overwhelmed my eyes. Parked cars formed a resting train below the leafy branches and one porch light along the avenue held a vortex of bugs against the night. Even inner-city neighbourhoods at this hour sometimes possess a deep rural calm. If a pampered house cat had been on the loose, I could have heard its tympanic paw-fall over the flower beds.

Instead, I heard only my own breathing as I hurried across the lawn to the cracked sidewalk. Of course, I expected to see no one – even intruders who linger strangely in open windows don't hang around to be caught and interrogated. So, the sight of a slight man in baggy trousers, a shirt of moonlight and an old-fashioned hat standing half a block away caught me unawares, to say the least. He seemed oddly familiar, though probably only because he stood no more than five foot five – my late father's height. Again, for some curious reason, my voice failed, as if I no longer had one. Instead, I waved my arms in what I intended to be a threatening manner, but the figure, whose face I could not make out, appeared to be waiting for me. As I came within fifty yards, however, the little man vanished. At that point, I took a deep breath and began to orient myself, to be the rational adult of the ultra-rational twenty-first century.

Dreams. Fancies. The phantoms and illusions brought on by stress. The truth was, I had slept fitfully for several weeks, as I generally did in advance of the university year when, as an itinerant lecturer in English, I steeled myself to meet a hundred young people and steer them, often against their will, down the corridors of syntax and through the abundant meadows of metaphor. It was pleasant enough work, but a shy middle-aged man with some talent for language is still a shy middle-aged man, and meeting humans for the shy is the same as it is for a spider or a coyote: a matter of no inconsiderable anxiety. But why cavil? I was a nervous, over-sensitive man who had reached an age of reckoning: I had more time behind me now than ahead, and the future looked increasingly untender, for my own three children and everyone else's. At almost fifty, I had become both disillusioned and anxious. So it was hardly surprising, then, that I should conjure up phantoms from the tangle of my nerve endings.

Yet, when I reached the end of the block, I already knew that the little man wasn't gone for good. And when the low growl sounded at my back, and the wild odour – a concoction of woodsmoke and salmon spawn – filled my nostrils as I turned, I understood that my world had shifted, and whether I still inhabited what the media considered reality didn't much matter.

Approaching the central north–south corridor of 99th Street – which was about as busy as a supermarket aisle after closing – I looked up and saw, forty yards away, my mysterious quarry. Except now he wasn't on the ground. He tiptoed, with astonishing agility, along a telephone wire, his absurdly large shoes flapping silently. He didn't even hold his arms out for balance. His shirt front blazed whitely against the faded confetti of stars. Oddly enough, there was no moon and no moonlight.

So, what had splashed into my bedroom?

With each step that I took, the little man took three; and as I increased my pace, he increased his. Soon we were both sprinting, my feet hardly more secure on the ground than his on the wire. How was it that he didn't fall? How was it that his tiny crushed hat didn't fly off? The houses of my neighbours slid away like trains on parallel tracks leaving the same station. By the time I stood, panting, under the 99th Street telephone wire, the little man had vanished again.

I looked to the south and back to the north. No one. And not even one moving car. I watched the intersection lights on Whyte Avenue change from red to green to yellow and back to red again. Then I watched the whole process once more. Strange – the signals blinking on and off without anyone to heed them. Like a movie running in an empty theatre without even the projectionist in the booth.

That was exactly how the knowledge struck me – not all at once, but in the meticulously timed cuts of the traffic lights. Was it strange that an image solved the mystery? Perhaps. But I had been a working poet for much longer than I'd been a father or a teacher, and the confluence of imagination, truth and mystery had never been an alien force in my life.

"Working? Fat chance, chum," grumbled a voice from right behind me.

I whirled around to find the same visual emptiness, but the wild odour took me under the armpits and almost lifted me off the ground. It wasn't an offensive smell exactly, but powerful as a river at freshet. Chum? I didn't speak like that, not even in my dream world. What was next, 23 skidoo?

When I turned back to the intersection lights, the red blazing like the torched eye of Polyphemus, I wanted desperately for the little man in baggy trousers to reappear. Because by now I knew exactly who he was, and I also knew I was as sane as any man in the twenty-first century can expect to be, dragging the bloodied pelt of the twentieth century behind him. The game's afoot, I would have said to Watson as I filled my meerschaum pipe, if I'd had a Watson to confide in.

But I had no companion in the summer dark except for the ghost of a long-dead funny man and a disembodied growl and a wild smell I recognized but couldn't name.

I turned and slowly retraced my steps, my body continually in the moving spotlight of the moon. But the strange thing was, the night remained moonless, and whenever I stopped and looked around for the little man, I saw only the shadows of trees and houses, and heard only a ghostly tinkle of breeze along the trembling tightrope where he had balanced so beautifully, up there with all the other lost voices.

1

BUSTER KEATON first entered my life in October 1964, when I was nine months old – nine months out after the nine months in. He arrived by train in the town of White Rock, BC, a few miles inland from the fishing town of Ladner, where I lay, all my senses on fire, my capacity for memory unknown. That autumn, Keaton was sixty-nine years removed from his mother's womb and a half-century removed from the vaudeville stage. After several decades of neglect, he was finally enjoying a small resurgence of fame. An international superstar in the 1920s, who directed and starred in a series of silent comedic feature films that made him both famous and wealthy, he was derailed by the advent of sound and its accompanying studio system in the 1930s and became a lost, forgotten, often-intoxicated figure throughout the 1940s and early '50s. The new medium of television saved him, gave him hope and work and kept him in the corner of the public eye until the public could be reminded of the genius of his early manhood.

After his fall from the heights of fame, Keaton took any job offered, no matter how trivial or cheap, and at one time proudly boasted that he worked more than Doris Day. But the work was mostly dreck over which he had no artistic control or input. Keaton fans – and there are thousands all over the globe – who like to debunk the idea that their hero's life was tragic simply do not understand what it means for an artist to lose the opportunity to employ his gifts. The same world of commerce that deprived readers of whatever greatness Herman Melville might have achieved after *Moby Dick* if he'd been encouraged is the same world that deprived filmgoers of the brilliance Keaton and Orson Welles might have achieved had their genius been celebrated and financed instead of quashed. But, as the poet Adrienne Rich writes, "no one tells the truth about truth." We all prefer legend and myth and illusion. We all prefer the movies. And why not? After all, we see what we know – which is what we remember – in silent, visual terms. If we recall a scream, it's the open mouth and the terror in the eyes, not the anonymous shrill cry, that comes to us. That Russian woman's horror at the runaway baby carriage in Sergei Eisenstein's *Battleship Potemkin* is all the more haunting because we can't hear it.

Back at home, I couldn't return to sleep, nor could I stop thinking about the little man on the telephone wire. Obviously, I couldn't go back nearly fifty years and see the real Buster Keaton on the railroad tracks at White Rock, at least not directly. But I could certainly see the screen image of the aged comedian there any time I wanted, because it appears in *The Railrodder*, a 1965 production of the National Film Board of Canada, and the reason why Keaton was in British Columbia at all. The film is memorable for two reasons: it is silent and therefore affords The Great Stone Face, as he was known due to his stoic onscreen expression, a final opportunity to resurrect the gags and gestures of his youth; and it captures the country I can no longer access with any of my senses, the country that is not a physical space but a vision and a time. How do we remember a feeling? How do we remember what the past felt like?

After making a press of dark roast, I slipped in the DVD and watched *The Railrodder*. Then I watched *Buster Keaton Rides Again*, the documentary shot simultaneously with the filming of *The Railrodder*, which is even more haunting in its depiction of a dying legend and a vanishing nation. And I stepped straight out of linear time – just like Keaton as the projectionist in his classic 1924 film *Sherlock Jr.*, who leaves his own body and enters the story he is showing on the screen – and arrived in the past where the light animates the dead and every shadow is a snarl of tape on the cutting-room floor.

THE SECOND time Buster Keaton entered my life, he was young, athletic, wildly creative and daring. He was also dead. This paradox – between the screen actor and the living man – haunted Keaton from a very young age. Born in 1895 in Piqua, Kansas, to theatrical parents always on the road, he first appeared on the vaudeville stage at the age of three, became a celebrity within a few years, and knew illusion and fantasy and applause as normal, and the world of school and boredom and institutionalized authority as abnormal. The stage *was* life. Everything else simply got in the way. No wonder, then, that the great illusionist Harry Houdini was responsible for giving Joseph Francis Keaton, aged six months, the name the world would always know him by. Houdini, working at the time with the Keaton family in a travelling medicine show, saw the infant Keaton fall down a flight of stairs in a boarding house. Rushing up, he cried out, "What a buster that kid just took!" According to legend, Keaton *père* – a long, lean Irishman of dubious talent also named Joseph and noted mostly for his violent high kick skills – responded, "Buster. That's what we'll call him then."

It's a cute story, and very likely only a promotional gimmick dreamed up long after the fact (once Houdini was famous and worth capitalizing on), but it nonetheless makes a critical point: the world of make-believe claimed Buster Keaton for its own almost from the start, and he would both star and suffer under that claim, like a mortal favoured by the gods of Olympus (or, in his case, the movie moguls of Hollywood).

But to return to paradox: the flesh-and-blood Keaton died on February 1, 1966, in Woodland Hills, California, not quite a year and a half after his visit to White Rock to finish filming *The Railrodder*. In the summer of 1969, in the sleepy fishing village of Ladner, one town over from White Rock, I saw several of the two-reel short comedies that Buster Keaton made in the early 1920s projected onto the mossy wooden side of a neighbour's house.

Imagine it. A sloped lawn, twilight dissolving to darkness, the scents of fresh-cut grass and brine and salmon mingled on the warm air, and a dozen wide-eyed children whispering excitedly as a genial middle-aged neighbour in horn-rimmed glasses arranges a giant praying mantis of a projector on the cracked sidewalk and sets it whirring. And there, at the far end of the shimmering, dusty swathe of light, running away from the police, in lifelong permanent retreat from the world inimical to joy and freedom, is a uniquely handsome, unsmiling, white-faced figure of madcap fun and something else, something a child of five would not understand but might very well intuit, a strange, intensely modern kind of angst, a furious helplessness of the kind that an insect exhibits in the hands of that unfeeling five-year-old. This figure, funny as he is while swinging over rooftops and diving through windows to escape his pursuers, is not funny in the same way as the Little Tramp of Chaplin, who also animated the side of our neighbour's house that summer, not adorable like Shirley Temple and not downright buffoonish as his co-star Fatty Arbuckle (who was nonetheless, like Keaton, a toy of cruel fate). There is something thoroughly original about this daredevil mime in the porkpie hat and slap shoes, and yet my child self recognizes him immediately as a kindred spirit. The world happens to him, and much merriment ensues, but he himself doesn't laugh; he doesn't even smile. Deep down in every child is an absolute sympathy for Buster Keaton's deadpan face, perhaps, again, because children intuit the real reason for it: that in the world as grown-ups construct it and know it, we are all outcasts.

The story of Keaton's stoic expression goes like this: on those early twentieth-century vaudeville stages, when vaudeville – that bustling mélange of live acts, everything from Shakespearean thespians to dog trainers to opera singers to ventriloquists – was the king of American entertainment, the child Keaton soon learned that audiences found him much more hilarious when he showed no emotion upon receiving his father's physical abuse. For The Three Keatons, as the family act became known, had quickly won a reputation as vaudeville's most riotous, rough-and-tumble turn. In brief, the gist of the show was mischievous son, aggravated father, innocent bystander mother. In even briefer brief, it was ad lib mayhem. Keaton's most thorough biographer, Rudi Blesh, describes a typical performance as "David and Goliath in the nursery," a violent farce that ended with little Buster literally being flung across the stage and into the wings.

Keaton himself in the late 1950s recalled one of the worst results of this type of planned but unpredictable violence. After one matinee, his father misjudged the distance when he kicked, and caught Buster in the head, knocking him unconscious, a state in which the boy remained for eighteen hours until the tireless doctors finally revived him.

On another occasion, Buster's father actually picked him up and hurled him at a heckler in the front row, breaking three of the man's ribs. Buster's slap shoes struck the man in the neighbouring seat, and broke two of his front teeth. As was normally the case, Buster went uninjured, mostly because he had trained himself on the right way to break a fall.

Meanwhile, in the midst of all this father-son roughhousing, which did indeed attract the unwanted attention of child welfare societies from time to time (because of his unbelievable comic talent, Buster was sometimes believed to be a midget, which helped legally and morally), the young Keaton learned the value of withholding his own expressions of mirth. He noticed that whenever he smiled or showed the audience any pleasure, they didn't laugh as much. So, on purpose, he started looking haunted and bewildered. Over time, he realized that other comedians could derive an advantage from laughing at their own gags, but that he simply couldn't. The public hated it when he tried. That was just fine with Keaton. He always claimed to be happiest when the folks watching him said to each other, "Look at the poor dope, wilya?"

The jury remains out – a long way out, in fact – on the relationship between Keaton's impassive mask and the abuse he endured at the hands (and feet) of his often-drunk father. How much of Keaton's legendary deadpan, for example, was the result of pure comic instinct and how much the result of his father's fierce onstage instructions? If you are six years old and being pummelled for laughs, and your towering father in a bald Irish wig and sidewhiskers hisses at you, "Face! Face!" in order to keep you from showing any emotion, how does this experience, repeated night after night until it's no longer necessary, affect your relationship to your own genuine emotions? Keaton himself always sidestepped the question. His parents loved him, he loved the stage: case closed. He would respond the same way when Joseph Schenk, his producer and friend who basically sold him out to MGM in the 1930s and effectively ruined Buster's creative life, was criticized for having been disloyal. Buster would have none of it, even though, as an intelligent man, he knew he'd been cheated and misused by Schenk. It was simply too painful to accept the truth. Face! Face!

Even by 1950, when Buster made a cameo appearance in Billy Wilder's *Sunset Boulevard* as one of the "waxworks," the deluded Norma Desmond's forgotten bridge players, he didn't openly blame anyone for what had happened to his career. Face! Face! But he drank, so heavily that at one time he wound up straitjacketed in an institution. What his features showed then are not part of the legend. The experiences Keaton lived between his father's hissing of "Face! Face!" and the two words he speaks in *Sunset Boulevard* – "Pass," and then, softly, as in final and permanent defeat, "Pass" – are the truth that contributed to the particular nature of his genius.

In short, Keaton's vision was darkly comic, almost entirely without popular sentiment of the kind found in Chaplin's work. And the darkness, without question, was allied to the deadpan.

Of course, I knew none of this in the summer of 1969 on the neighbour's lawn sloped like whaleback under the buttery stars as I watched, spellbound, the quick, lithe figure walk, then walk faster, then sprint and leap from one calamity to another. All I understood then was the hilarity, but some part of me must have registered the melancholy and tragic vision. Why else should Buster Keaton haunt me nearly a half-century later? Middle age, the death of loved ones, the challenge to stay positive in a world awash in cynicism, materialism and grotesque sentimentality. Who whispers "Face" to us, and what face should we reveal before we look glumly into our hand and mutter, "Pass"?

3

As the early September darkness continued to melt like chocolate around the house, and the world of mortgages and bills and social noise required me once again to enter a classroom and stand at the head of it, I put on my Buster Keaton deadpan mask in order to hide my mounting anxiety, in order to keep the cornered animal from snarling and lashing out. Meanwhile, the encounter with the little comedian kept returning me to my own beginnings, as if some ur-projectionist had reversed the reel.

I spent my entire childhood in the same small bungalow, literally a stone's throw from the banks of a great river, the wild, 850-mile-long Fraser. My immediate family – parents, two much older brothers and a slightly older sister – made a subsistence income in the salmon fishing industry. It was not as unusual a profession as vaudeville, perhaps, but it was unusual enough and afforded a certain amount of freedom from the nine-to-five rat race, which, in the 1960s and early 1970s on the west coast, didn't seem like much of a race. Our town was gull-haunted, sleepy, steeping under the lunar changes and the persistent rains like an ever-darkening tea bag. The neighbourhood I grew up in was the most haunted, condensed part of that intensifying darkness. Within a few blocks of my house, in every direction, lay ruins of some kind: stove-in fishboats and moss-sagged net sheds along the river; a whole row of empty, condemned shops on the little main street; at least five crumbling two-storey houses from the Georgian past, abandoned after being bought up by real estate companies waiting patiently for an upturn in the economy that never seemed to approach; and, believe it or not, a mile in the opposite direction, an entire vegetable canning factory filled with silent, greasy machines just waiting for a ghostly hand from Hollywood's silver age to set them in motion again.

My entire childhood world was a Buster Keaton film set, circa 1924. When I look back on it, and imagine the sunlight and the flowering abandoned orchards that had been planted by the pioneers who had built the abandoned houses – all those plum and pear, cherry and apple trees thriving in forgetfulness along with the untended blue-joint grass and the great coal-smoke blackberry bushes – everything quickly becomes black and white and intensely silent. When I see myself, either in memory or in the photographs so rarely taken at the time because to develop them cost money that our family couldn't spare, I was a serious child, even in play – especially in play. As Keaton himself routinely remarked about his legendary deadpan, "I was concentrating so hard that I wasn't even aware that I wasn't smiling." Between our town's one flaking totem pole with the rain-gnawed raven, bear and raccoon, and the grey, pyramidal, granite World War I cenotaph with, ironically enough, the names of two Aboriginal soldiers engraved on the sides, I lived the five years of my greatest innocence and watched the ten years of Buster Keaton's most inspired genius.

That the man himself, in the fall of 1964, so close to his own material death, should approach within a few miles of that perfect film set and of the infant who would perform on it seemed at once eerie and joyous. It was as if he had arrived to direct successive generations in the art of the tragic vision, and his most inspired directorial touch was to withdraw.

Fighting sleep, drinking coffee, I saw him there again, outside of the image on the screen – I saw the real man. No, I see him. He's both young and handsome and old and drink-ravaged, and he's looking through the complicated camera of every blue heron set up in the marsh, standing on the rusted rails of the tracks that still ran through town to the riverbank but no longer carried any trains, hovering in his huge mime's face over the slack tide and those sleepers in the houses who, as children, would have watched his films when they first appeared, back before Hollywood had the bureaucratic bit firmly in its glittering mouth. I was not a religious man. I believed in a human fate in human hands – and yet the image of Buster Keaton on the edge of my childhood came close to a vision of God. It was right that this should be so, for what is a vision of God if it isn't an acknowledgement of life's gravity and an intense avowal to keep the faith? Every day in North America life is sold to us as a trivial, passing entertainment, and death as a horror whose spiritual and emotional meanings are to be avoided at all cost.

I would not buy the trivia and I could not turn my eyes from the horror. Keaton was making cold laughter out on the tracks and in the marshes, in the attic rooms of abandoned houses. He was the god of the black and white, of silence, and he was approaching even as he withdrew – like a more famous god of the human imagination, he was visible nowhere but present everywhere. No, but wait – he is visible. There he is, on the side of Mr. Atkey's house in the summer of 1969. He is a spoiled rich boy somehow alone with a spoiled rich girl on an ocean liner somehow floating out to sea at night. And that ocean liner floats straight off the side of the house and onto the Fraser River, and drifts past the silt islands in the mouth where the lumber baron, H. R. MacMillan, once entertained Keaton's even more celebrated peers, Mary Pickford and Douglas Fairbanks, for pheasant-shooting parties.

There could no longer be any disbelief: Keaton was the god of time and art, and he was as cruel and merciful as the most credible of gods. I placed my bare neck on the altar. While I did not smile, my whole body prepared to laugh.

4

I DECIDED THAT a Buster Keaton film marathon might help alleviate my gloomy condition. Perhaps existential comedy could trump existential angst. Perhaps Keaton's ghost had appeared precisely to lead me back to his great work. It was worth a try. I decided to start with the shorts and proceed to the classic features of the mid-1920s. But I wouldn't keep going to the talkies. As James Agee so beautifully expressed it, Keaton's "dark, dead voice, though it was in keeping with the visual character, tore his intensely silent style to bits and destroyed the illusion within which he worked."

Ideally, this marathon filmfest would take place on a grassy slope under the stars. There'd be a faint scent of salmon and river mud and wet springer spaniel on the air, and my father would still be alive. But I had long ago put away childish things, including desperate attempts to reclaim a vanished world. Even so, I was a man, like Keaton in the early 1930s, seeking escape – from Time's winged chariot, from the inevitability of grief, from the nagging sense that everything turns to ash and dust in the end and that no amount of human creativity can divert that cold and hard trajectory. Suddenly, one dark night of the soul as I approached my fiftieth year, the world turned dangerously cold, and I could not melt the ice from my eyelids. But I was not Buster Keaton. Drinking binges leading to an ill-advised marriage to a mentally unstable nurse were not the answer for me. (They weren't for Keaton either, as he would find out.)

Keaton's art, however, could be an answer. Looking back, it was astonishing that I'd ever seen any of Keaton's films as a boy. They weren't shown in regular theatres, they weren't often shown on TV and there was no YouTube. I must be one of the few adults of my generation, in fact, who had the revolutionary experience of seeing the young Buster Keaton in action while I was still a child myself. And just how did this happen?

It was as simple as it was unlikely. Our neighbour in 1969, Ken Atkey, worked as a Paramount film rep in Vancouver and somehow he had access to rare copies of silent movies. (Over ninety percent of the silent movies ever made have vanished, due to the deterioration of the nitrate stock with which they were made.) Mr. Atkey was the sort of man who, like Keaton, loved toy trains. Indeed, he had constructed a complicated papier mâché layout complete with mountains and tunnels and tiny figures of people and animals that took up the entire top floor of his house. Perhaps some sort of gadget involving trains woke him up every morning, as in *Pee-wee's Big Adventure*, the 1985 film starring Paul Reubens (a kind of Keaton throwback, who American society threw back after police caught him masturbating in an adult theatre). I didn't know. But I did know that Buster Keaton as a middle-aged man so loved toy trains that he set up a system in his Hollywood home whereby a train delivered drinks to his guests. Oh, yes, and the single most expensive shot in the entire history of silent film production occurred in Keaton's *The General*, and involved the blowing up of a real engine as it crossed a trestle bridge. As critics point out, only a few of Keaton's films do not have trains or water.

I was fond enough of trains, but not so fond that a toy set would help me forget my teaching anxiety, the increasing worldwide gap between the rich and poor, or the mysterious haunting of the September night. Perhaps watching Keaton's entire silent oeuvre, including the late silent promotional film he made in Canada the year I was born, would help. It certainly couldn't hurt. At least I didn't think so.

I made my vague plans more concrete: since I did not wish to have a toy train or a robot wake me up each morning à la Pee-wee Herman, I would, every night before going to bed, watch a Keaton film. And I would keep a record of the experience, tracing how the intersection of Keaton's life and my own might tell something true about a thinking, feeling human's plight at the beginning of the twenty-first century.

But teaching started later that morning; "the toad, work," as Philip Larkin called it, squatted on my life.

Ah, but don't give up on me, Buster, I cried. I won't let you down. "This was no playhouse," Robert Frost writes, "but a house in earnest." Life *is* funny, but there's a reason we don't smile about it. As Shakespeare points out, "there is nothing / either good or bad, but thinking makes it so."

I vowed that I was not going to think about income-earning middle age, or the cynical, false, life-denying, pornographic, materialist world. I was going to watch *The Navigator* again, and retreat.

5

THREE O'CLOCK. If anything, the world had gone even deeper into its womb. My coffee was cold, and I lacked the energy to get up off the couch and put the kettle on again. Every five minutes, despite my conviction that I would honour the little comedian's appearance by *not* working that day, my heart clenched like a jellyfish poked with a stick. Responsibility. To slough it off was to slough off the very fibre of my being. I couldn't face – "Face! Face!" – my own wild hunger. After all, those young strangers out there in the city night rightly expected a basic level of mid-life maturity from me. The low growl I kept hearing must have simply been the appetite of my childhood self that I had lost the ability to satisfy.

A clatter of trash cans suddenly broke through my self-absorption. I tensed, hoping that whoever was out in the back alley would stumble on to the next household. Even as I hoped – the way Scrooge in *A Christmas Carol* hopes that the spirits will just leave him alone – I realized that I needed to investigate.

The moment I opened the door and stepped outside, the neighbour's security light turned the backyard into a World War II airfield. Shielding my eyes, I shuffled towards the alley and right into a cloud of wilderness stench. If I'd been wearing two spawned-out salmon for slippers, the smell could not have been more potent. Gagging, I continued to the edge of the alley, just in time to catch a large shape – most likely a coyote – rising from the garbage cans and turning in my direction.

It wasn't a coyote. I shook my head and looked again. I could have sworn that . . . no, those animals didn't prowl around the centre of Edmonton. Just then, the shape snarled, dropped a garbage can it had somehow hugged to its coat and lumbered away. On two legs, though what kind of animal besides a man . . . Cautiously, I approached the spilled garbage, only to find that both cans were in their proper place with their lids on. The rotted autumn stench had also evaporated.

Unconvincingly putting the incident down to a lack of sleep, I returned to the house and, with mounting desperation, popped another Keaton disc into the machine. Seconds turned into minutes, and the old magic of cinema soon cast its spell again.

As always, Keaton's persona delighted me, even when the particular work didn't quite satisfy. I watched two films: *Our Hospitality* and *Sherlock Jr.* My reaction to each film could not have been more different.

Our Hospitality, which is often cited as one of Keaton's finest efforts, involves a tired (even in 1923) Hatfield and McCoy storyline. Buster plays a young man raised in New York who inherits a Southern estate (which turns out to be a hillbilly shack). He also inherits a long-standing feud and, when in the South, winds up being shot at and chased around by his blood enemies, who turn out to be the father and brothers of the love interest he'd made the acquaintance of on the journey down. The film's not exactly boring, but it's slow. The first twenty minutes involves some silly melodrama about the history of the feud, followed by one long, not very amusing joke that makes fun of how slow and rudimentary early train travel was (the film is set in the early part of the nineteenth century). For example, Buster's dog runs along under the train all the way from New York to the South and then greets him as he disembarks. The middle portion of the film is funnier. Buster finds himself in the mansion of his enemies, who can't kill him indoors because their code of hospitality forbids it, so he conspires not to leave. As his hosts see him to the door, Buster sneaks an opportunity to toss his famous porkpie hat under a chair. Then he claims that he can't find his hat and a search ensues. Alas, his faithful dog keeps retrieving the hat for him, and he keeps surreptitiously tossing it away. Eventually his hosts see him with the hat in his hands and the jig is up. In the end, Buster escapes from the mansion dressed as a woman (as popular a gambit in the silent film comedies as it would be for the Monty Python troupe in the 1970s), and *Our Hospitality* concludes with a justly famous action sequence involving Buster and his love interest (his real-life wife, Natalie Talmadge, whose two glamorous sisters were huge silent film stars) in peril on a rapidly running river.

In later years, Keaton would always happily discuss the physical risks he took in making his films. He was justifiably proud of the fact that he performed all his own stunts, which explains why there are so many long, continuous takes in his work; he wanted the audience to know he wasn't using cheap camera tricks to avoid putting his body at risk. That's really him in the river, hurtling at high speed towards the rapids, grabbing an overhanging branch that breaks. That's really him going under.

And yet, while the river scene in *Our Hospitality* is admirable from an athletic point of view, the film is dull. Never mind that in its first week at the Capitol Theatre, a big Broadway presentation house, it equalled the box office record for the chain and nearly tied the record in hundreds of other theatres. Popularity then, as now, is no true indicator of quality. Keaton himself was disgusted that a dud MGM film he appeared in called *Parlor, Bedroom and Bath* greatly outgrossed a marvellous film like *Sherlock Jr.*

What redeems *Our Hospitality* is what redeems every single one of Keaton's films, and especially the weaker ones: the man himself. I have exactly the same reaction to Woody Allen's comedies. When he's on the screen, I'm engaged, delightfully tense with comic anticipation; when he's not on the screen, I lose interest. It's that way with Keaton, too. There's so much life and energy in his persona, so much barely repressed vitality, so much obvious acting confidence and athletic grace. The only way I can sit through a film like *Our Hospitality* is by concentrating on Keaton.

That is exactly why *Sherlock Jr.* is as wonderful, fresh and engaging as the earlier feature is dull, stale and tired. In the entire forty-five minutes running time (*Our Hospitality* is a painful thirty minutes longer), Buster is rarely off the screen. He *is* the film. And what a lively, inventive, clever and entertaining film it is. How much fun Keaton must have had making it; you can feel the joy of creation just flowing off those black-and-white faces. Buster plays a lowly projectionist in a theatre who dreams of being a famous detective. Falsely accused of stealing a watch from his love interest's father (played by Keaton's real-life father, who looks exactly like the abusive drunken roughneck he was), Buster sadly returns to work, starts the projector whirring and promptly falls asleep. What happens next is cinematic history, pure genius, the reason why

Keaton is held in such high esteem fifty years after his death, eighty years after his greatest period of fame.

A ghostly dream-Keaton steps out of the body of the sleeping projectionist and stares at the screen of the running film. The film characters suddenly become the characters of the real-life story: there's the love interest, there's the lounge lizard who framed Buster and who wants to get his girl. Alarmed, the dream-Keaton tries to wake his sleeping self, but to no avail. Desperate, and with no other choice, the dream-Keaton rushes down the aisle of the theatre and launches himself into the action on the screen. The villain immediately boots him back into the theatre. We see all this from the viewpoint of the projection booth, over the heads of the audience. Uncowed, the dream-Keaton clambers back into the movie. Now the real fun begins, the director Keaton's giddy expression of his love for his medium. On the screen within the screen, the editing process rapidly transfers Buster from one perilous moment to another. As he approaches a door, the image cuts and he's in a garden. He decides to sit on a garden chair, but the image cuts to a busy street and he sits down backwards, somersaulting into speeding traffic. He starts to walk along the street and suddenly finds himself teetering on the edge of a cliff. Looking down, he stares into a lion's mouth. In rapid succession, he's almost hit by a train, then winds up sitting again, but the shot cuts to an island. He dives off into the sea but lands headfirst in a snowdrift, legs kicking helplessly in the air. Eventually he finds himself back in the garden. All of this happens with the breathless, unpredictable leaping of metaphor, which explains why James Agee described Keaton as a poet. And from this point on, the pace of *Sherlock Jr.* is relentless and the narrative gripping.

The screen within the screen disappears, and now the movie version of the dream-Keaton's experience is all we see.

All we see is a dizzying succession of chase-and-escape gags, with Buster as the famous detective, Sherlock Jr., outwitting the villains. Among the many remarkable stunts – including the wild ride on the handlebars of a motorcycle without a driver – is the legendary waterspout incident. Buster – hot on the trail of the lounge lizard (also known as the tea hound or the sheik) – is trapped in a railroad refrigerator car by the villain. He escapes by emerging through a trap door on top of the train, then proceeds to walk across the cars from right to left as the train begins to move, the camera panning expertly to keep him in the centre of the shot. Remember – the real man, Buster Keaton, is actually doing this, as a kind of stunt double for his dream double. Finally, he leaps off the last car, grabs the chain of an overhead waterspout and, his weight bringing down the chute, gets doused by a tremendous torrent of water, so powerful that he crashes hard to the track. The entire sequence is continuous and unfaked.

Perhaps its beginning is an even more delightful, if less dramatic, display of athleticism. When Buster trails the villain, he *really* trails the villain – right on his heels, mimicking every move, right down to tossing a cigarette butt over his shoulder after he'd puffed on it (he had caught the one just tossed by the villain). All his years of vaudeville training came to the fore here – no athlete in the history of sport has ever required more timing and revelled in the requirement. No comedian ever understood the gag power of repetition and duplication better than Keaton. What makes the trailing so funny, in fact, is the situation, which relies heavily on characterization. Already, as a viewer, our sympathies are with the boy-projectionist; he's the wronged one, the underdog, and he's vulnerable and awkward and trying so hard to be otherwise that we recognize him immediately as our double, the doppelgänger of the human condition. That isn't funny, though; it's too serious. As biographer Rudi

Blesh accurately exclaims, "Keaton did not do the serious picture because he is too serious and because he is an artist." What is funny about the duplication/replication is that the villainous lounge lizard is tall and debonair with a graceful waxed moustache, while the would-be detective is short, decidedly unsophisticated and sports a fake moustache – not the double, but the opposite. And, of course, the gag of the amateur detective trailing job is so common and overused now (every sitcom on TV has used it, ad infinitum) that to see one from 1924 that remains so witty and fresh is a revelation. What is revealed is Keaton's incredible physical ability, borne out of his long, do-it-yourself vaudeville training. That waterspout scene? The idea was that, using the rope to swing to the ground, he'd open the spout. Well, the volume of water shooting out was much greater than anticipated and struck Keaton with such force that he lost his grip on the rope and fell backwards onto the track, his neck snapping down on the steel rails. As Keaton ruefully explained decades later, "Conditioning is the one thing, I suppose, that can enable a man to walk around unaware that he has a broken neck."

Neck, schmeck. Keaton was long accustomed to such mishaps; in fact, they've become, or rather they already were at the height of his fame, the stuff of legend. How about the unbelievable day in July 1898 when he was not quite three years old? A sweltering Kansas afternoon, and Buster's parents, busy on stage, had left him in the care of the landlady of the boarding house. In quick succession, though not quite as quick as the editing work in *Sherlock Jr.*, the toddler Buster jammed his fingers into a clothes wringer, hit himself in the head with a rock and, most dramatically of all, was swept out of the boarding house's second-floor window by a cyclone. After the same doctor had amputated half of little Buster's jammed finger and stitched the gash in his temple, the legend really takes off. The cyclone-enveloped Buster is whirled high over the trees and houses and set down unharmed in the middle of the street four blocks away, where his relieved parents find him. Apparently, this too-astonishing trinity of mishaps settled the matter. No more babysitting landladies; from that day on, little Buster was a part of the act.

Twenty-three years later, the risk-taking and the accidents took centre stage again, leading to the short film *The Playhouse*, which leads to *Sherlock Jr.* Keaton was making *The Electric House*, which involved mechanizing the set to suit the title and setting up numerous gags. At one point, Buster caught one of his floppy slap shoes in the escalator, which had unpredictably sped up, and his foot jammed at the top. Snaaap! His ankle broke, the slap shoe tore off and he fell ten feet to the studio floor. To summarize, Keaton had to wear a cast for the next seven weeks. So *The Electric House* was shelved as he convalesced. Bored and restless, unable to work, he decided to take the train to New York and get married (more on that ill-advised decision later). Finally, with the cast just off, Keaton was ready to make movies again, but, with his recovering ankle, he simply couldn't do the usual falls and chases. What he came up with as a substitute is typical of his genius. "We don't need falls and chases," he told his crew. "I'll be the entire cast." He then detailed his vision of a picture in which only Buster Keaton appears, in hilarious multiples. "The whole picture is a visual gag. I hardly have to do anything."

I hadn't come to *The Playhouse* in my movie marathon yet. I was still under the spell of *Sherlock Jr.* In fact, I had enjoyed it so much that, despite the late hour and my own fatigue, despite the fact that I knew I would eventually go off and rejoin the responsible world, I decided to watch the film again.

I made it to the waterspout scene and began to fade. My head dropped, then snapped back. I saw the rapid black-and-white images as if they were part of a dream: a man was running along the top of a moving train; he was bouncing along on the handlebars of a speeding motorcycle; he was crashing through the window of a shack and colliding with another man. I left my own body on the sofa, and blinked down at it in curiosity. Who was this almost fifty-year-old person asleep with a DVD remote spilled from his hand? Why wouldn't he wake up when I reached out and shook him?

I could see that it was no use. I had broken from the cocoon and would be, for as long as the illusion lasted, the man I was born to be – not a detective, not an acrobat or an actor or a teacher, but a human worker with exposed nerves borne back ceaselessly into the past.

I WOKE WITH a crick in my neck and a mouth as dry as laundry lint. The TV screen was frozen to the menu of a DVD. The tinkling piano so often associated with silent film played the same refrain over and over until I had no choice but to flap my hand around, grasp the remote and hit mute. Then I sat in the silence and let the world creep across my consciousness, the way sound and booze had crept across Keaton's in the 1930s, the way the cop's flashlight beam had crept across Paul Reubens in the adult theatre. Outside it was still the late summer of 2012 – noise, speed, the adulation of money and power. Outside, linked together like boxcars and stretched from coast to coast, were endless classrooms of bored teenagers holding gadgets of ineffective distraction in their hands. Outside, Keaton and my father were dead.

With mounting panic, I checked my watch. Five-thirty. In

five and a half hours I'd be standing in front of a room full of strangers, as prepared as anyone's ever prepared for fate. There was no point in going to bed now. I decided to shower and head out early to a café to put together some kind of introductory lecture. The thought unsettled me. All my nerve endings twitched. In thirty years I'd be seventy-eight, my father's age when he died, eight years more than Keaton managed. So why this anxiety now?

I hit play, then fast-forward and the black-and-white images flew by, faster than the jumped-up speed silent movies always played at for decades after the glory days had ended. When I hit pause, there was Buster in the projection booth, twitching and falling off his chair – the dream over, the film within the film over, normal, regular life resumed. But was it? The girl rushes in. She tells him that she knows he's innocent, that he was framed. All is forgiven. Now Buster has to make his move. Confused, he looks to the movie screen for help. Up there, the original detective-hero takes the original girl's hand. Buster does the same with his girl. The hero kisses the hand. Buster follows suit. Next, a long, passionate kiss. Buster delivers a peck on the cheek. Finally the screen cuts to an image of the hero-detective holding two babies on his lap. *Sherlock Jr.* ends with Buster's legendary face, frozen and yet pregnant with meaning. He blinks and blinks. So *this* is life, *this* is what it comes to? The expression on the comedian's face offers no clear insight. Fatty Arbuckle would have winked at the camera; most comedians today would find some obvious way to suggest that this fate was a death knell for a man. Keaton suggests this, but good-naturedly. After all, he's young still himself, he's been married for a brief time, he's the father of two little boys – where's it all leading? He doesn't know. What he does know is that life won't ever be the same; that time marches on; that the dream, the illusion, must give way to reality.

He blinks, he picks up his briefcase, he enters a classroom and says, "A complete English sentence must contain a subject and a verb." He says, "A complete human life must contain loss and gags." *Buster runs.* That's a complete sentence. *Sherlock Jr. tails the villain and Buster Keaton never makes a feature film of his own after 1928.* That's a complete life. Or, *Buster Keaton films* The General, *one of cinema's greatest accomplishments, and receives a twenty-minute standing ovation at the Venice Film Festival the year before his death.* An old man, he blinks and blinks, tears in his eyes. Soon, illusion and reality as he knows them will be gone. That's also a complete life.

And it's full of fragments.

I couldn't rise from the couch. I started *Sherlock Jr.* again. It was only forty-five minutes long, one of Keaton's shortest features, apparently because audiences at the preview screening found the concept either confusing or disturbing, so a lot of footage was cut. I had forty-five minutes; that was slightly more than one minute per one year of my life. Surely I could afford that much.

I settled back into the illusion with a sigh. That face! That iconic face looking up over a book on how to be a detective, except there's a thick Victorian moustache where there should only be white skin. The gag, always the gag – even in a strait-jacket after a bad case of the DT's, even forgotten, even after Natalie left him and changed the boys' names to her own and he was just an old waxwork muttering, "Pass. Pass." A man could put his faith in the gag, because his faith had to go somewhere. And if it didn't . . . Clyde Bruckman, gag man extraordinaire, Keaton's co-writer almost from the very beginning, killed himself in 1962. Killed himself with a gun he'd borrowed from his old pal, Buster. How funny is that? Is it real or an illusion? I settled back to revel in the gags of a suicide. When I was done, when I had showered and put on clean clothes and brushed my teeth, when I had quietly left the house so as not to wake my family, I simply did not know how I would continue to the completion of my sentence and my life.

IT WAS STILL DARK but approaching light, just as in a movie theatre in the seconds before the curtain draws back. Or at least in those older kinds of theatres. I hadn't been to a mall-o-plex ad-orgy, or whatever modern first-run theatres were currently called, since about the time Pee-wee Herman's bike was stolen. And yes, I was certain Paul Reubens, the actor who played Pee-wee, had the classic 1948 Italian neo-realist film, *The Bicycle Thieves*, in mind. It wasn't a comedy, but bicycles – as anyone familiar with Flann O'Brien's brilliant novel *The Third Policeman* will attest – *are* funny. Indeed, when Keaton first appears on screen in *Our Hospitality*, he's riding a penny farthing, an ancient contraption of a bike with a gigantic Ferris wheel of a front wheel – it's a delightful image in an otherwise overrated film.

Normally, I ride my mountain bike to campus. It's a pleasant journey, one Keaton would have loved, for, halfway through it, I pedal over the High Level Bridge, an impressively high, coal-black girdered railroad bridge built in 1912. In fact, as I pick up speed as I reach the span, I often forget to change gears and I pump the pedals as rapidly and ridiculously as any silent screen comedian ever did until my momentum returns me to the twenty-first century and the real world of finger-giving drivers and impatience and the terrible class struggle that no one's even allowed to acknowledge.

I wasn't going to campus, at least not yet. It was only six-forty, and I didn't have my first class until eleven. I stood under a huge, overarching Dutch elm, its branches as black as bridge girders, and listened to the absence of birdsong. I knew that songbirds, like so many other things, were dying out, but I was rarely up at the hour when the absence was so obvious and, well, unnerving. The natural world was giving us a new silence, but it wasn't art. I suppose it was the silence of death, but that idea wasn't going to help me face my life, or even my day. So I shook it off, the way sparrows in my childhood shook raindrops off their wings as they perched on telephone wires.

Of course I didn't really shake it off. North America constantly shakes the idea of death off, but I was intent on shaking North America off. And Keaton was obviously the key; Keaton was the pilgrim's guide through hell. I could only hope there'd be a paradise at the end of the journey.

I began to walk through the dark wood, musing, half-plotting, remembering. Edmonton had been a stop on the vaudeville circuit – not a glamorous, big-time stop, but vaude-villians were, by and large, down-to-earth folk, unfussy and practical; they'd follow the money, go where the work was. The Three Keatons very likely came through Edmonton, at a time when my own family – my paternal great-grandparents and their children – lived here. Maybe they even saw the legendary act and one of the world's greatest filmmakers in the flesh. It was certainly possible. My grandparents were long dead and my great-grandparents were barely even photo-graphic images. As for Edmonton's most famous vaudeville theatre, it had vanished along with every other building from that era. But I knew where the city's missing and sparkling tooth had been. Right downtown. Vaguely, I turned my body and its double lenses in that direction, all the while keeping one lens wide for the reappearance of the silent little man on the telephone wire.

A bus approached as I neared the stop at 99th Street. In the dark, its silent and empty glide of light struck me as cinematic. Here was the modern *Sherlock Jr.* projectionist, almost asleep at the wheel, dragging a cut scene from filmdom's glory days behind him. A city of strangers, boarding one by one in the darkness, perhaps in twos or threes, paying their admission at the booth, would animate the old, forgotten world. The projectionist at the camera would come alive; he'd peer into the faces for clues to the great mystery as the horizons widened and the noise and colour and perplexing heaviness of the inescapable reality of the unreal future rushed in. The knife-scored theatre seats and the daylight like a shabby velour tapestry creeping over the stillness of the watchers. Watching what?

The old magic slowed for me. I clambered out of the orchestra pit of the self and into the illusion of art. No one kicked me back over the footlights. The projectionist barely stirred as I dropped my coins in the box and was offered a transfer by the little machine. And where exactly was I to transfer? Must we pay now even for our daydreams? It was like a ticket stub, so I accepted it fondly. I moved on and found myself become a child again, early at the matinee, with a whole theatre of seats from which to choose. Selecting one near the middle, I settled in comfortably and waited for the flow of images.

My hometown appeared, circa 1969. A slickness lay over the streets and lawns like the slickness on the scales of a just-caught salmon. I counted seventy-two masts sticking up from the harbour, four steeples sticking up from the tradition of belief and not a single tombstone sticking up from the moist earth. Imagine – a town so lightly built on water that there wasn't enough depth of ground for a cemetery. We had death, of course, but we had no dead. The morning sun and the twilight moon changed their lights only for the traffic of the living. In the little theatre next to the dry cleaners next to the Daisy Dell grocery next to the shadow of the stray mutt sleeping at the bakery store curb, another projectionist readied the film, looping the tape into the reels.

The mist on the river flowed into my eyes, for I remembered the loss, the closure of the local movie house a few blocks from where I lived, the day the laughter stopped, to use Keaton's phrase to describe the effect of the Arbuckle rape case on Hollywood. The theatre vanished within a month or two of my grandmother's death, which was my first death and the only time in my childhood that I ever saw tears in my father's blue eyes. His silence, for he was a silent man with a Keaton-esque mask, was different then; a deeper, more resonant chord sounded in the orchestra as we drove to the higher ground of Vancouver to lay my father's mother under the cool shadows of the evergreens.

The theatre lurched to a stop. A brightly lipsticked woman in a pastel skirt, and a grubby, unshaven youth in a Charon hoodie cut across my vision of the screen. "Modern times," to quote Chaplin. The day of the remaining days. I always tell my students, do you know, in the history of our species, there are far more dead than there are living? Do you realize that by the very act of sitting here, listening, breathing, yawning, just exactly how rare you are? Nine billion, and rare. They blink; they stare into their digitized hands; they google to see who this lunatic is and whether there's another section of the course they can take. Maybe a half dozen look up with fresh attention; I give them my transfer for the incubus and insert some change for the succubus. What else can I do? They're on their way to the places I've already been, the places that have worn me down at last. My father's dead without a grave; who will give me back my hours of fiercest watching?

It was too late. The mist evaporated, the bus filled with workers and I stood in the downtown core of North America, cattled among the chains and franchises, the terrified flesh of power on one side, the terrified flesh of money on the other. Cattle chute and spawning stream – so much life on the way to death, forced and natural, panicked and driven to fulfillment.

I sighed and walked a few blocks west on Jasper Avenue to the corner of 102nd Street.

Here, almost exactly a century ago, on May 12, 1913, the vaudeville business mogul beautifully named Pericles Pantages (though he went by Alexander, for Alexander the Great) opened what was billed as "the most northerly high class playhouse in North America." In partnership with an Edmonton businessman, the not-so-beautifully named George Brown (he went by George, for George), Alexander the Great recognized that Edmonton was large and thriving enough to join his chain of western North American theatres. And so the Pantages Theatre was born – and what a palace it was. Built from classical inspiration with Italian Renaissance touches, Pantages was a $250,000 explosion of culture in Hicksville, all bevelled glass and Grecian marble panels with an interior boasting a proscenium arch, Corinthian columns, delicately moulded carvings, a vaulted ceiling with a domed light, and ivy, gold and rose auditorium walls. The auditorium walls were finished with panelled red damask silk, imported from Peking, and the boxes, balconies and draperies featured deep gold fabric trimmed with handwoven embroideries. It was like walking inside a whale that had just swallowed centuries of European high culture. And the effect it must have had!

According to the *Edmonton Bulletin*, a crowd of sixteen hundred gathered outside for the grand opening, many without tickets, as crews inside worked feverishly to put on the finishing touches. The opening was delayed fifteen minutes, then a half hour, then forty-five minutes. The crowd swelled. All darkly clothed with charcoal silent-film eyes full of romantic longing and immigrant hunger, the crowd stood on the titanic deck and sang to themselves the song of the coming god of entertainment, "Nearer, My God, to Thee." Escape! An hour late, the doors finally opened. Rush into the whale's mouth! Pushing, jabbering, sweating, the rich and the poor together, first class and steerage, on the hunt for magic. Who's got a ticket? Where's your ticket? Oh never mind, let it go, it's the wave of the future and we're all on the crest, no icebergs anywhere.

One hundred years later, I stood at the corner of Jasper and 102nd Street and tried to count to one thousand six hundred. It didn't take long; the big commute was emerging from darkness into dusk, the human flow was accelerating like the river at the end of *Our Hospitality*. I ballparked sixteen hundred people and put them in a mob and milled them outside the Pantages Theatre on opening night. It almost worked; I could almost pull the present that far into the past. But the present, as it must, resisted. I yanked the history rope. The present yanked back. I yanked again, my eyes closed against the clamouring day. Just when I thought I might not win, I remembered my own history in this place, I saw my ancestors in their youth and the rope turned to taffy in the delighted pulling of a child.

They had come west by train, with their bees. I'm not sure even Buster Keaton would have dreamed up quite so unusual a gag. He always maintained that an effective comic feature film could not be ridiculous, that it had to be constructed on a platform of believability in order to hold together. In the early days (not long after Edmonton's Pantages opened, in fact) when he worked with Roscoe Arbuckle, Keaton had only one disagreement with the rotund, ill-fated funnyman that he loved so well, and that disagreement involved this question of artistic integrity. Arbuckle claimed that movie audiences had the intelligence of twelve-year-olds, so why not mug for the camera, why worry about structure and believability? Keaton saw no sense in this argument at all. But then, he was an artist who had just discovered his medium. The movie camera fascinated him. Unlike any of the other great comedians of the silent era, unlike almost any actor in the film industry from its beginnings until now, Keaton had an intense technical interest in the camera. Immediately upon leaving the stage to work for Arbuckle in the movies in 1917, he asked if he could take a camera apart and study how it worked. Buster Keaton had never spent more than a day in school, but he had a curious, searching intelligence; some might even argue that he had that intelligence *because* he'd avoided school. Whatever the case, one point was clear enough: there is no beekeeping in any of Buster Keaton's films.

But there are plenty of trains, of course. The elderly Keaton in the fall of 1964 crossed Canada by handcar in the same direction and on the same tracks as my ancestors had done in 1905, heading west from Ontario with the family's precious bees in their luggage. Well, they thought they might need them in their new life. And as it turned out, they did. My great-great-grandfather, an expert carpenter, had built a special case designed to bear the bees in secrecy. As Great-Aunt Gladys pointed out in a privately printed little family memoir, "Imagine what would have happened if the porter had discovered that we had bees in our luggage!" At this point, Keaton, the real or the dream version, would have glided in with all of his comic imagination on fire, suggesting this gag, that stunt, directing the swarm of bees to chase him across the tops of the moving boxcars. Or perhaps he would have directed the porter to toss him out of the moving train as it passed the town of . . . oh, let's say, Rivers, Manitoba, if there was a Rivers, Manitoba, in 1905. Here, in the west, which isn't really the west if you're from it, towns come and towns go. Keaton's own birthplace of Piqua, Kansas, for example, was blown off the map by a cyclone shortly after his arrival and almost-immediate departure to the next vaudeville stop. And the Hollywood of the silent film era, that glittery, romantic town where the money men some-times gave geniuses absolute creative control, vanished too.

I wavered on the sidewalk outside the twenty-storey, phallic Enbridge Place skyscraper and peered through the black-tinted glass. A security guard sat up high behind a massive desk. A sign on the glass read, "All visitors to this building must report to security." I wanted to put some bees in my pockets and stride in with Keatonian insouciance, just as my grandfather and his four siblings had strode into the grand lobby of the Pantages Theatre on May 12, 1913, without tickets, as eager as the rest of the crowd to see the inside of a theatre that had cost a quarter of a million dollars to build. I wavered. Even now, in the second decade of the twenty-first century, I would have to teach fifty sections of introductory grammar and rhetoric in order to make $250,000. Years of work, over a decade's worth. It was a lot of money, and a king's ransom in 1913 – my grandfather and his siblings must have goggled at it. Alexander Pantages, however, was a business king by 1913. He'd eventually build an empire that, at its peak, included thirty vaudeville houses scattered across the north-west, including Vancouver and Winnipeg. Sixteen years earlier, he'd been a penniless Greek immigrant toiling as a waiter in the goldfields of Skagway, Alaska, dreaming of ways to make it big without having to sweat and labour like a prospector. What better way to separate the miner from his poke than to set up shows and watch the gold nuggets and dust pour in?

Eventually, he hooked up with Klondike Kate, the legendary dance-hall girl, and together they established the Orpheum Theatre in Dawson. Kate became Pantages's mistress, and then he left her, virtually at the altar. There was a breach of promise suit with a delicate violinist as the other woman. The strings played. It was all in black and white but very colourful. Over a century later I stood in the chill winds of time and death and ruin and fumbled in my pockets for admission. My grand-father, who, perhaps not incidentally, was born the same year as Keaton, had no ticket. Neither did I. But I had a fierce love of the past and a memory soaked in nitrate and honey. Here's a handful of dust, Mr. Pantages. Or perhaps a handful of pollen. Open the doors and let me in.

It's a *Sherlock Jr.* moment. I'm in a fan-shaped auditorium blinking up at a great asbestos curtain of deep gold. The walls to my sides are panelled with real damask Chinese silk. Giant Corinthian columns. Panels and cartouches. I look around. I look back, my eyes full of a great plaster relief of crossed swords supporting a torch. Lion heads, dolphins, garlands, scrolls. Lion heads! Suddenly I'm teetering over a great hole in the earth, and a wrecking ball swings straight at me. It's 1979 and the Pantages is being razed.

I jump, and land in a plush theatre seat. The mayor of Edmonton is giving a speech from the stage to honour the grand opening. I lean forward to watch the evening's enter-tainment, which begins, in a disturbing act of foreshadowing, with a moving picture. Then, according to historian John Orrell, comes a "trio of equilibrists, a singer of ragtime songs, a one-act skit called 'The Police Inspector,' a comic duo known as Coogan and Cox, and a group of dancers known as the Alisky Royal Hawaiians." Three months later I'm still sitting there as the Marx Brothers parade around in their anarchic fashion, and three years after that I'm still there when The Three Keatons take the stage. Open-mouthed, I watch the young Buster work hard to cover up the timing inadequacies of his increasingly drunken father as his almost-always-written-to-the-wings mother tootles on a saxophone. Within a year, Buster and Myra will walk out on old Joe and end the act, and Buster will hook up with destiny (in the roly-poly form of Fatty Arbuckle) and begin co-starring in the Comique Film Corporation's short films in New York.

I stand and approach the stage. It changes to a speeding

train on which I glimpse a family of beekeepers heading towards my own modest production in 1964. Then the image blurs completely, and I'm standing on the corner of Jasper Avenue and 102nd Street on September 4, 2012, the day's commute in full swing, my nerves jangling, my stomach a swarm and not even my immediate destiny known.

7

HEEDING THE order "Go west, middle-aged man," I walked along the avenue, thinking that I ought to pick up something to go for my lunch. As I strolled, I continued to muse on the rapid pace of North American progress.

Vancouver – that sexy metropolis of reckless real estate speculation – demolished the oldest Pantages vaudeville theatre in North America in 2011. And when the wrecking ball crashed into the side of the grand old playhouse, what sound came out? The long, mournful cry of the railroad whistle of the trains that carried the vaudevillians around on the circuit, Winnipeg to Calgary to Edmonton to Vancouver – all those bridge games in the club car, all that cigarette smoke, all that scenery! And the granite railroad hotels, those glamorous tombs of opulence. The very British stationery, the promotional postcards sent from Jasper and Banff, the royal family's royal visits, I say, jolly good what! But, so much more than all that, the very real, very moving link between so many vanished lives and their vanished aspirations.

One example: my mother, born and raised in poverty in Toronto, left in October 1945, at the age of eighteen to start her married life on the west coast. How did she travel? By train. She was the youngest of my grandparents' eighteen children, only six of whom survived birth and infancy. Obviously, she and my stout Irish grandmother were very close. I believe my mother's shabby luggage was drenched with peat-black Irish tears, I believe my mother's cedar hope chest was lined with tear-sodden Irish lace. Well, the story ended a few weeks later. My grandmother, sixty-five, died of a stroke, and my mother couldn't afford to travel across the country again. She lay, a new bride, in a little, rainy fishing town full of strangers, and listened to the trains cry across the salt flats. It was the sound of her mother calling to her. It was the sound of her childhood, which was gone forever. It was the sound of human history, and what else is a country if it isn't just that?

Money? I beg your pardon. For a moment I forgot where I was and who I was, out in the relevant urban jungle, child of the cold Scottish till, walking west along Jasper Avenue on the morning of my first day of classes. As it happens, my great-grandfather might have done the same in 1905, though his labour was different from mine. He worked for the railroads. But then, who didn't work for the railroads in Canada a hundred years ago? It *was* unifying, in its way. Why else should a British-born filmmaker named Gerald Potterton make a railroad promotional film in 1964? Why else would he go to the inspired trouble of travelling to noisy New York to persuade a faded screen legend that riding a motorized handcart across a massive land mass in autumn would be just the ticket? It was unifying, the railroad, and the reach of its tracks was long, long enough to touch the imagination of Buster Keaton. The romance convinced one of the world's greatest artists to come here near the end of his life – why would he bother to come?

Of course, it always boils down to work and money. Keaton came for romance, perhaps, but mostly he wanted the opportunity to work. He made no distinction, in fact, between life and work. His attitude was very much akin to that of the Spanish poet, Juan Ramón Jiménez, who believed that the greatest joy in living was to work – but that's only if your work calls to the deepest parts of yourself. Another poet, the stereotypically miserable Englishman, Philip Larkin, famously asks, "Why should I let the toad *work* / Squat on my life?"

I looked into the faces of the men and women walking past me on their way to work, whatever kind of work it was. I tried to guess who would be passing the security guard in the Enbridge Tower and who would be putting on latex gloves to make sandwiches at Tim Hortons. Perhaps that rather handsome and intense middle-aged Asian woman served on the board of directors of the Edmonton Opera Association, or perhaps she was a dentist or a cashier at Shoppers Drug Mart. I smiled a limp smile, which she did not return. Was that a toad squatting on her life?

And what about my life? I had a toad worthy of a Macbeth witch on my shoulder, a toad the pale green colour of American money. It was a wonder that all of Edmonton didn't turn at the sound of the terrible croaking. I walked faster, longing for the whistle of the train to drown out the toad's monotonous harangue. I thought of an interview Keaton gave near the end of his life, in which he explained that he would have been a millionaire if he'd cared about money and business the way Chaplin and Harold Lloyd did. Chaplin, who loved to play at being a communist, was a consummate capitalist, just as Mick Jagger, who loved to play at being a rebel, was a proud graduate of the London School of Economics. So the world goes, full of illusion, like the movies.

Life isn't the movies, especially if you have an uncertain income, no benefits or security, and few prospects for anything better. I thought of the thirty teenagers now rising from their more optimistic sleep and getting ready to commute to my class. It might be the first class of their first day at university. My God, they deserved better than me, they deserved a teacher who didn't stagger in with a twitch in his left eye and an amphibious right shoulder. "Canada, land of the train," I cried, "don't fail me now!"

It didn't. But it saved me, or at least offered salvation, in the only way that it could, with an almost vaudevillian turn, as moving and sad as Keaton's few minutes on screen in Chaplin's 1952 film, *Limelight*. When I crossed 109th Street, the dark had almost lifted, but I still dragged the heavy chains of Labour Day behind me; the cold, grasping, Jacob Marley rattle of money. Between the squatting toad and the rattling chains, I made a sorry sight, which was probably why the sun made no hurry to climb over the horizon and rest its yellow peepers on me. It was over four hours until I was due to take roll call, and that fact turned me south, toward the North Saskatchewan River, over which a magnificent iron railroad bridge, constructed a century before, soared. Water and trains.

Was it any wonder that the ghost of Keaton finally reappeared to walk along just ahead of me? I saw him there, kept my eye on him. Keaton rarely walked for long before he broke into a run, and if he ran, well, I was going to follow. By now, I figured he cared as much about me as I cared about him. When you come right down to it, death is really just a state of mind.

No! Of course it isn't! Should a man who has such thoughts really be responsible for any part of any young person's education? How could I possibly help them to secure solid financial advice? Death is death, movies are movies and a train is not a streetcar, not quite. I stumbled upon the northern terminus and read the little sign that proclaimed the schedule. The streetcar operated right through September, making its fifteen-minute run across the High Level Bridge to the neighbourhood of Old Strathcona, where I lived. I had travelled on this charming blast from the past many times before, always delightedly staring out from yesterday at today, as if the boy in me looked out at the man. Were there tears in those eyes? Of course. But a man's tears, not a boy's. Today I vowed I would ride the streetcar in a new way, for a new reason: I would ride it with Buster Keaton, and I would ride it to escape.

But not until my first working hour. I needed another strong cup of coffee to help me and Buster bide our time.

8

I WANDERED BACK to Jasper Avenue, my mood expectant yet wary. The sky's flush of light disturbed me somehow; it was like the colour coming back to the cheeks of Lazarus. And – deny it if you will – there's always a Lazarian quality to a morning rush hour. How many of these ordinary Edmontonians that I now passed, who now passed me, were Buster Keaton heading to the film set in 1920? How many were Philip Larkin heading to the main library at Hull University in 1964?

The curious truth is most people must work for a living, yet we live in a culture that celebrates only the escape from work. The way most of us spend our lives is scorned and dismissed. Is it any wonder, then, that we should rise as if from the dead to take up our toil? Why, even the desire to work harder has negative connotations – several of these sober-faced citizens are probably workaholics throwing themselves into the busyness of labour in order to avoid the emotional, psycho-logical and domestic aspects of their lives. The Great Stone Face himself, who claimed he never smiled when he acted because he was working and concentrating so hard, very likely took any job he could get after 1935 because it kept him off the booze. Workaholic alcoholic – the former often drinks to come down from working so much, the latter is despised partly because he loses the ability to function as a worker. North American society is nothing if not confused. Think of it: most of us will spend our lives working, and working hard, as our parents did before us and as our children will do after us, and yet the very activity is belittled. What is the first and usually lasting public response to any labour dispute? Blame the workers, blame those who are seeking to improve or protect their own condition of suffering! Why has the word *union* become so demonized? The unseemliness of workers banding together in their immigrant garlic sweat and general misery to complain about what we all must endure. Labourers. Workers. Unions. What has this to do with the dreams of who we really are? Yes, I have a job, but I'm not a labourer. That was the slightly stifled cry I saw in the eyes of the working masses on Jasper Avenue. Masses? Nonononono. The individuals who will one day own the franchise where they currently sell crullers to the Enbridge executives who will one day be the CEOs. And what of the thirty teenagers stir-ring now and preparing for their first day of university? They expected to work but not to be workers. They would relax on the Labour Day long weekend, but they were not labourers. No, they were on their way to the professions, to the wearing of the white collars not the pink and the blue, not those colours we happily give to the newborn girls and boys they so recently were. Confused? This is only the beginning.

At Jasper and 107th Street, I came upon a mass of exposed nerve endings muttering away in his sasquatch stink. He stood beside a shopping cart bulging with blue recycle bags full of plastic bottles. The bags were piled up like cumulus clouds; they hung off the sides of the cart like ballast that couldn't quite keep the man connected to our more sensible version of earthly existence. Yet the recycling bags bulged with empty bottles and cans. Clearly this scrap of human flotsam had worked to gather what we had tossed away. He probably had a route that he worked every day, garbage can to garbage can, Dumpster to Dumpster, in the pre-dawn hours, battling the cold and the competition as fierce as any in a boardroom. But for what stakes? For the stakes to survive another day, for the common human stakes.

I didn't meet his eyes. I didn't stop and speak with him. Studs Terkel was dead, and who would walk through the twenty-first century urban jungle with the ghost of Studs Terkel at his side? I wasn't a lunatic. Indeed, I was a product clanked out of the machine of my place and time. To step out of the body of the daily lot, as Keaton stepped out of the body of the lowly projectionist, was to be a filmmaker, an actor, an artist of sublime imagination and daring. I had stepped halfway out; I had one foot on the platform, the other foot on the train (okay, the streetcar, and I wasn't going back to New Orleans, even if I *was* wearing a ball and chain), and I knew I had the sympathies of many. I could feel the common human will pounding in my breast even though I knew the idea of poetry was anathema to my culture. It was the Great Escape; it was freedom before fifty-five; it was living so differently that you didn't even have to come up with the expected third part of the trinity structure of the metaphor. Studs Terkel was no kind of escape at all. Way back in the 1960s and '70s, he authored a number of bestselling tomes about the lives of ordinary working people. If he tried to do that today, he'd wind up like this urban balloonatic, shyly picking bottles out of the city's sleepy shadows. And what about James Agee, the film critic who helped resurrect Keaton's career? The book that brought Agee – and still brings him – attention is ironically titled *Let Us Now Praise Famous Men*, ironic because it is a portrait study of the desperate lives of southern sharecroppers. Not even J. K. Rowling could sell such a pitch to the multinational conglomerate publishing companies of today.

Still on the sidewalk, I stood and let the great Thoreauvian tide swirl around me. Henry David Thoreau, nineteenth-century American who stepped out of the mainstream in order to live simply at Walden Pond and then write about it, author of the famous line "The mass of men lead lives of quiet desperation." The quiet desperation flowed and pulled, but I held my ground. And the balloonatic, with his blue ballast, held his just a dozen feet away. I closed my eyes. Now my stillness and my shut eyes separated me, for it takes very little to disturb the sane balance of North America in its contemporary hurry. And though the passing masses, the walking commuters, couldn't see it, I had risen free of my own body again, and was playing the film of the mind and spirit in which, this time, the real-life Buster Keaton starred.

IT WAS EARLY IN 1917, and the Three Keatons were in turmoil. Papa Joe, who had been miserable about growing older for at least the past half-dozen years, now drank so much that the family rough-and-tumble act was an embarrassment. Buster, by then a young adult of twenty-one, tried to hold everything together. First of all, he petitioned the owner of the Pantages west coast circuit (the Keatons had been blackballed out of the big-time eastern circuit due mostly to Joe's belligerence), Alexander the Great, that tough old Greek, to let the family do two shows a day instead of the contracted three. Buster explained how gruelling the Three Keatons' performances were, what a physical toll they exacted. No soap. As Buster himself put it, Pantages's "experiences in the Frozen North had not made him very benevolent." Indeed, like many bosses who have risen from nothing, he had a lovely, self-serving hypocrisy about him. "You signed to do three shows a day," he informed Buster, "and that's what you'll do." Never mind Klondike Kate and that old breach of promise suit, never mind that the tough old Greek agreed to love for a lifetime and then skipped out with his pretty violinist. This was business, not personal life; the separation goes straight to the heart of North American society.

So, Buster soldiered on, covering up for his drunken father's vanished timing. Finally, there was nothing to do but break up the act, which Buster did in Los Angeles. Along with his mother, who had never really cared about performing, he travelled by train to New York, leaving Papa Joe to emerge from his drunken stupor, accept the truth and then subside not uncomfortably into his drunkenness at the family getaway in Muskegon.

Now what? Buster decided he would have to go solo. This was no easy matter. Oh, it was easy enough, because of his fame, to get work. Almost immediately he signed on to a popular Broadway revue at two hundred fifty dollars a week for six months. The problem was, he couldn't quite figure out *how* to do a solo act. He had worked all his life with his father as a foil, and now he had to come up with a different version of onstage fate to struggle against. Of course, he was also facing the practical challenge of the imagination at the same time he was dealing with the psychological and emotional turmoil of having abandoned his father (but Keaton *never* spoke of that). So there he was, in a New York hotel room, desperately setting up chairs and falling over them, working out the pratfalls; he had stepped out of his father's drunken body on the wooden vaudeville stage, yet there was no waiting reality for him to step into.

Then, one day, he began walking the streets, looking at the window displays without seeing them. He turned a corner, his head down, and someone called his name.

"Hey! Bud!"

Bud? I searched the Keaton biographies in my mind's eye, but could find no typo. In fact, *Bud* was a pretty significant typo for *Buster*. Then I felt a tug on my sleeve, just as a swirl of cigarette smoke, booze and sweat-stink assailed my nostrils. I opened my eyes.

The homeless man, detached from his floating balloon of nonconformity, stood beside me on the sidewalk, his bloodshot eyes tossing like a pair of burning dice.

"Hey, bud," he repeated, his voice nasally as if he'd found just the tiniest bit of helium in a Dumpster and ingested it. "You got kids?"

Why is it that homeless men so often seem to address strangers as Bud or Pal? Is it because these terms are blue-collar, originating in the working classes where, once, a very long time ago, the common struggle made every stranger a buddy or a pal? Wasn't the theme song of the Great Depression called "Buddy, Can You Spare a Dime?" Come to think of it, didn't the down-and-outer of that still haunting ballad have something to do with railroads? Yes. "Once I built a railroad, now it's done. Brother, can you spare a dime?" Brother, not buddy. But brother implies an even greater closeness, as if we were all carved from the same ur-stone.

"Er, yeah," I said, blinking away the New York of 1917 and trying to focus on the Edmonton of 2012. "Three kids." The Three Kids. What an act it was, but with certainly more than three performances a day. They routinely brought the house down.

Almost shyly, he handed me two objects out of his cart. The first was a toy plastic horse about the size of a small loaf of bread. It was grimy and a large crack ran from its mane to its hindquarters, but from a considerable distance away (in time, in time), I began to recognize it. How could I not? For the horse's insides – its skeleton and organs – were visible. It was one of those transparent models that taught the science of biology. I might have owned one as a boy, or perhaps a friend did. I seemed to remember a human version, as well. Suddenly I was relieved that the balloonatic wasn't handing me a miniature version of my own vascular system.

As I pondered the horse's dim, dirt-hidden heart, the homeless man pushed the other object into my free hand. This was heavy and also a toy, a cast-iron piggy bank, except it wasn't in the shape of a piggy. It was a magician with a black top hat and a green coat. The colours were surprisingly sharp. Looking closer, I admired the details of the magician's face, right down to the waxed goatee and red lips. But the most intriguing quality of the bank was, much like the transparent horse, how it worked.

"You gotta use small change," the derelict muttered, gently taking the bank from me and placing it on the busy commuter sidewalk. We knelt together. Do you think that any of the dozens and dozens of rushing pedestrians also stopped? No, but many of them looked. They flowed around us like water going around a rock in a current.

"A loonie's too big," he continued, and pulled a nickel from somewhere out of his malodorous rags. He placed it on a little circular depression on the table in front of the magician, which served as the base of the bank. Next, he pushed a spot somewhere behind the magician, and the magician doffed his top hat, covered the nickel and – clank – the nickel disappeared. Fantastic! My heart, which no one could see, not even a biology professor, gave a little doe-leap.

"That's really something," I murmured, and set the transparent horse down, found a coin in my coat pocket and tried the bank myself. Clank. Five cents to be admitted to a surprising moment in a lifetime of moments. The Keaton story flowed past. What was it Buster's decidedly wrong-footed, high-kicking father had said to squelch his son's first chance at a movie career in 1912? Responding to the wealthy William Randolph Hearst, he of *Citizen Kane* notoriety, who wanted to put the Three Keatons in the movies, Papa Joe had said, "We work for years perfecting an act, and you want to show it, a nickel a head, on a dirty sheet?"

I had some genuine sympathy for Old Joe: technologies could hurt, and right in the pocketbook. Hadn't my own writing career suffered financially because publishers now sold thirty-dollar print books as ten-dollar e-books? I was no accounting genius, but twenty-five percent of ten is considerably less than fifteen percent of thirty. *What? I work for years perfecting a text, and you want to show it, a ten spot a head, on a flickering screen?* Joe Keaton was wrong in 1912, and perhaps I was just as wrong a century later. The technologies, in any case, were going to win. "Stay green, never mind the machine," wrote the poet R. S. Thomas. "Live large, man, and dream small." The words were powerful, and, whether on vellum or a plastic screen, they hit hard. But what exactly did it mean to live large in the twenty-first century?

Well, my situation wasn't the Keatons' in 1912, nor Buster's in 1917. In the first place, no multi-millionaire business moguls were offering me a contract for the e-text of my next book. I didn't even know any moguls. In the second place, I wasn't anywhere close to famous and successful. By the standards of North American society, I was on the brink of complete failure, unable to face – or at least contemplating avoiding – my only source of semi-reliable income.

"Hey. Bud."

He turned a corner. Someone called his name.

Hey, Buster!

It was 1917, and a great artist was about to meet his fate. Perhaps I was a great artist, too, and this homeless man with his Dumpster-bin treasure was my fate.

My mind cut like an edit. Medicine show to vaudeville to silent film to sound film to television – and Buster bows out. Television to computer to home computer to the Internet – will I bow out, or will I survive? From 1917 to the late 1920s, Keaton revelled in silent film just as a generation before, Van Gogh had revelled in paint. In New York City where, if you can make it there, you can make it anywhere, someone once called out, "Hey, Buster!" and a period of genius began. When sound came to the movies, bringing structural and economic changes, lye was thrown in the artist's eyes. Keaton himself became a major victim of the technological shift, primarily because his onscreen inability to communicate with the world was the whole basis of his comedy. According to film historian Walter Kerr, Keaton was like "a man from an alien world, quite unaccustomed to human logic and foibles, he floundered around, overlooking the obvious, harnessing the equipment of the world to his own ends." Like a man from an alien world, floundering around, overlooking the obvious. That sounded about right. That sounded just about too damned right. Then again, what was art, how was it made? Uniformly, efficiently, by machine?

"A penny for your thoughts, Bud."

I blinked into the homeless man's face, which was as close to me now as a bee's feet to a loaded sunflower. No more overlooking the obvious, I vowed. He was a man approaching fifty, like me. White, like me. He even had my full lips, and there might have been some watery blue between the bloodshot

{63}

streaks in his eyes, as in mine. But he wasn't my long-lost twin, or doppelgänger; we hadn't stepped out of each other's bodies à la *Sherlock Jr.*, and entered a new reality, unless every moment is indeed a new reality, which it probably is. No, this man, this urban misfit, bum, panhandler, vagrant, down-and-outer, tramp, hobo, jungle bum, drifter, derelict – he wasn't me. I didn't know him from a hole in the ground. I didn't know him from Adam. I didn't know him from Adam standing in a hole in the ground. He was just a human being old enough to know the expressions I'd picked up in my childhood. A penny for my thoughts? A penny? The federal government had just discontinued the little brown circle – how long would it take for those millions, perhaps billions, of tiny brown eyes to stop blinking out at the twenty-first-century sky? Most of them had vanished already.

"Oh, I was just thinking I'd better get going, that's all." I leaned back from his face.

He nodded understandingly. "Late for work, huh?"

Not yet. Not yet. Then it struck me. The man was roughly bearded, the hair the colour and texture of mange. Where the skin showed, it was dark, as if some street artist had charcoaled parts of his face. Now that I had noticed this, I couldn't overlook it. As I couldn't overlook the crisis in my life, a crisis he'd no doubt already been through. I simply couldn't face the face of suffering humanity because I couldn't begin to take its measure. Suffering might not have been his condition at all, of course.

The commuter morning had grown louder, as if the cars, like birds, had to greet the rising of the sun. It was time for business, and the homeless man, the man from an alien world, got quickly down to it.

"I'll take a toonie for the both of them."

I believe his spine even snapped to corporate attention as he stood.

Despite everything, I was a man of my culture, and I knew a bargain when I heard one. The magician bank was old, solid; they didn't make toys in China out of cast iron. That whole burgeoning nation was awash in plastic, right down to the fish and the lettuce now shipped in their chemical tonnage to sit on our local grocery shelves. I suddenly felt the kind of magnanimous generosity that a man feels when he's on the verge of a seismic change. Here, have my whole life, all the silent memories worth a penny a head on the dirty sheet of Time.

I pulled out my wallet, and hesitated. Did the homeless have Interac? Did they take Visa? I never used the former, and I didn't have a pin for the latter. How long would it be before actual paper money disappeared? That time would certainly come, and sooner rather than later. There was no sense in overlooking the obvious. Ah well, given the prime ministers we've had over the past few decades, I'd prefer not to see their smug corporate mugs every time I pulled out a ten. Then again, maybe one day we'd have the CEOs of Shell and Apple and Walmart plastered across our plastic cards. But one day wasn't this day. I gave the bum the purple bill, told him to keep the change, and took my little horse of guts and my magician in my hands and began once more to walk the streets.

The derelict, who had not tugged on his forelock and exclaimed, "Bless ya, guvna," returned to his floating balloon of blue recycling bags. I looked back once and saw him shuffle away, rather splay-footed. There was, in fact, something familiar about his gait, something as antiquated as his language; it didn't fit the twenty-first-century day at all. But there was dignity in the way he moved precisely because of that. The dignity of the downtrodden. Jesus, where *had* I seen that kind of movement before?

The answer came to me when I stopped at an intersection and scowled nonchalantly at the faceless rush hour masses who stole glances at the Secretariat and Houdini dangling from my hands. Chaplin. Charlie Chaplin. His Little Tramp, still more famous than Keaton's persona, walked exactly like that. All the balloonatic needed was a bowler and cane.

Suddenly I wanted my ten dollars back. Suddenly I felt cheated. For I'd never really liked Chaplin all that much. Or, at least, I'd lost my taste for him over the years, just as I'd lost my taste for candy – Chaplin's sentimentality hurt the teeth of my spirit, you might say. But what it really boiled down to was the difference between manipulation and art – Chaplin could be phony where Keaton was never that. Here's Keaton himself on the fundamental difference: "Charlie's tramp was a bum with a bum's philosophy. Lovable as he was, he would steal if he got the chance. My little fellow was a working man and honest."

I stared at the intersection's pedestrian light, and there appeared Keaton's little fellow, much more lovable to me than Chaplin's Little Tramp. And Keaton's little fellow was, like the pedestrian figure, just as white and pure, right down to the way he walked.

Keaton's walk always suited his particular filmic needs. In *Sherlock Jr.*, for example, that incredibly agile quick step he perpetrates right on the heels of the villain is a masterpiece of comic timing that rises directly out of a gag. Whenever I think of Keaton walking, I think of humanity walking; there's such an ordinariness about his stride as he breaks from a saunter to a quick step and, inevitably, a hell-bent-for-leather run. The combination of slightly controlled panic and defiant optimism was, in fact, all around me on Jasper Avenue this morning. Chaplin's iconic gait, however, existed only as a shadow in one street person, and probably only because that person felt that he had just gotten away with murder by earning ten bucks for a skinless horse and a piggy bank without the piggy. The point is, people move like Keaton all the time, and nobody ever moves like Chaplin. As Geoff Nicholson points out, "by the time a walking style has become recognizable it has also become absurd." But then, Nicholson, like me, was no Chaplin fan. He finds the Little Tramp's walk unbearable because of "its cuteness, its faux humility, its feverish attempt at ingratiation." He then defends his position by referring to a contemporary opinion, that of Wyndham Lewis, who, in 1928, published a novel, *The Childermass*, in which characters in the afterlife are forced to perform routines from Chaplin's movies. Lewis, who remains largely unknown, but who is probably one of the most clear-sighted and truthful writers of the twentieth century, loathed phoniness.

As I walked along the avenue, trying not to be self-conscious about how I walked along the avenue, I observed how others walked along the avenue. Purposeful, mostly. Yet is there not always a degree of the false in our sense of purpose? Just how important were all these destinations? These dozens upon dozens of human bodies, male and female, moved like salmon on the way to the spawning beds. No, of course salmon don't walk. I mean the urgency, the sense of following a star-charted course. Ah, but surely some of these people felt about the world as I felt about it, surely they had come to question the wisdom of the stars. That tall, skinny man there, with his bony jaw slightly raised – did each long stride of his not contain some of Keaton's fundamental cosmic hesitation? And what of the many men and women whose walks had been slowed by the technologies in their hands? The little screens reduced their walking speed but did not divert their purpose. In fact, these people were doubly purposeful in the disturbing way of sleepwalkers, who inhabit two worlds at the same time – yes, like Keaton's projectionist in *Sherlock Jr.* Except, here, on the avenue, these walkers had stepped out of their real lives without even leaving their real bodies. Perhaps they were watching videos of themselves walking somewhere else, somewhere that wasn't on the way to work. Perhaps they were watching *Sherlock Jr.* Anything was possible.

Just then, I noticed the sunlight. It was ambery, klieg-intense, and I stepped straight into it, bearing my strange material and psychological burden. Do you know, in *The Wizard of Oz*, when Dorothy leaves black-and-white Kansas behind, the black-and-white cyclonic Kansas of Keaton's birth, and lands in Oz, and the whole screen blazes out in Technicolor? I marvelled at the change, and then I marvelled at being marvelled. As long as a heart and spirit can still lift at the presence of the sun . . .

"Hey, Buster!"

He was walking along Broadway, "down along Eighth or some place," and an old vaudeville actor named Lou Anger called his name. It was a Monday morning, dark, windy, cold and full of rain. The newsboys were shouting headlines about the war that America hadn't entered yet. Gloom and pressure. Keaton's walk was just human, like anyone else's. He looked up.

"I'm heading for the studio," Anger said. "It's just a few blocks over on Forty-Eighth. Why don't you come along?"

He did. He came along to the magic of the motion picture, to his art and his fame. It was as if someone had said to Vermeer one dreary seventeenth-century Dutch morning, "I'm heading to this shaft of sunlight. Why don't you come along?"

They proceeded to the Schenk Studios, an old warehouse between First Avenue and Second. They stepped out of the dark and the rain and the sinking of ships and the bicycling of cablegrams to the parents of slaughtered young men. They stepped out of the black-and-white of history into the black-and-white of art. There, in a great barn-like loft, a space still dark but oh so different, three movies were being produced. The klieg-light islands floated along in the unquiet hush of making. Keaton was seduced immediately. He passed one island, then another and finally reached the Island of Riotous Racket, with a set representing the interior of an old country general store. Here, the company was filming a two-reel slapstick short. Bodies sprawled all over. Then the noise stopped. Someone shouted, "Break!" The bodies disentangled and stood. A slate emerged from the light. On it was scrawled "Butcher Boy Scene 3." Keaton looked past the words to the famous figure heaving into view, the two-hundred-sixty-pound hilarious mass of Roscoe "Fatty" Arbuckle.

The rest, as they say, is history. But who are *they*? I was not they, because history is as unreliable as it is undeniable. In some versions of the Keaton legend, Fatty Arbuckle is walking along with Lou Anger down Broadway, and it's Arbuckle who invites Buster to the studio, but not on that morning. Keaton gave an interview in 1958 in which he says that Arbuckle invited him to come to the studio the following Monday. A whole week in between! That's certainly not as dramatic as heading straight over to the studio and stepping out of the rainy, history-torn dark into film legend's glorious lights.

But, one way or the other, Keaton did walk into that studio, and it was a defining moment. As he puts it in his autobiography, "It was like being in a great entertainment factory where different shows were being manufactured at the same time." Even when remembering, Keaton always spoke like a worker. Factories and manufacturing. His little persona who'd struggled so often with machinery came from the imagination of a man who was fascinated by machinery. In fact, Keaton's only regret about his unschooled upbringing was that he'd never had the chance to pursue the other career that intrigued him: civil engineering.

So he went along to the Schenk Studios, accepted Fatty Arbuckle's invitation to do a bit in *The Butcher Boy*, and his destiny changed; he left the past behind and boarded the train for the future. And this wasn't just a professional turning either. That same day, or so the legend has it, he also met his future first wife, Natalie Talmadge, the least famous of the three Talmadge sisters. From that meeting, his two sons would emerge, stepping out of the sleeping body of the life that got away from him in the late 1920s. But that tragic sadness did not appear in the klieg lights in 1917. Even if it had, Buster's eyes were too full of the flour from the huge sack that Arbuckle hit him with in *The Butcher Boy* to notice. Indeed, Buster Keaton's eyes were always too full of his art for him to notice much else. Or, if he did notice, he chose to look away. How else to explain what happened to his money and his first marriage? This is so often the artist's fate – when a spider spins its web, the rest of the spider's life naturally falls into place: the living and the mating, the whole being of the creature, are not separate from the wondrous spinning skill. Not so for us humans. By the time Keaton made *Sherlock Jr.* in 1924, as intricate and delightful as any arachnid performance, he was no longer sleeping with his young bride. Natalie's powerful stage mother, and the girl's interfering, famous older sisters, continually undermined Buster's authority, eventually to the point where his sons would be stripped of his name, redubbed Talmadge and removed from his presence for most of their childhoods. As biographer Rudi Blesh so succinctly puts it, "Even from a distance there is always a deep sadness about the old, foolish, tragic scenes of the human comedy."

The divorce and the advent of the talking picture and the alcoholism – the three straps of the straitjacket not even his intense vaudeville observations of Houdini could help him untangle – lay more than a decade ahead. In 1917, covered with flour and molasses, Buster was in his glory. His vaudeville skills translated so smoothly into film that his first-ever celluloid take, his first appearance in *The Butcher Boy*, exists as a permanent piece of cinematic legend. And perhaps, given what would befall Keaton eventually, it makes a logical, circular, comic sense that his introduction to moviemaking would involve him taking a heavy sack of flour straight to the face and being knocked to the floor. There he is, a customer who walks into the general store just as a yokel fight breaks out. Arbuckle heaves the sack, from a six-foot distance, at another actor, who ducks, and – wham! – Keaton's childhood of slapstick on the vaudeville stage becomes his young adulthood of slapstick in the silent movies. The transition, though violent, was smooth. For a considerable cut in pay (the Broadway revue paid him two hundred fifty dollars a week; the movie work for Schenk Studios started at forty dollars a week), Keaton chose to throw in his lot with the art of the "dirty sheet" that his father so despised. His mother wrote to him shortly thereafter, "Glad you're in the movies. Should have done it a long time ago."

It wasn't a simple case of transferring the rough-and-tumble of slapstick to the rough-and-tumble of the comic two-reeler. Or, rather, that simplicity wasn't the point. Keaton immediately grasped the greater possibilities of the film medium. Oh sure, in *The Butcher Boy*, he got bit by a dog, and spent a hilarious, madcap time trying to retrieve a quarter from a bucket of molasses, an escapade that had him and Arbuckle and co-star Al St. John smeared with the sticky sorghum. But, in a way, that was old hat, and Buster was on his way to the future legend of his crushed porkpie hat. Between his first film appearance in 1917 and his direction of *Sherlock Jr.* in 1924 – a mere seven years – Keaton transformed himself into a genius. He owed the transformation to film. As he says in his autobiography, "The greatest thing to me about picture making was the way it automatically did away with the physical limitations of the theatre. . . . The camera had no such limitations. The whole world was its stage."

No wonder, then, that on his very first day as a film actor, Keaton asked Arbuckle to explain how the camera worked. Together, the two comic legends took one apart, and Arbuckle showed Keaton how film was developed, cut and then spliced together. The first technical steps on the way to the technical brilliance of *Sherlock Jr.* had been taken. The art of the film, like the art of the spiderweb, begins in the guts. Gags were the strands; film was the instinct that spun them.

I STOOD ON Jasper Avenue in the sunlight and considered the horse's guts. I knew nothing about a horse's anatomy, let alone my own. If you take a man apart, piece by piece, you'd learn nothing. Even if you take his life apart, as so many try to do with the famous, like Keaton and Arbuckle, you'll still learn very little. What have all these material lumps and twists and turns to do with the power in a horse's gallop or the ferocity in its eyes? Idly, I tried to locate the bladder.

A horse couldn't be so very different from a goat, and it was a goat's bladder that gave the world the term *slapstick*. Indirectly, anyway. For in the early vaudeville days, the comedians used a curious prop, a goat bladder stretched on a stick, in their acts. One comedian would hit another with it, accompanied by a loud noise, and the other would fall. Not exactly sophisticated, but the human race is not exactly sophisticated. The simplicity

– even primitivism – of slapstick still has mass appeal. Just consider TV shows such as *America's Funniest Home Videos*, where the laughter stems directly from physical humiliation. The clichéd gag of the unsuspecting walker slipping on a banana peel bears investigation in this regard: what does it say about us? Most people – let me make this clear – do not enjoy seeing others get hurt. However, who among us doesn't at least chuckle inwardly if we see some stranger trip on a curb and almost fall down? And just add a loud, unexpected splatting noise to the image – God swinging His slapstick – and Buster's your uncle. Why, even if it's an old person who falls, we'll laugh (inwardly), as long as it's obvious that Grandma or Grandpa isn't really hurt. The sudden, random humiliation of others – we enjoy it to the point of cruelty. When Fatty Arbuckle was falsely accused of rape in 1922? Oh, the fun the public had in ripping his fame apart, whole mobs of men and women yelling at the fat man they had loved so much a few weeks before, "Murderer!" "Big fat slob!" "Beast!"

But then, the fun had been replaced with a different kind of pleasure: viciousness. Keaton referred to the Arbuckle trials as "The Day the Laughter Stopped," which is accurate, but, true to his nature, he does not dwell on what moved in to take laughter's place. There's nothing very funny for very long about a pool of blood around a banana peel tossed on the cold sidewalk of the human condition.

We don't live in the world of goat bladders and banana peels anymore. On this crowded rush hour avenue it's urban everywhere now, which means a greater distance from the base material of animal bladders and fruit skin than an old vaudevillian such as Buster Keaton could have ever imagined. Can people slip on a plastic Starbucks coffee cup? Would that be funny? What if I hit that smartly dressed young woman on the head with her iPhone and made a loud bone-cracking noise? Ha ha ha.

I located only the horse's heart, the ventricles and atriums forming what resembled a tiny bagpipe. Staring at it, the loneliness rushed in and tightened around my own. A century before, horses – their power, grace, musky smell – would have been familiar here on this avenue, though their time, even then, was ending. Now we're haunted by equine ghosts, those of us who love history, or, rather, attend to its quiet music. A steam engine huffs up to a station, a horse lifts its head in a meadow, the meadow buzzes with the sound of gathering bees, an unschooled comedian hand-cranks a Bell & Howell camera. Husha, husha, we all fall down. And there isn't any sound at all.

I entered a Second Cup, and, with the transparent horse tucked under my arm, the magician bank in my other hand, ordered an Americano. The woman before me had ordered something that sounded like a milkshake with a bit of coffee breathed onto it. The drink was so large it needed a runway to arrive safely on the counter. I super-gulped as the woman hefted the frothy concoction to her red lips and sipped. At that rate, it would take her until the next rush hour to finish, and the idea made the toad, work, croak on my shoulder. It was still several hours until my first class, and to the first run of the streetcar. Despite my desire to escape, despite the silent urgings of my complicit Keaton Sherlock, I still couldn't step out of the heavy body of the responsible man. It was a burden, one not easily unburdened. In James Thurber's comic story, "The Secret Life of Walter Mitty," the protagonist exists in a wild imaginary world of daydreams, but is a henpecked husband and obedient citizen. For the life of me, I couldn't recall the ending. Hadn't Walter Mitty somehow imagined his way into a different life? I remembered something to do with fantasized episodes of heroism while he trailed his wife around a department store, trying to shut out her nagging. And then what?

So there I stood in the Second Cup, trying to imagine the imaginary world of a fictional character while I clutched my Dumpster-bin toys. All around me the responsible century gazed into its laptop screens and fiddled with its earbuds. I sleepwalked my way to a table, set down my horse and magician, and let the full force of the coffee-spout crash me to the metaphorical tracks. When the voice spoke, I did not think it addressed itself to me at first. And then, when I realized that it did, I thought the voice belonged to Walter Mitty's haranguing harridan of a wife.

It didn't. It belonged – and I swear on the box hives of my apiary Edmonton ancestry – to a three-hundred-pound man with a babyish face in a tight-fitting chocolate-coloured suit. He was young, crewcutted like all the young men today, in or out of the military, and wore a gold watch that cost more than a first edition of *Tess of the d'Urbervilles*; it clanked like a snapped handcuff as he reached his hand out to my transparent horse.

"I had one of these when I was a kid." His grin was genuine and joy-making. I thought perhaps a genie might emerge from the gap in his teeth. "That's the large intestine, that's the small."

"Really?" What I meant was, you had a transparent horse as a kid? The man couldn't have been more than twenty-three or -four. Were they still making transparent horses? What about transparent men? And by they, I meant the grim-faced Chinese peasantry, of course. I was certain they, meaning we, didn't make toy horses, piggy banks or any other toys on this continent anymore.

"Oh yeah. I had the transparent man, too." He looked at me with what appeared to be compassion. "It wasn't the jockey. The horse and the man didn't go together. Can I?" He reached hesitantly towards the horse.

I nodded, still gobsmacked by his face, a large blancmange in which the features of Fatty Arbuckle and Winston Churchill had been mixed. If he had announced, "This is our finest hour," and then pushed his forefinger into a dimple and winked coquettishly, I would have saluted and chuckled. While he revolved the horse in his huge, doughy hands, I considered him more closely. His hair was Prince Valiant black and heavily gelled, and, like many young people, he sported a tattoo to express his individuality – in his case, a heron-blue-and-lizard-green Chinese dragon flew on his bull neck from the right collarbone to an ear whose lobe dangled like a flapper's art deco earring. It made me think of that dragon guarding the treasure in *The Hobbit*. What was it called? Smog? Suddenly I felt overwhelmingly sad that I couldn't remember the last time I'd read *The Hobbit*. Had I even read it to my kids? While the fat young man's dragon flew, the stressed middle-aged man's toad croaked. Yet neither of us was transparent. We wore our flesh like goblin armour. I fought off the urge to call my uninvited guest Roscoe, to tell him, "For heaven's sake, whatever you do, don't go to the St. Francis Hotel in San Francisco for the Labour Day weekend. Stay here and talk about horses."

As if he'd heard me, the big man loosened the dark tie at his throat and announced, "A horse can outrun a train." Then, placing the toy gently on its four hooves, he added, "But a man can't outrun his fate."

No, he didn't. What he said was, "Why do you have these things? Do you own a toy store or something?"

A toy store! To own a toy store. Was that even possible? I knew that somebody sold the toys that the Chinese peasants sweated over, but it wasn't a single man, transparent or not, who owned Toys"R"Us and Walmart. Small business, if it exists at all, doesn't exist the way it did when I was a boy. A pang of admiring melancholy for the adults of my childhood washed over me, those men and women who, together, owned toy stores, shoe stores, convenience stores, bakeries, dry cleaners – and, yes, tack and butcher shops – those men and women who, knowing hard times, gratefully made a living and did not dream of expanding into franchise millionaires. They took the keys out of their pockets every misty October morning and unlocked the doors and turned the Closed sign around to Open. And then, in the misty late afternoons with the foghorns and the horns of the coal trains blowing somewhere behind Time, they turned the signs back around and locked the doors. They're locked forever now. Knock as hard as I can, I can never get in.

The past is so close, so intimate. It connects us, generation to generation, and then, abruptly, the chain breaks. The butcher shop of my fifth year in 1969 still had sawdust spread on the floors. The butcher always snapped a raw wiener out of a link and handed it to me. The giant head and antlers of a moose presided over the doorway. In would come Mrs. Hatt, the tall, skinny widow. She wore cloche hats and hose the colour of wet English sand and had teeth like a horse. One day I'd learn that Mrs. Hatt, when she was a little girl in London, watched Queen Victoria go by in a carriage. Queen Victoria! 1969. We reach out for history; we touch the fresh gravestone of Neil Armstrong who, denying death, will always take a small step. My brothers – senior citizens now – drove their Valiant and El Camino as teenagers to the beach at White Rock to see an old vaudevillian walk slowly along the tracks.

What had the big man asked me? Oh, yes.

"No. I don't own a toy store. I just bought these things." And then my age showed, as clearly as my underwear would have if I'd stood and dropped my pants. "For a lark."

His eyes, I noticed then, were pigeon-breast grey, soot soft and set far back from his surprisingly small nose. I supposed he was processing what I'd said, but his computer didn't quite go that far back. For a lark. That was Keaton and Arbuckle talk. Lord love a duck. Heavens to Murgatroyd. For Jiminy's sake. That was my parents' talk. Betsy and Pete probably owned the butcher shop that sold veal cutlets to the old lady who'd stared after Queen Victoria's horse-drawn carriage. My sigh was like the cosmic silence after the *Titanic* slipped under the icy Atlantic.

"Hey. Can I try the bank?" The chubby boy he had been suddenly bloomed to life in his face. As if to vouch for his character, he introduced himself. "I'm Charles Sleep." We shook hands.

"Tim Bowling," I said. And when I did, I saw the old Ladner Lanes again. I hadn't seen them in such a long time. The skinny Ouevray twins were pinsetters. They crouched out of sight behind the pins and, when you left a dreaded split, they magically cleared the rubble from the gap. Meanwhile, the whole town came out to bowl. Everyone kept their own scores, chewing on pencil ends, shading in the strikes and spares, working out the math. Shrouds of cigarette smoke. Laughter. Chants of "Hecky! Hecky! Hecky!" as my father readied to throw the last frame of a perfect game that did not end in perfection. One year his average was almost 300. His average! Come back and bowl me another game, Dad. With your grandson. He's fourteen, and his average is 150 and climbing. There aren't any pinsetters, though. Computers keep the score. You still have to take the bowling balls in your hands, and they still look like storm-battered versions of the planets. Come and bowl Jupiter one more time through the vapours.

"Are you all right?" Charles Sleep asked with genuine concern.

I brushed my eyes with the base of my palms and smiled. "Go ahead. Give it a try."

A few people at the neighbouring tables looked up from their laptops and phones to watch. The big man named Sleep stood and plunged his hands into his pants pockets. He grinned sheepishly.

"I don't have any coins."

This magician didn't take plastic. He was cast-iron through and through. By now, I longed for the past to stop knocking behind my eyelids and heart valves. Yes, yes, money itself would soon be gone, but it was only symbolic anyway. I put a dime into Fatty's palm and he grinned without any sheep appearing this time. Fatty put the dime on the magician's table, pressed the mechanism, lowered the top hat, vanished the dime and cried, "Cool." I saw the blood in his neck pump the dragon's wings.

A woman with long hair the colour of washed-out celluloid asked if she could try. I reached for another coin, but she had her own. Of course, she was probably a little older than me. The magician again performed his magic. The woman's smile would have melted the iceberg that sank the ... "Can I try?" A young woman with bright red glasses this time. Then a thirtyish black man in a UPS uniform, then two older men in grey suits, then one of the gals who worked at the Second Cup. Human beings were gathering en masse, just like all those brides in Keaton's *Seven Chances* who want to wed a millionaire. Coins clanked. Laughter. How about that? I sat there in stunned silence, feeling sorry for the little transparent horse whose transparency had become invisibility. The magician offered illusion, but the horse stripped illusion away and revealed the trick that gave the horse its power. We don't really want that degree of truth, and yet we live in an age of science and reason. The paradox rose up and died away in the random delight of ordinary humanity. What brought these people to my franchise table had brought my grandfather and his siblings and thousands of other Edmontonians in 1913 to the grand opening of Alexander Pantages's vaudeville theatre. The broken chain relinked.

As I watched a dozen strangers laugh and fumble with coins, suddenly a lovely silence enveloped them; they became actors on the screen, circa 1921. Now I was truly the boy projectionist, watching not the distant past but rather the entrancing present. Yet I could not stir my spirit self to rise and join the fun; it was too heavy with material experience, the way a field of grass in autumn can't stand tall until the sun has burned the frost away. I sat there, so close to life, and all my apprehensions about the day and months and years ahead would not let me close enough to live. I knew it, and I fought myself, in fierce silence. According to Socrates, the unexamined life is not worth living. But what about the too-examined life? I let the merrymakers of illusion burn the frost from my eyes as the sounds of the franchise coffee shop returned – the prepackaged, programmed, market-tested music; the grinding of the espresso machine – and the workday punched its clock with a fist like a fetus. Why was the capacity to enjoy life to the fullest so fraught with the feeling that defeats enjoyment?

Buster Keaton filmed *Sherlock Jr.* with all of his senses on fire – no young man has ever been so fulfilled. Fatty Arbuckle, that prince of a giant man, threw the most lavish parties. Together, the two comedians pranked their way through the halcyon early days of the little town called Hollywood. Everything was fun. "In the silent days we could try anything at all, and did," Keaton said. "We were not supervised by business executives who lacked a sense of humor.... In the early twenties we also had a whale of a time for ourselves after working hours playing practical jokes." What they did on the set, they carried over off the set: impersonating city workmen to threaten a millionaire actress's cherished lawn with picks and shovels, impersonating chauffeurs to give a visiting studio boss a terrifying madcap ride, impersonating butlers to make a dinner party hilariously unforgettable. Once, they constructed an elaborate gag involving fake Belgian royalty and a fake state dinner that was so well orchestrated and acted that the duped host of the royal visitors didn't know he was the victim of a practical joke until he was told three months later. For Keaton and Arbuckle, there was almost no separation between work and life. It was just as if I lived the stories I wrote each day. Youth! Freedom! Humour!

Then it all came crashing down. Overnight, Arbuckle was ruined. Within a decade, so was Keaton. The frost deepened on my eyelids as Fatty's face put on a perplexed scowl and the laughers around him darkened to a mob. Only it wasn't the face of Fatty Arbuckle; it was the face of Charles Sleep, and his living hands were shaking my little magician.

"You jammed it," a woman said plaintively.

"But I didn't." Charles Sleep looked desperately around at the scowling faces. His cheeks were tinged red, his brow looked slick. "I didn't do it. It wasn't me." Suddenly he met my eyes. "Honest. I wouldn't."

The older woman with the celluloid hair gently took the bank from Sleep's hands. "Let me try."

Clank. Clank. It was no good. The top hat would not lift. She tried to slip a finger underneath the brim. The UPS man tried next. The girl in red glasses made a suggestion. Charles Sleep's face pulled back like the moon that had seen too much horror on the earth.

A voice said, "You put a quarter in. It was too big." There was a palpable sense of disgust. Charles Sleep blinked feverishly, all little boy now, bewildered by a vicious, adult world he couldn't understand. I had to give him his illusions back. I had to give my own back.

I smiled. Like any decent man in the tangible world, I yoked my material and spirit selves, and then sailed into the fray. "It's all right. I'm sure you didn't do it. The toy's old. It's probably just rusted. A little oil and . . ."

The mob wasn't buying it. They crouched like trolls under a bridge, waiting for the clatter of goat hooves. I took the bank in my hands, pushed my forefinger under the top hat and closed my eyes to conjure up the laughter. Remember *The Butcher Boy*, I told myself. 1917. New York City. Keaton's first screen appearance. He goes to a country store to buy a bucket of molasses, and he drops his coin into the molasses. Fatty tries to help him get it out. Somehow Buster's hat gets stuck to his head. Fatty yanks at it. Mayhem! The silent comedy, which is every bit as much a part of the human condition as . . .

It was no use. The fun was over, the crowd drifted away, the wrecking ball crashed into the side of the Pantages Theatre. Charles Sleep simply didn't know what hit him. The sweat on his brow now turned to tears of frustration in his eyes. It was just after Labour Day in 2012, the Enbridge Tower of humourless executives towered over us, and Charles Sleep, a man of his time, offered up the solution of his time. Though he wasn't guilty, he offered to pay, not with his career, not with his whole jocular and trusting self, but with money, our age's plastic Shroud of Turin.

"I'm sorry," he said in a hoarse whisper. "If I hadn't asked to look at it, this wouldn't have happened. Listen, I was going to ask to buy it anyway. How about a hundred bucks? Will that do?"

Immediately, as a man of my time, I gulped like a bullhead at the dangled profit bait. Then my humanity flooded in and I wondered if I could find the homeless balloonatic and really make his day. At last, the waterspout of humanity broke open and crashed me to the tracks. Who could make a young man named Sleep pay for the end of all illusions? Not me. Some things are not for sale.

I reached out and shook his trembling, sweaty hand, but not to close a transaction.

"I know you didn't wreck it. It's an old toy and it's lasted a long time. The coin will come loose." I suddenly realized that the magician and the transparent horse could never be separated, the way the elderly Keaton could never really be separated from the young genius. "I want to take it home for my kids."

"Are you sure?"

Then Charles Sleep did two surprising things. He reached tremblingly into his coat's breast pocket, the way Elisha Cook Jr. always reached for his gat in John Huston's *The Maltese Falcon*, and extracted a small card, a business card. It read: Charles Sleep, Unit Manager, Systems and Protocols, Enbridge Corporation. It was the address that really caught my eye. No, it more than caught my eye; both my eyes were spiderwebbed and fixed in a kind of disbelieving horror that was so close to pleasure that the ghost of John Keats coughed blood mildly in the mists of Parnassus. Charles Sleep worked in the Enbridge Tower!

I didn't know why this information shook me to the core. After all, hundreds of people must work on those twenty floors that don't have a thirteenth floor, and most of those hundreds were probably milling around these few Jasper Avenue blocks before cracking the workday's whip in earnest. But you must understand: I was a solitary individual, and I didn't generally engage with strangers at all, except in the most fleeting of instances. That I should meet a fat man who looked like Roscoe Arbuckle and worked where Edmonton's Pantages Theatre once stood didn't just defy the odds; it put a rent in the universe. The card throbbed like Braille in my hand. I felt the long sidewalk of time tip very briefly back into the past.

Then Charles Sleep, in a few quick motions, spoiled everything. He pulled a mobile device from his capacious wardrobe, pushed a few pudgy fingers across the little screen, paused, his face wearing that very contemporary mix of intensity and boredom, and finally announced, "You might really have something there. Shit. I sure hope it's not wrecked." He held the screen out on his palm like the host of a god he believed in but didn't pray to.

And there, in the magical, multicoloured conglomeration of pixels, appeared my cast-iron magician bank. One just like it was listed on eBay.

"There's a few of them," Charles Sleep mused as he laid his phone down and took up the bank. "Some are reproductions, worth only about fifty bucks. But if this is an original . . ."

Days. "Days are where we live." So says Philip Larkin. But I didn't generally live in days anything like this one.

"Here's one going for seven grand." He had somehow retrieved his phone. I hadn't seen him or it move. Perhaps, I thought, the technologies had caught up to *Star Trek*'s beaming powers, at least for small objects. It was certainly possible. Being a man who didn't own a cellphone (I couldn't shake the association with prison, and that movie moment when the unjustly accused gets one call to a lawyer), I tended to lag behind the contemporary pace of change. Well, more than lag.

"Seven grand?" Now my tongue was as spiderwebbed as my eyes. I couldn't articulate the impact of that sum. I made barely five thousand dollars to teach thirty teenagers the rudiments of grammar for four months. To think that some homeless guy had just handed me six months of teaching income! "Strange days have found us," to quote Jim Morrison of The Doors, who also sang, "people are strange when you're a stranger." And when are we really ever anything else, even to ourselves?

I WAS NO cavalier Buster Keaton when it came to money. I cared about it, I cared a great deal. Money was freedom, and freedom was . . . it wasn't a fast car or a tropical holiday or an Italian villa in the Hollywood hills. "Whatever else poetry is freedom," wrote Irving Layton. And freedom, then, must be poetry. One rises spirit-like out of the body of the other. There's no escape, not really.

I recalled one of my favourite works of short fiction, "In Dreams Begin Responsibilities," by the poet Delmore Schwartz. The story occurred to me just then, the way that sweet childhood flavour occurred to Proust's narrator in *In Search of Lost Time*, except that my memory immediately released the curious wild stench of rotting salmon that I'd been smelling since the middle of the night. Proust put his mouth to a memory hidden in a madeleine, while I ignored the stench and pressed every intellectual and emotional substance of my being against a written text, the *memory* of a written text. Was that itself a kind of dream? If so, how was I responsible?

Schwartz's story is about a man who watches, on a screen in a movie theatre, the history of his parents' courtship. It *is* *Sherlock Jr.*, except darker, colder. Schwartz was a little boy when Keaton made his brilliant, out-of-body marvel – had the film influenced him?

The story opens, "I think it is the year 1909. I feel as if I were in a moving-picture theatre." The narrator then describes watching a scene from a silent film. After a few sudden jumps and flashes, the action begins. It is a specific June day in Brooklyn. The narrator sees his young father walking the streets, "once in a while coming to an avenue on which a streetcar skates and gnaws," and jingling the coins in his pocket. *This* is interesting. Schwartz writes, "I feel . . . I am anonymous. I have forgotten myself: it is always so when one goes to a movie; it is, as they say, a drug."

Drugged, we watch the narrator's father enter the house of his future in-laws, meet his future wife and take her on a date to Coney Island. All the while, we are given psychological insights into the characters of these two young people; both are playing a part dictated by their time and circumstances. As the date progresses, as the couple strolls along the boardwalk and gazes at the ocean, the narrator can't bear the inevitability of their fate. He starts to cry, stands up and, stumbling over the feet of the other people in his row, goes to the men's room. When he returns, the film's still running, but several hours of screen time appear to have passed. His parents are dining at one of the best restaurants on the boardwalk, and suddenly, the narrator's father proposes. The woman, who, remember, carries the possibility of the narrator deep inside her, sobbingly, joyously accepts. Now the story shifts to a fiercer, more heartbreaking gear. The narrator stands up in the theatre and shouts, "'Don't do it! . . . Nothing good will come of it, only remorse, hatred, scandal, and two children whose characters are monstrous.'" The whole audience, annoyed, turns to look at the narrator. An usher appears, waving a flashlight. The old lady in the neighbouring seat tells the narrator to be quiet or else he'll be put out. So the narrator shuts his eyes. But only briefly. He cannot stop watching the film, and, of course, neither can we, especially not after what he's just shouted.

The date continues. The couple has a photo taken in a photographer's booth, and then they begin to argue about whether or not to go into a fortune teller's booth. Finally, they enter. The fortune teller appears. The father says it's all nonsense; he tugs the mother's arm but she refuses to budge. Angry, the father strides out, leaving the mother stunned. Horrified, the narrator rises again and shouts, "'What are they doing? Don't they know what they are doing?'" This time, the usher not only appears, he seizes the narrator's arm, begins to drag him out and says, "'What are *you* doing? . . . . You can't carry on like this, it is not right, you will find that out soon enough, everything you do matters too much.'"

There is no moustached villain to trail here, no lounge lizard and butler to outwit. Yet the story concludes with the same disappearance of illusion. The narrator is dragged "through the lobby of the theatre, into the cold light, [where he wakes up] into the bleak winter morning on my twenty-first birthday, the window-sill shining with its lip of snow, and the morning already begun."

It's a terrifying story about tragic fate, and I felt it rush through me, the words and the images whirling, as if I was the theatre and the narrator, and the film was playing and the story being written inside me. It seemed that Schwartz's fiction had stepped out of the body of Keaton's movie. A cold wind gusted through the Second Cup. The magician bank was like a block of ice in my hands. Silent movies, streetcars, coins. At one point, the narrator's parents even ride the horses on a carousel! But it's the riders who are transparent – and yet the horror of the vision, the horror of all tragic vision, is what are we seeing when we see? I trembled in the sudden cold, and my shaking intensified when I heard the low growl and smelled the wild odour of my distant youth. But when I looked around the café, I saw only the day's ordinary beings.

When I looked back, Charles Sleep still held the little screen of his phone in front of me. I focused on it again, all sense of real time lost. Had minutes passed, or only seconds? Eternity breathed down my neck. And the breath smelled of woodsmoke and salmon spawn.

"I think it could be an original," he said. "You ought to take it to an expert."

An expert? Take *what* to an expert? Dreams, tragic visions – how do you take them anywhere? And besides, we're all experts. Heavily, heavily, I fought my way back from art to life.

"You work in the Enbridge Tower?"

My question took him aback. He withdrew his phone, and nodded slowly.

"If you don't mind me asking, what sort of businesses are in there?" I didn't expect – or even hope – for him to say, "There's an antiques dealer who specializes in old toys," but I also didn't anticipate the blunt answer.

"Just one."

My jaw must have dropped like the magician's top hat onto the table.

"It's all Enbridge," Charles Sleep explained dully. "It's a big company."

"One?" I simply could not fathom the idea. One company occupied the whole tower, all . . .

"Yep. All twenty floors. I'm on the eighteenth."

I almost blushed. Once again, I felt like an alien in the twenty-first century. Approaching fifty years old, and it had never even occurred to me that a single company could occupy an entire skyscraper.

"But . . . but what does Enbridge do exactly?"

It was as if I'd let all the air out of Fatty Arbuckle's fame. Suddenly, I had given him his regular workday morning back; taken away his childhood of transparent horses and replaced it with management systems. It wasn't even that Charles Sleep didn't enjoy management work; he might have found it wholly rewarding. But this morning in the Second Cup had been a change, and change is always exhilarating.

He cleared his throat as he slipped his phone back into his clothing. "Oil and gas. It's Enbridge Pipelines. Resource extraction and transport."

I wanted to ask him, specifically, what his own job involved, but he no longer seemed as receptive to conversation. Besides, no matter what people did at Enbridge, there wouldn't be as much variety as what humans had done at the Pantages Theatre. After all, another term for vaudeville *is* variety. Opera singers, magicians, acrobats, comedians, sword swallowers, tap dancers. A disorienting image flashed into my mind of all these vaudeville acts entering the Enbridge Tower, showing their passes to security and rising on the elevator to twenty storeys of little theatres. Maybe Delmore Schwartz would be waiting in one of them with a bag of popcorn. Maybe he would shout at Buster Keaton as he entered in his slap shoes, "'What are *you* doing? Don't you know you can't do things like this, you can't do whatever you want to do. . . . You will be sorry if you do not do what you should do.'" Maybe the shout was directed at me.

Charles Sleep spoke softly, as if he did not wish to wake me up. "Please let me know what you find out. I'm curious. My phone and email are on the card."

What should we do? That is a very large question, a question for philosophers and artists, but philosophers and artists are also workers who live in the world. In the world, what we should do is take the old toy bought off the homeless guy for ten bucks, sell it for several thousand and invest the difference in Enbridge shares. On the expectation that oil prices would rise again, creatures from the black lagoon. I'm not being facetious. The world is the world. Delmore Schwartz – did I mention? – was a manic-depressive schizophrenic who died penniless and forgotten, after great fame and success in his youth, in the hallway of a seedy hotel. No one claimed his body in the morgue for three days.

Charles Sleep had turned and walked away. Without even thinking about it, I followed him, astonished all over again by his uncanny resemblance to Fatty Arbuckle. Both were large men who wore their pants belted high at the waist, as if to accentuate the surprising thinness of their lower halves, the almost balletic delicacy of their movements. I didn't quite fall into step with Charles Sleep, the way Keaton as Sherlock Jr. fell into step, beautifully and hilariously, with the villain, but I was aware of the parallel. I was even more aware of the sudden lead-like heaviness of my own movement, which reminded me, in shocking succession, of two things: the first line of Delmore Schwartz's most famous poem, "The heavy bear who goes with me," and the heartbreaking fact that, when Keaton, at the age of forty-five, learned of his mother's death, he walked the streets of Paris alone for five hours. Never mind genius: a man who loved his mother enough to walk in grief for five solid hours, carrying that heavy bear and all her lifetime of cubs on his back, is a man I respect and can relate to.

As I followed Charles Sleep along Jasper Avenue towards

the old Pantages Theatre that was now a skyscraper housing a single oil and gas company, I vowed to call my ninety-year-old mother as soon as possible. Before my five solid hours of walking and bearing, which would probably not occur in Paris, I needed to do as much living as I could. The wet and heavy and tattered fur of my mid-life sensibility would, one way or another, be shed or skinned, but the pumping, psychological placenta that binds us to the body – no, the bodies, for the father is there, too – of the life that gave us life has a much different existence. Fatty Arbuckle, I recalled, lost both his parents as a child, when his father abandoned him and his mother died. I heard the sound of gumboots sloshing through starlight and tears. And the sound, as sound did to the great silent comedians, caused me to lose my way. Or, rather, caused me to lose Charles Sleep in the commuting crowd.

It was just as well, since I had no idea why I was trailing him. Perhaps I wanted something magical to happen; perhaps I wanted to wind up on the handlebars of a motorcycle speeding wildly through the streets of 1924. Instead, I stopped dead on an avenue of the new millennium, clutching my perhaps valuable magician bank and my transparent horse, and pondered my next move. I didn't need a watch to tell me what time it was; it was fast approaching the time to address the future, the future in the form of thirty pairs of blinking teenaged eyes. They opened before me, then, an audience in a small theatre, poised between silence and sound, waiting for my pratfall, waiting to see how I would handle this straitjacket they would likely one day, in one form or another, inherit. I had stopped dead, except I wasn't dead.

The heavy bear who went with me sat cowed and compliant on the cement, like a collared creature from the Elizabethan age who no longer rose to the bait. I blinked and blinked, willing the image away. But it wouldn't go – and somehow I knew I had added one more ghostly companion to my day, one more sensory overload, a heavy bear who, quite naturally, smelled of forest fires and rotting salmon. I decided to name him Delmore.

"It's about time, too," the suddenly visible animal snarled. "You'd think a poet could take a hint. Maybe you're not much of a poet." He reared up on his hind legs and pushed his snout into my face. His breath was the smell of my hometown fishing canneries combined with a hobo's wet woollen socks. "Besides, my mother named me, not you, boychick. She gave me this ridiculous name, so don't you go claiming that dubious honour."

"What's so ridiculous about it?" I took a step back as he dropped onto all fours with a grunt.

"Delmore Schwartz? What kind of name is Delmore for a Jew? You're a Gentile. And your name's a hundred proof Gentile. What the hell's mine? A bad marriage, that's what. Like my parents' marriage. Why do you think I wrote that story you love so much? Why do you think I made up characters with names like Shenandoah Fish?"

I had no useful response, mostly because I was so taken aback by the immediate intimacy of this new relationship. It already seemed as powerful as the intimacy I shared with Keaton's ghost. And Delmore Schwartz, after all, had published a book called *Vaudeville for a Princess and Other Poems*. Even more to the point, Delmore Schwartz had taught at several universities, and he had never felt entirely in his element there. In fact, he survived in the way that Keaton himself survived – he tried to enjoy the comedy in his situation, at least until mental illness deprived him of his gifts. Once, in class, a female student had misread T. S. Eliot's line from "The Love Song of J. Alfred Prufrock," "Shall I part my hair behind?" as "Shall I part my bare behind?" Well, even the most philosophical, existential, woe-laden man has to get a chuckle out of that!

Once again, the walking commuters flowed past me. And once again, I commanded only a mild and glancing notice. The difference, in a city, between a distracted man with toys standing on a busy street and that same man sitting in a café is oddly considerable. It's as if we just don't believe that a lunatic or a derelict will sit calmly down to drink a coffee. If he does, it will probably be at a McDonald's or a Tim Hortons, not a Second Cup – lunatics aren't sensible enough to drink coffee, and derelicts can't afford a second cup, not unless they find and sell a magician bank worth seven thousand dollars.

The thought warmed me and cooled me at once, the way money does. My possible astonishing good fortune collided with my nagging sense of morality that would insist upon finding the balloonatic and sharing the windfall. So much of life turned on the taps of two temperatures simultaneously, as if we must constantly wash our souls with our faces. As F. Scott Fitzgerald famously wrote, "The test of a first-rate intelligence is the ability to hold two opposed ideas in the mind at the same time, and still retain the ability to function."

Delmore, lumbering along at my side, grumbled, "Don't remind me. I always meant to write a book on Fitzgerald. My problem was that I held about six opposed projects in my mind at the same time and could hardly function at all. I was still a genius, though. The Great Gadfly." He chuckled at the witticism, or at least he made whatever sound a bear makes when it's amused.

As for me, I stood at the crossroads of that Fitzgerald intelligence sign, exactly where Buster Keaton stood in the early 1930s at MGM, when it became obvious that the glory days of his creativity were behind him, that he could not push through the wardrobe into Narnia ever again. For nearly two years he lost the ability to function, as the opposing freedom of the past overwhelmed the cold, systemic present. He drank, and drank hard. He describes this period bluntly and briefly in his auto-biography, in a chapter entitled "The Chapter I Hate to Write," as the worst two years of his life. During this period, Keaton spent time straitjacketed in an asylum and ended up marrying the private nurse who had been assigned to look after him. The marriage was a disaster, with the best thing about it being that it didn't last long. That second wife, as so often happens to people who become footnotes in the lives of the famous, suffered a tragic and mysterious fate: she was committed herself on several occasions, and eventually just vanished, never to be heard of again, one of the millions of humans for whom there is no clear final chapter.

Which of these commuters walking by, I wondered, would suffer the tragic fate of Mae Scriven, Buster Keaton's second wife? I shook the thought off, and returned to what was left of practicalities.

There were still hours to go before my first class, a class I knew I couldn't teach. At eleven, I planned to be on a streetcar heading south with Delmore, Buster's ghost and my Dumpster-bin treasure. Yet I had not lost all sense of responsibility. I decided to go to campus, to my classroom, and write in big bold letters on the chalkboard (which is no longer chalk), CLASS CANCELLED TODAY. Then . . . well, what then? Unlike Keaton, I had no team of gag men to help me plot my next feature move, no technical whiz like Fred Gabourie who, after *Sherlock Jr.*, announced with breathless excitement to Buster that he'd just found a huge ocean liner that they could buy and use as a prop (the result was *The Navigator*, one of Keaton's greatest films). I had an imaginary bear who wept, a silent film ghost who remained true to silence, and my own sense of reality, which might either have been slipping away or speeding straight at me like an express train, depending on how you define reality. One fact was clear enough: the more I taught, the less I would write. And if I did not write, what would keep me out of a straitjacket? Yet what I wanted to write didn't pay me enough to support a family of five. I couldn't expect street people to go on supplying me with vintage treasures four or five times a year, nor could I take a management position up on the eighteenth floor of the Enbridge Tower with Charles Sleep.

Oh, but that was only equivocation. I knew well enough what the real trouble was: I had reached the age when, everywhere I looked, I saw the tears in things. I also knew well enough what the passing, practical world would say: "Get a grip, pal, you hardly have problems – you have a job, shelter, enough to eat, a loving family. You're damned lucky." These were the same people who belonged to Keaton's fan club, the Damfinos, and who insisted, again and again, that Keaton's story wasn't tragic. They had no idea. None. If you're an artist like Keaton who had, for over a decade, complete artistic freedom *and* commercial success, anything that comes after, no matter how pleasant to the ordinary world, feels like failure. From 1997 to 2010, I worked full-time as a literary author, produced twelve books and supported my family. Now I needed to teach more and more to survive. I thought of Delmore Schwartz, and then I thought of the ferociously practical Robert Frost. Very likely the most celebrated and successful American poet of all time, a four-time winner of the Pulitzer Prize, who even read a poem at the inauguration of John F. Kennedy, Frost didn't achieve any kind of success until he was into his forties. Perhaps that's why he had such a calculating attitude towards fame and money, an attitude that Keaton did not have as a young man but very much developed as the decades put him through the financial wringer. Frost's attitude comes across powerfully in "Provide, Provide," a poem that might very well have been written with the whole silent film era in mind, a poem that refers to a former "picture pride of Hollywood" who falls to the lowly condition of a cleaning lady. "No memory of having starred," Frost writes, "Atones for later disregard / Or keeps the end from being hard."

Keaton could have related. The speculation is that he worked so much in the last decade of his life, never turning anything down, because he wanted to provide for his much younger third wife, who was as good for him as his second wife had been bad. As for Keaton's first wife, Natalie Talmadge, she had basically compensated for the lack of a film career rivalling those of her famous sisters by spending Buster's money as fast as he could earn it. She often spent nine hundred dollars a week, and the Italian villa itself, the large mansion she so desired, cost $250,000, as much as it cost Alexander Pantages to build the lavish vaudeville theatre in Edmonton. All this wealth and spending couldn't save the marriage, especially once Keaton wound up miserable, his creativity fettered, at MGM. Natalie Keaton's bitterness toward her ex-husband remains one of the great mysteries in Keaton's biography. She so loathed him that she wouldn't let him see his two sons for most of their childhoods. In the last decades of her life, she wouldn't even let Buster's name be spoken in her presence, and died in 1969 just as bitter as she'd been at the time of the divorce in 1932. Not a single one of Keaton's biographers, and certainly not Keaton himself, ever adequately explained Natalie's gargantuan hostility, except to suggest that her controlling and interfering stage mother poisoned Natalie against Buster. But such a suggestion seems an inadequate explanation. One point remains clear about the marriage, though – Natalie loved to spend, and Buster, as he admitted many times, wasn't interested in money.

But he became interested. And I had become interested,

too, more and more as I stumbled into mid-career and found that, as my imagination flourished and my skills increased, recognition became a scarcer commodity. At the same time, living expenses, the basics required to raise a family, increased. Where once I happily made do on little and the eternal promise for more, I now found the cold winds of the world blowing through my empty billfold. The romantic faith that I would be sufficiently rewarded materially if I did good work had been shaken to its foundation. I stood on Jasper Avenue, like Keaton on the dusty street in *Steamboat Bill, Jr.*, and waited for the front of the house to crash over my head. For Keaton, everything in the film had been measured to inches, and he survived the dangerous stunt when the open window of the house front passed right over him. For me, the house with all its unpaid mortgage payments crushed me, and the blood that ran out of my skull had no poetry in it; it was just blood. Hemingway claimed that the world breaks everyone, and that if you don't break, the world will simply kill you. "It kills the very good and the very gentle and the very brave impartially," according to Papa, who added that if you are none of these, the world will still kill you but with no particular hurry.

My goodness and bravery were, admittedly, small scale, but I possessed them. I had tried to be true to my artistic vision by living on my wits, and now I was sitting on the set of a bad studio comedy, miscast, and weeping for the minor triumphs of my youth. The world was in a hurry to crush me, as it was in a hurry to crush everyone. It didn't matter that I wasn't famous like Keaton, or that I'd never been wealthy. I had published a few good books, and I wanted to build on them. But what I had done could not save me from the chill intimations of mortality, the painful knowledge that I couldn't protect my children or anyone else's from the hard truths of the human condition. Provide! Provide! If Robert Frost was such a wise old soul, why couldn't his poem help me? Why did the image of Keaton as a cigar-store Indian in a 1960s beach movie drive such a sharp dagger into the base of my cerebral cortex? I didn't even have to sing to the passing commuters, "Don't cry for me, bourgeois Canada." Who would cry? Most of my fellow citizens would sneer, hurl abuse or look away in perplexed embarrassment. My plight would be unrecognizable to them, but no less real for that – oh no, it was all too real, and the isolation only deepened the coldness of the reality.

I moved my chilled body towards the chill in the risen late summer sun. Frost's "Provide! Provide!" dredged Henry David Thoreau's advice up from my memory banks, the only banks that had ever been kind to me. In *Walden*, Thoreau urged his fellow citizens to slow down and live less complicated lives. He wrote, "Simplify, simplify." And Keaton, the discarded waxwork in *Sunset Boulevard*, muttered, "Pass. Pass." I simply did not know what to do.

How cold was I then? Colder than I'd ever been in my life, but not as cold as the body of Delmore Schwartz lying unclaimed in the morgue for three days. No, where there's smoke, there's fire, and where there's fire, there's hope for warmth. I decided to let the day unfold. I would cancel my first class, I would find a pay phone and call my elderly mother, and then I would conduct my curious entourage to my own little streetcar named Desire and, with all my spirit and imagination, shout silently from the middle of the High Level Bridge, "Bus – ter! Bus – ter!" As plans go, it had the virtue of difference, and difference means what metaphor means in a poem: surprise. There was no surprise for Delmore Schwartz's corpse. I pointed my heavy compass to campus.

And the heavy bear named Delmore stirred his big black flour bag of tears and came with me, mumbling through his sobs a few lines from the poem that kept him, and his creator, alive: "That heavy bear who sleeps with me . . . / Howls in his sleep because the tight-rope / Trembles and shows the darkness beneath."

"Never mind, Delmore," I consoled, knowing how terrified he was. Then it occurred to me that I should include another viewing of *Sherlock Jr.* somewhere in my day. After all, Keaton had made his homage to film because he deeply appreciated the power of film to hide the darkness beneath. And Delmore Schwartz had depended on film's ability to do just that. As he wrote in another short story, "Screeno," which takes place almost entirely in a theatre: "Drenched by such a tasteless, colorless mood, there was only one refuge, one sanctuary: the movies."

11

WE SLEEPWALKED the ten minutes to Grant MacEwan University, though I did note the large grey towers on the horizon, an architectural anomaly that always made me think of J.R.R. Tolkien's *The Lord of the Rings*. But I rarely felt a sense of magic or fantastic escape as I approached. This morning was no different. The bodies and the faces, as usual, grew younger as we neared the campus; it was as if the falling autumn leaves had burst into spring life on the way down off the branches. Youth! How much promise and time and hope – yet who is more woe-laden than the young? Their strong, vital bodies so often house the hearts of marble statues. I looked away from their faces. I had none of that vampiric desire some teachers have to suck on the jugular of youth's spirit. In fact, I had always been extremely careful to maintain a strict professional distance with my students –

the importance of the comma splice, not the vastness of the darkness beneath, was what I taught. I could help with the former; with the latter, they were, along with the rest of us, mostly on their own.

Even so, I felt the atmosphere lighten around me as the concentration of the franchises gave way to a single small food court selling fat and sugar to the stressed-out scholars. But it was early September, and there was still more optimism for the beginning term in the air than anxiety. Delmore chuckled. "Shall I part my bare behind?" I shushed him, but smiled despite myself.

Not at all to my surprise, he wasn't about to let me off the hook.

"You're laying it on just a bit thick, you know. Try being a Jew in an Ivy League college. Those bastards really had it in for me." He grimaced, and I could see the slobber hanging off his fangs. "Besides, what exactly are *you* falling from? I had letters of praise from Eliot before I was thirty. I was featured in *Vogue* for Chrissakes. I looked exactly like Apollo, too. Everyone said so." Breathing hard, he tilted his great ursine head towards the sun, as if he was Hamlet holding Yorick's remains aloft. "The nobility of my head, that's what did it. Why do you think I exist in the afterlife as a goddamned bear?"

I blinked at him, not sure if he was serious. "Because of your poem. The heavy bear who goes with you, et cetera."

"No." He extended and retracted his claws. "Because of the impressiveness of my head. And because of my power and fame. The Jewish Robert Frost, that's what I was. Though it's more accurate to call him the Gentile Delmore Schwartz."

We had reached the hallway outside my classroom, and reality rushed in again: the lecturing to indifferent faces, the terrible faux-god marking and grading, the desperate stand-up act under the scalding administrative lights. By the time I stepped through the door to my windowless classroom with its bare walls, all the stultifying weight of the institution had crashed over me. Delmore, who had refused to pass through the door, held his great shaggy head in his hands and cried, "No no no no no."

I turned back to see him with his paws over his eyes.

He wailed, "The stage fright, the stage fright! I was a grotesque before every class. Worse than a polka clown, a burlesque queen. No no no no."

His behaviour didn't help, nor did Randall Jarrell's claim that the gods who had taken away a poet's readers had given him students. Jarrell meant this to be a cause of some celebration. But then, he and his second wife liked to dress up in costumes and act out parts of their favourite fairy tales. I stepped into the room and glanced at the seats rising in a half-ring, like a Greek or even a vaudeville theatre, and sighed with relief that I would not be performing the next show. With a coloured marker, I began to write, but had managed only CLASS CANCE when an excited voice stopped me short.

"Professor! Hey, Professor!"

I whirled around, my heart in my mouth. No one – no one real, that is – had spoken to me since Charles Sleep had said goodbye, and he had looked so much like Fatty Arbuckle that I didn't even feel as if the twenty-first century had been a part of his dialogue. At first, I couldn't locate the source of the cry. It had seemed to come from directly behind me, but no one was there. I must have rubbed my glasses or somehow looked confused, because the voice – which I had recognized as female – now cried, "Up here!" Sure enough, in a corner of the highest row, tucked in against the blank taupe wall, sat a blurred shape that slowly assumed the form of a young woman.

"I'm way early," she said, and plucked the earbuds from her ears as if her head was a switchboard and she was about to leave on her 1956 lunch hour. When she descended the rows towards me, I couldn't shake the disturbing impression that she was about to widen her eyes, turn dramatically sideways to make a prow of one shoulder and announce, "All right, Mr. DeMille, I'm ready for my close-up." From the doorway, Delmore whispered, "Teaching is vaudeville," and I saw the ghost of Keaton, just beyond, framing the classroom with his index finger and thumb over one eye. I looked back to the young woman, and it seemed that the film had jumped, for she already stood at ground level. There was a quality of rushing water to her, and I flinched, as if about to be knocked hard to the railroad tracks of *Sherlock Jr.*

"I'm totally into this course," she said, and I thought she referred to her own watery motion. "English is my best subject. Well, so's home ec. I love to cook, but I love to read even more. Maybe I should read more cookbooks. But I don't think there's an English teacher anywhere who'd assign a cookbook." She laughed.

The young woman was just like all young women to me – so close to my daughter's age that I had to fight the urge to say, "Hi, kiddo." It wasn't a matter of disrespect; I simply couldn't lose sight of the age gap between me and my students. They were all starting the day shift as I was punching the night clock. Out of courtesy, I forced myself to look at this young woman. Caucasian, round-faced, light red hair pulled back into a short ponytail. Her face had a filmic quality, but not an archival one from the silent film era. This girl was too present to be anywhere but the exact moment that we inhabited together. Yet why did I feel as if we were suddenly cut adrift on an abandoned ocean liner headed for 1924?

Her voice – clear and cheerful but with a decided streetwise edge – returned me to the world. "I'm Chelsea. Chels. Everyone calls me Chels. Hey, what's up with the horse?"

I looked at the desk where I had placed the Dumpster-bin toys.

"Oh . . . uh . . . I just bought them this morning." My voice trailed off.

She narrowed her eyes at me, and the sharp blast of her confident intelligence almost made me gasp. It was so direct and honest and . . . well . . . genuine. I felt that I had just swallowed an intellectual breath mint.

Delmore, who had lumbered up behind me, shoved his snout into my neck. "Intellectual breath mint. That's not half bad."

"This morning?" the girl asked. "Really? Where do you get your morning coffee? The Timmy's where I go doesn't sell transparent horses or . . . what is this, a bank?"

The heavy bear's mulchy breath crept up my nape to my scalp. He growled, "Not half bad. All bad."

Chelsea touched the magician's top hat and clucked delightedly. With every second that passed, I grew more and more uncomfortable. I stood there, a full container of toxins on the shore of a salmon-spawning stream.

"It's jammed," I said softly, happy to ignore Delmore and to avoid the subject of where I'd purchased the toys.

She nodded, then turned her attention to the horse. She held it on its side, in both hands, and I could feel the intensity of her gaze pouring like smoke off her mind. "I used to ride horses. Well, I did for a while, when my mom had the money. But I never thought about what was *inside* of them."

"No," I said stupidly, for want of anything else to say. For what could I say to this girl's quick, inquiring spirit, except "Flee!" There ought to have been a skull and crossbones on my face.

Delmore sighed. "Ah, yes, they flee from us who sometime did us seek."

"Shut up," I hissed out of the side of my mouth. "She's a child. What the hell's wrong with you?"

He just shrugged, which I hadn't known a bear could even do.

The girl placed the horse down gently on its four legs, and smiled. "I've read some of the essays on the syllabus already. I thought I should before things got too crazy."

Too crazy? Child, I thought, you have no idea. In an effort to avoid her piercing eyes, I dropped my own. Doing so, I noticed her clothes. She wore a cardigan, of all things, a tan, brown-buttoned cardigan about a size too large for her. Even though I understood it was a matter of style, the tectonic shift in chronology intensified my disorientation.

"That's very sensible," I said, loathing my professor voice, feeling the cold sweat form on my brow. "Term does get busy pretty fast."

Fast? Medicine shows to vaudeville to silent film to sound film to TV – *that* was fast. Vinyl discs and gramophones to cassettes to CDs to iTunes – *that* was fast. My father alive to my father dead – everything was a cyclone blowing everyone's Piqua, Kansas, right off the map. We stand in it, and shiver, but do not move, except in the inexorable motion of age.

"Oh, yeah, that's what I figure," the girl said. "And because I'm working a couple of jobs, too, I figure I need to read ahead. Well, to be honest, I sometimes read on the job when it's slow. But that's a different kind of reading, you know? I mean, I can't exactly *get* some of these essays at work. It's hard to concentrate at a Wendy's even on your break."

I treaded the pulling waters of memory, struggling to stay afloat in the present. "A couple of jobs? What else do you do?"

She rolled her eyes. I noticed, then, the incongruity of her presence: though delicate in the face, Chelsea wasn't a small person. Her shoulders were surprisingly broad, and her hands looked large enough to grip a regulation-size football. Perhaps her mother had been a cheerleader who had married a line-backer.

Delmore sniggered. "Maybe her mother was the line-backer. I knew this one dame at Wellesley ..."

I glared at him, and he just grinned in return, his sharp teeth surprisingly white.

"Oh, just shit jobs," she replied. "Minimum wage service stuff. Nothing interesting."

My legs pumped furiously in the dark vortex. Come on! Come on! "And you like to read? What sort of –"

"Tons of stuff. Fantasy's my favourite. When I was a kid, I read all the Harry Potter books about ... oh, I don't know ... at least ten times. And Susan Cooper. You know, Dark is Rising, that whole series."

I didn't know. But it certainly didn't surprise me that the darkness beneath would rise. What else could it do? This kid, who thought she had stopped being a kid – my God! – was on a journey, a lonely journey. Books would help, a little. Even Harry Potter. I glanced at the magician bank, hoping that some vaudevillian ta-da would transport me from the dreary world of muggles or, as humans are called in another series my own kids enjoyed, Children of the Lamp, mundanes. Mundanes is better – I think I would hit it off more with that author than with J. K. Rowling.

"I read other stuff now. The essays for this class. There's some really good ones. I mean ..." Chelsea bit her bottom lip. "I like some much better than others. The one about Dumpster diving. That's really great. How he talks about it like it's serious, like doing it can be ... like there's more to it than just being grossed out."

Had the girl blushed? It was hard to tell under the glaring institutional fluorescents. Certainly her manner was engaged. The essay she referred to was "On Dumpster Diving" by Lars

Eighner, an odd piece by a sort of intellectual street person, which explains how to go about eating food out of Dumpsters. Despite my morning's experience with the toys, I had forgotten all about Eighner's essay. After all, it wasn't on the syllabus until November. And this day had turned out to be its own syllabus, its own full degree – I sensed I'd be paying off these student loans forever. Even so, I tried to remember the essay. There was a list in it of all the things the author had found in Dumpsters besides edible food – books, dead pets, birth control devices. He might just as well have mentioned transparent horses and magician banks. He didn't. But he did comment that there was good material to be had in the Dumpsters near university campuses. That much I remembered. The young, with their penchant for dramatic mood swings and changes of plans, often wasted perfectly sound goods.

"Yes. Students seem to enjoy that essay." Any more hollow and my voice could have housed a family of woodpeckers.

But the girl suddenly exclaimed, "You're cancelling the class!"

I followed her gaze to the letters behind me. CLASS CANCE. I didn't know what disturbed me more: her obvious disappointment, or the letters CANCE, which I naturally – or perhaps unnaturally – concluded as CANCER. No, not that I was a class cancer, poisonous to students, or that I was somehow turning against my own bourgeois status as a university instructor. What struck me then must have been the ominous silence around the missing R, a silence that made me search for Keaton in the doorway. He had died, too soon, a victim of lung cancer at the age of seventy. He hadn't even known that he'd had the disease. His young wife and his doctors had kept the information from him. But why? Was the great clown really such a child that he could not face the darkness inside? Perhaps he had faced it enough by then, and it would have been cruel to make him face his end just as the work of his most creative period was being remembered and celebrated. Let him watch his beloved World Series on TV and play with his toy train set.

CANCER CANCELLED.

"I'm not feeling too well," I explained, and the sweat on my brow was heavy and cold as morning dew, except it didn't feel like morning.

"You don't look so good," Chelsea said.

I smiled weakly, despite myself. "I should have stood in bed today."

Delmore grunted appreciatively. "I always liked Yogi Berra. You know, me and your little white-faced pal have that in common, too. We're both nuts for baseball."

Ignoring him again, I apologized to the girl's perplexed expression and searched desperately for a change of subject. My eyes landed on the toys.

"You should take echinacea," Chelsea said. "I swear by the stuff. As soon as I feel something coming on, I take a pill. And green tea with ginger. That's good, too." Her voice, genuinely sympathetic, almost broke me. Any sign of compassion from a stranger, especially a young stranger, tends to make me weep for all the lost potential of the planet. But I rallied.

"I got those toys from a street person. He probably found them in a Dumpster. And the bank . . . there's a chance it's valuable."

"Really?" She took it in her large hands. "It's heavy."

Yes. The heavy bank that goes with me. I tried to control my shivering. Maybe I was sick; maybe I had picked up some strange germ off the flank of the grimy horse. "It could be worth thousands. If it's not a replica."

She whistled and placed the bank down gently. "Have you looked it up on the Net?"

I almost answered, "Yes. With a big man named Sleep." Instead, I just nodded. "But it's hard to tell for sure. I need to take it to an antiques dealer."

"And you say you bought it off some homeless dude?"

I could tell from her slightly suspicious tone where she was headed, and I was pleased. A sense of justice in the young is the only hope we have.

"For ten bucks. But if it's a real antique, I'll try to find him. I'll give him what it's worth. If I can find him."

"Well, half." Her tone softened. "Half is fair. How much could it be worth?"

"A bank like this," I said quietly, "has sold for seven thousand dollars."

"Holy shit!" She jumped back, again as if the film had been cut, and then immediately covered her mouth. "Sorry about that. But . . . wow . . . that's a lot of cash." She whipped out her phone so quickly that I thought she might shoot me with it and run off with the toy. A very special kind of bank robbery. For all I knew, phones could shoot bullets now. Surely some American company had patented and manufactured that gem of an idea. Why not? I wouldn't put anything past this culture except the past.

"Past the past. Nice one, genius." Delmore winked at me, then returned to casting perfect little statues of salt from his eyes.

"Hey. You really don't look good. How are you feeling, Professor?"

Chelsea's voice was as soft as the fontanelle of my first-born, so soft that I let the "Professor" pass. I lacked a PhD, and could not profess to profess, which was just as well. I stood always before the young only as a mister.

"I'm fine. That is, I'll survive."

"There's an antiques dealer just north of here. We should

go." This time, I was certain the girl blushed. "I mean, you should go. You should drive over there and find out. Aren't you dying to know?"

Today I was dying *from* knowing, but I wasn't about to go into that. And, in truth, I was curious. Then my lack of transportation deflated me. "I don't have a car," I explained, which, in North America, is often akin to saying, "I don't have a life."

The cheerleader almost hit me with a metaphorical pom-pom. "I do! I can drive you!"

Delmore laid a heavy paw on my shoulder. His voice had more glee in it now. "She's like this student I once had. A kid named Lou. He ended up forming some rock and roll band. The Velvet something or other. Underworld, I think. Ever hear of them?"

"Underground," I almost said aloud.

Delmore heard the word anyway. "Ah, I get it. Dostoevsky. *Notes from Underground*. Yeah, Lou was a clever kid. Of course, he would have picked up the Dostoevsky from me. I was always talking about Raskolnikov. Sometimes, when I couldn't face lecturing, I'd just read to the class. Probably read a lot of Dostoevsky."

"It's no big deal," Chelsea added. "I mean, if you're cool with it."

What about the class, I thought. If I was healthy enough to visit an antiques dealer, I was healthy enough to teach. Besides, it was the twenty-first century. A university instructor didn't go around fraternizing with students. Apart from being obviously unprofessional conduct, such behaviour was usually a sign of massive insecurity. Yet I wasn't a real professional instructor, and I understood myself well enough to know that *carpe diem* in this case posed no harm to the young woman. I would spontaneously self-combust before I ever acted irresponsibly towards a student. So, against my better judgment, and because the day was already so strange, I accepted her offer.

"Yes!" Chelsea slipped her phone back into her cardigan. "This is great. I'm parked a few blocks away." She hesitated. "Are you okay to walk?"

It wasn't possible to insult me, so I simply smiled and said I was. Chelsea raced back up to her desk and pulled on what turned out to be a kind of army duffle coat. She was back and through the door in a matter of seconds. Nervously, I turned and shakily added the LLED and TODAY to the board. Gathering up the magician and the horse a few seconds later, I left the campus with a student who wasn't even my student yet.

A T FIRST, I simply could not believe her lemon-yellow Pinto, forty years old but in remarkable condition. I hadn't seen one since the original Trudeau lived at 24 Sussex. A memory about the car immediately dolphined to the surface of my mind – they often exploded if you put them in reverse. Or was that the Gremlin? Some funny little vehicle from the seventies used to blow up in reverse. I gaped at the Pinto's hyperbolic burst of lemony ridiculousness. Chelsea, who was no doubt used to the effect her car had on others, sighed like Herman Melville looking over his last royalty statement.

"My granddad gave it to me. He bought it for my grandma, but she died not long after and never drove it. Then he couldn't sell it because it was a present to her. So it sat in his garage. Finally, he gave it to me. Because I'm just like her, he said.

Sorry about the mess."

The front and back seats appeared strewn with guts. I had to move some clothing with discreet delicacy before I could sit down. Chelsea hastened to help, taking the clothes and tossing them in the back with the rest of her wardrobe.

"It's mostly uniforms from work," she said, and gunned the engine so suddenly that my heart did a Keaton pratfall. Then she squealed the tires as she pulled out into traffic. I tried to relax into the slightly sour smell of polyester fabric, but the angle of the bucket seat in relation to the curve of the windshield was so unfamiliar – yet strangely familiar, too – that I seemed to be strapped into a rocket hurtling away from the earth. But Delmore was quite content. He had curled up in the crumpled uniforms and had started to snore in rhythm to the Pinto's engine. The ghost of Keaton, meanwhile, grew excited by the speed and clambered onto the roof. I couldn't see him, of course, but he was in his element, standing up there, wind-blown, holding his porkpie hat tight to his head as he waited to duck neatly under overpasses and telephone wires.

I didn't even need Keaton to remind me of Keaton. The drive was pure *Sherlock Jr.*, all high speed and near misses at intersections – with one striking exception: it wasn't silent. Chelsea conducted an almost non-stop commentary on other drivers, punctuated three times with a loud, "Come on, jerk!" followed by a sheepish, "Sorry, Professor," and a rapid-fire explanation of how the dude (it was always a dude) either cut her off, wouldn't get over to let her in, drove too slowly or ran lights (which she also did, to my dismay, but the hypocrisy was unremarked upon). Eventually, I had to shut my eyes and trust to the Fates. After all, as Jordan Baker points out to Nick Carraway in *The Great Gatsby*, "it takes two to make an accident." And, when I thought about it, I saw that there was a kind of independent flapper quality to Chelsea, a daring and a promise of excitement. But she clearly wasn't rich, spoiled or bored – and my instincts told me that she wasn't dishonest. No, she wasn't a flapper, so perhaps she was more like one of Keaton's leading ladies? Absolutely not. While Keaton's onscreen co-stars, such as Kathryn McGuire in *Sherlock Jr.* and *The Navigator*, and, most famously, Marion Mack in *The General*, occasionally exhibited flashes of spunk, they were mostly props, functionaries of mild prettiness conventionally present to serve the male plot lines. My classroom experience had certainly taught me that, despite the feminist movement, there were still plenty of young women around willing to be co-stars in title only. But Chelsea clearly wasn't one of them; she lowered her athletic shoulders and drove straight into the world.

Somehow or other, we survived the journey. Perhaps we had even driven along a bridge under construction that conveniently collapsed just as we reached the end of it. I was too rattled to know. I had already decided that this out-of-character outing was a mistake that I'd bring to a conclusion at the first opportunity.

"Here we are," Chelsea announced, and jerked the Pinto to a stop. Gently as an autumn leaf, the ghost of Keaton tumbled down the moon-wide windshield, landed on the street, stood, brushed off his baggy trousers and waited for us. Not at all gently, Delmore shoved my seat forward, grumbling, "The ego isn't always at the wheel; sometimes it's in the passenger seat," as he forced his bulk past me. Still trembling, I managed to reach the sidewalk, the toys once again like ballast in my hands.

We were definitely not in an upscale part of the city, but somewhere north and west of the downtown, which I rarely ventured out of, regarding any part of Edmonton that wasn't within a few minutes of downtown in the same way that the characters in Huxley's *Brave New World* regard the savage zone. We stood smack dab in the middle of North America's main contribution to civilization: a four-lane highway next to a little strip mall. This mall consisted of two dingy fast-food franchises, an even dingier dry cleaners, a couple of empty shops with For Lease signs in the windows, a supremely sad pet store with a pair of lugubrious rodents – perhaps guinea pigs – dozing on sawdust behind grimy plate glass and, just beside that, a decidedly unpromising-looking shop called, believe it or not, Better Times Antiques. For a long ten seconds, we stood there, breathing in the diesel and fried fat fumes. I wondered whether one of the guinea pigs would move first, but they just lay there like a losing boxer's gloves.

"Here we are," I mumbled.

Chelsea laughed. It was a powerful, rolling kind of laugh, and I waited for the pins to crash and for her to boom out "Strike!" Instead, she did what the young are so good at, what I used to be so good at: she headed for Better Times.

"I strive to be fed," Delmore grumbled. "You know, 'the scrimmage of appetite everywhere,' and all that."

"'Provide, provide,'" I said, and watched him rumble off on all fours towards a big blue Dumpster, one of the hundred million of his kind.

By the time I entered the little shop, Chelsea was already talking with the tiny, bespectacled, elderly man behind the counter. He was nodding like one of those syrup-filled, long-necked novelty birds so popular decades ago, and I wondered if Chelsea had met him before. They resembled conspirators. Perhaps the girl had led me here to her unassuming accomplice, who probably held a very modern weapon under his grey vest. Seven thousand dollars was seven thousand dollars. Then it struck me all at once: what the hell was I doing? No one knew where I was; I didn't even know. I had gone off with a student, a young woman still in her teens, to get an old toy I'd bought off a street person appraised. Why? I was a respectable man, a teacher, almost fifty years old. What the hell did I think I was doing? I knew what was illusory, what was real. Delmore, the ghost of Keaton, my own memories and terrifying darkness: if I had stepped out of my familiar body, I hadn't lost control of the medium in which I performed. The gross world of heavy bears, fast-food franchises, work and death remained all too real, even as I longed for magic. While I stood there, uncertain, the contents of the shop helped to settle my nerves.

It wasn't a large space, but it was absolutely crammed with the survivors of changing fashion. High shelved like a university library, Better Times, conveniently enough, seemed to specialize in toys. Right away, my eye took in a huge green pogo stick, one of those punching-bag dolls with sand in the base (this one was Bozo the Clown), a couple of hula hoops, some Peanuts figures and what might have been an original Monopoly game. Small lamps with tasselled lampshades, a walnut filing cabinet with at least thirty tiny drawers, some Lionel trains (Buster will glom on to those, I thought) and a Disney poster from when Disney and everything else at least appeared innocent. And then my eyes faltered in the dim light, which seemed no stronger than what stars give off in puddles. It occurred to me then, with mild excitement, that there might be something related to the silver age of cinema in the shop, perhaps a *Photoplay* magazine or Erich von Stroheim's monocle; I wasn't hopeful enough to imagine that serendipity would grant me some Keaton memento.

Suddenly, Chelsea was at my side, whispering. "It's like Ollivander's wand shop." She paused for my reaction. When I didn't have the appropriate one, she added, "From Harry Potter. The owner's just like what I always imagined Ollivander would be like."

Well, I didn't know what she meant exactly, but I got the

gist of it. Despite the musty smell and the cramped quarters and the unusual absence of music (which I had just noticed) – or possibly because of these – magic was in the air.

"He seems like a good guy," Chelsea went on in a hushed voice. "I think he'll give you the straight dope."

The straight dope? Had she found that expression in the glovebox of the Pinto? I didn't have time to mull over the girl's diction, though. Eagerly, she gestured me towards the counter, past a head-high iron birdcage that looked strong enough to trap a woodcutter's child.

The air around the owner of the shop smelled of snuff and roasted chestnuts. The man himself seemed as indistinct as a grey and wispy column of smoke, except for a pair of prominent front teeth, which, ridiculously, made me think of George Washington, who, as legend has it, had worn a set of wooden choppers. The owner appraised me carefully – his head to one side, his pencil end tapping his front teeth – and must have found me wanting as an antique. I almost expected him to say, "He's original, but not in very good condition." Instead, his eyes lit on the bank I clutched to my chest, and noticeably widened.

"Ahhh, what have we here?"

His long, thin-fingered hands, more veins than flesh, reached out with a little boy's greed. I gave him the bank, and the three of us closed around it like Astor, Greenstreet and Bogart around the dingus in *The Maltese Falcon*. For a few crazy seconds, I even wondered if the bank was solid gold under the paint. Nervously, I fingered my gat, until I realized I was only scratching my stomach.

"Yes, yes, yes," Mr. Ollivander murmured, in a voice that should have had a Hungarian or Romanian accent, but sounded unmagically Ontarian. "J. & E. Stevens Company. Of Connecticut."

Unless I was hearing things, and of course I was, he had pronounced the middle *C*. I had never heard anyone do that before. I looked at Chelsea to see if she had registered this verbal oddity, but she had her elbows on the counter, her jaw cupped in her hands, and was gazing raptly into Ollivander's face, which hovered like a waxy moon over the magician.

"Is it real?" she asked cautiously, as if her words might break the toy or Ollivander's Dickensian bifocals.

"Undoubtedly so. I do not even have to look. It carries the patina of time. And besides . . ." He straightened up, adjusted his glasses and fixed the smoky lenses on me. "After so many years, one can feel the spirit in an object, just as in a person. This magician . . . ah, he has not lost his magic, let me put it that way."

I couldn't get over his voice. All the inflections were eastern European, but the tone was flat-out southern Ontario. It was disorienting, but Chelsea forged ahead with the bluntness of youth.

"What's it worth?"

Ollivander's irritation didn't surprise me. A man doesn't speak of the spirit and then happily plunge straight into the material. Well, perhaps a televangelist does, but not many others.

"Young lady," he said, but looked at me, "patience is required in such delicate matters."

Ollivander didn't let the silence linger, despite his comment. He turned his pewter lenses to Chelsea.

"You see here? What he is wearing? I'll bet you don't know what kind of shirt this is."

Chelsea shrugged. "White."

"Yes, white. And the paint is original and still so fresh after over a hundred years. But the shirt is something else." He glanced at me, but I had barely followed the conversation.

"Boiled!" Ollivander announced it like a spell, with a flourish of one hand and a following chuckle that was halfway between a giggle and a snake's hiss. "It is a boiled shirt. I'll bet you've never heard that before, young lady."

Now it was Chelsea's turn to be impatient. She sniffed, said, "Nope," and quickly followed with, "We saw one on eBay selling for seven grand." Again, her phone flicked out and she ran her fingertips over it.

Ollivander pursed his lips. "eBay. Ach. Junk and more junk." Almost in desperation, he addressed me. "You have heard of boiled shirts, I am certain? You have worn one, perhaps, on special occasions?"

A boiled shirt? I'd heard the term before, but I couldn't describe a boiled shirt for the life of me. Before I could respond, though, Chelsea thrust her phone in front of the antiques dealer. His eyes flickered, the whole mist of his body thinned. "Very nice." Then he touched his own fingertips to the magician's face. "Look at the goatee. As pointed as the day it was made. And the eyebrows. Might I ask, sir, where you obtained this handsome fellow?"

"Private purchase," I somehow managed to say, not looking at Chelsea.

"The mechanism is jammed," Ollivander went on, "but..." He made a few deft movements with his pencil. "Voila. Perfect again. May I?"

When I nodded, he placed a nickel on the magician's table, pressed the lever, and down came the top hat and away, with a little click, went the coin.

"Flawless," he murmured. "Really quite remarkable. A private purchase, you say? Recently, or ..."

"Today!" Chelsea's answer was like a blow to the forehead. The dealer and I briefly exchanged hearts, then returned them to each other. The unRomanian Ontarian did not quite recapture his professional calm, however. Strangely, he seemed to chill as he grew more heated. He became a column of fire with ice cubes for eyes. But his voice – did it tremble slightly now?

"Today? In Edmonton? Might I be so bold as to ask what you paid for him?"

Chelsea slipped her phone into her coat pocket. "Sorry. That's a delicate matter."

I didn't know whether to admire her spunk or to be horrified by it. Certainly he had been patronizing, so . . .

He bowed and forced a smile. "A hit, young lady, 'a very palpable hit.' I commend you. However, I have been patient, and the time for business, if you operate a business, always comes." He turned the ice cubes, which hadn't melted in the least, on me. "The bank is valuable. And I know collectors, especially collectors in this city. More to the point, I know their collections."

What was his insinuation? That I was a thief? Somehow I couldn't muster the energy for umbrage. But Chelsea had no such problem.

"Big deal. If you think the professor stole it or something –" The girl was spluttering, and on my behalf. As if realizing that she'd grown too emotional, she lowered her voice. "He's a professor. He doesn't need to steal." The light was too dim to tell if her cheeks blushed, but her tone certainly did. I felt embarrassed for the world that encouraged her innocent belief in my professor-hood.

"You misunderstand me," Ollivander said, neatly placing his pencil on the counter and making a teepee with his fingertips. "The point is, none of the collectors here own such a bank. I would most certainly know if they did, even if they did not tell me. Word, you understand, gets around."

A sudden wave of curiosity crashed over my discretion. "I bought it off a derelict this morning. He likely found it in a Dumpster."

"A derelict?" The shop owner returned to quivering smoke. In fact, he looked very much like a tiny, elderly man who'd stepped into the presence of his god. "You bought this, *this* bank, for . . ."

"Ten dollars," I said. "Oh, and that included the horse." I placed my hand near the visible heart.

"Horse?" Ollivander shrank even more as he stared at my hand. Then he began to laugh, like an engine getting up steam.

Chelsea widened her eyes at me. Together, we asked, "Are you okay?"

"The horse! That included the horse! Oh, that's good, that's very good."

He chuffed and plumed a few more seconds, then composed himself with what seemed a tremendous effort of will.

"You are fortunate that you came to me. I am – for my sins, and Heaven help me – an honest man, an honest man in a world of the eBay. This little man is worth a great sum of money."

Chelsea and I were leaning forward, pointing ourselves like golden retrievers.

"Yeah?" she said. "What's a great sum?"

An entire century tightened around us. A hundred plus years of getting and spending and laying waste our powers, millions upon millions of people earning paycheques and paying bills, all those hands handing over bills and coins and holding pens to ink signatures. I thought of my father, a salmon fisherman who scraped a living out of that dwindling resource and who often had to drive a tractor in the potato fields to make ends meet when the fishing season had been poor. And my mother, a pogey child in the Toronto of the Great Depression, who was once farmed out to a wealthy doctor's family in the country to improve her nutrition. I thought of Keaton, too, once a millionaire star at MGM, reduced to working as a gag writer for the same studio at one hundred fifty dollars per week. But, of course, I thought of myself. Ollivander's answer might buy me a few hours each week to work on my own writing. Even after I'd found the derelict and given him his fair share, I might still have a hundred fewer student papers to grade.

"You won't believe me," the old man said.

"Oh, come on already," Chelsea replied.

The answer had to come bluntly when it came, and so it did.

"At auction, as much as thirty thousand dollars. Perhaps more."

The pause was long, the silence like the silence around a deathbed, or like the silence over the ocean after the *Pequod* sinks. Silence itself became silent. At last, Chelsea exploded the grandeur. "No shit!" And she punched me on the shoulder. Hard. Her grin had widened like the Grinch's when his heart grows bigger.

I had shrunk along with the antiques dealer to a miniature size, and was sitting on the table under the magician's top hat, listening to the world go clunk. It was inevitable, however, that the mundane world would replace the magical one.

"Mechanical banks," Ollivander explained, "are highly collectible. Recently, at auction, one with a pair of ice skaters sold for $130,000. It is a matter of scarcity and condition." He touched his long forefinger to the transparent horse. "This is not scarce or in good condition, and it is worth about what you paid for it."

Thirty thousand dollars! Six courses, thirty students per course, four essays per student. My mind whirled with the figures. Seven hundred twenty papers I wouldn't correct and grade! Thousands and thousands of comma splices and dangling modifiers I would never see. And what would take their place? My own sentences, sentences that never had comma splices or dangling modifiers because I had worked hard all of my life to learn how to avoid them, sentences potentially rich and flowing and dramatic, sentences that could change someone's life and sentences – o cold world – that needed to be financed. I wanted to weep tears of joy and sorrow on Delmore's shaggy shoulder, but he had not returned from the Dumpster behind the fast-food franchise. Maybe he'd found another vintage toy; maybe this day was determined to self-destruct with marvels.

"If you wish to sell," Ollivander went on, returned to his business self, "I can offer my services as a broker. For a percentage, of course. And the auction house would take a percentage, too."

I couldn't concentrate. I needed air and time.

"Just for the hell of it," Chelsea said, "what would you give for it right now? I mean, if the professor didn't want to go the auction route?"

"A fair question, young lady. It would require me to secure some capital, but I am confident in the appraisal. Normally, a dealer in antiques will offer fifty percent of an item's value."

"Fifty!"

"Normally, I said. You see, young lady, not everything sells right away. The proper buyer must be found. In this case, however, I believe that resale will not prove difficult."

The shop owner picked his pencil up and started to tap the end against his picket-fence front teeth once more. Then he stopped.

"Tomorrow, if you wish, I believe I could write you a cheque for twenty thousand dollars."

"What do you think, Professor?" Chelsea didn't wait for my answer. "If it was me, I'd save all the hassle and take the cheque."

Were me, I thought absurdly. If it were me.

"I'll need to think it over," I said above my pounding heartbeat. "Tomorrow . . ."

"Here is my card." The dealer held it out to me with his

Ichabod Crane digits. "Please. Take very good care of him. He is a survivor and deserves our greatest respect."

My mouth was dry, but I managed to ask about the subject that had started this unlikely chain of events.

"Do you have anything from the silent film era? Any Buster Keaton . . ." I couldn't find the right word, and ended awkwardly, "stuff?"

"Buster Keaton?" Ollivander spoke the name with mild surprise but also with pleasure, or with as much pleasure as an Ontarian could allow himself. "Yes. I have a few posters. Not originals, I'm afraid. Reproductions."

A fierce desire to have an image of Keaton consumed me. The great comedian himself had kept two framed photographs in his house all his life; one was of Roscoe Arbuckle (those who knew him *never* called him Fatty), and the other was of Joseph Schenk. The good man who'd been falsely accused of rape and ruined, and the hugely successful film mogul who in his old age paid starlets, including an unknown Norma Jean Baker, for oral sex and left absolutely nothing in his will for Keaton. Justice and injustice, failure and success, ten bucks and thirty thousand bucks, reality and illusion stepping out of each human existence. I followed the dealer to a corner of the shop where he kept posters on a swinging rack.

"I am very selective," he said defensively, "when it comes to posters. No James Dean, no Marilyn Monroe. But Keaton . . . you have a favourite film?"

"*Sherlock Jr.* I just watched it last night. Well, this morning."

"Ah, your lucky day is not all luck. I do not have an image from *Sherlock Jr.* Here is one from *The Cameraman*. And another from *The General*." He held the rack open.

There was Buster, at his creative height, his hair long, his dark eyes blazing, as he perched precariously on the cow-catcher of a steam locomotive, a locomotive he would eventually crash off a bridge in the single most expensive shot of the silent film era. And there, too, was Keaton's ghost, at the end of the aisle, not saying anything, not crying, not smiling. His expression was iconically enigmatic. Perhaps my own was, too. I said I'd take the poster of *The General*, and the dealer nodded.

"A wonderful film. Such fidelity to history." He spoke the phrase as if it summed up his whole life's ambition. "I will bring it to the counter."

Chelsea, in the meantime, had been looking at some jewellery in a glass case. It was something my teenaged daughter liked to do, and for a moment I almost mistook Chelsea for my daughter again. I had a sudden urge to buy her a pair of earrings, but, of course, that was impossible.

The transaction completed, I gathered up the bank, the horse and the poster, and turned to go. Ollivander said, almost desperately, "Tomorrow. And be careful with him."

His words stirred Chelsea back to the less material jewels of her young life. "Hey, thanks a lot," she said. "You've been a big help."

13

THEN WE were outside, in the cool and gritty fried-food air of North American strip mall reality. The light, as light so often is, was almost blinding. We stood in it like Vermeer figures, though, for my part, not at all serenely. Chelsea, however, didn't appear to share my unease.

"Thirty thousand bucks. Woo hoo!" She didn't punch my shoulder again, but I flinched anyway. "So? Are you going to sell it to him for twenty?"

"I don't know. I'll have to talk it over with my wife. It's a big decision."

"No kidding! Hey, I meant to ask, what's up with the poster?"

I was reluctant to answer, but – trust me, Buster – there was no way out.

"It's Buster Keaton. I like his movies."

She squinted, frowned and said she'd never heard of him. I wasn't surprised. My students often hadn't heard of less recent celebrities. Marilyn Monroe? Probably. James Dean? Probably not. Delmore Schwartz? Fatty Arbuckle? Robert Frost?

"Do you want to use my phone?"

I blinked.

"To call your wife?"

"No, no thanks." The phone was so small that I was sure I wouldn't be able to read the numbers without removing my glasses. And whenever I removed my glasses, I felt as vulnerable as Piggy in *Lord of the Flies*. "I'll ask her when I get home."

When Chelsea offered to drive me there, I realized I didn't want to go. Not yet. I thought the miraculous day might end once I walked into my house, and the idea leadened my spirit. Then I remembered.

"The homeless guy. I have to find him." Just then, Delmore appeared, a McDonald's bag flapping at his throat and then spinning away like froth. He certainly wasn't lugging a mechanical bank, which was just as well, since he'd have had to walk on his hind legs to free his paws, and that wouldn't have been a pretty sight.

"More with the Keaton, huh?" He nodded at the poster. "You know, I wrote to Chaplin asking for a blurb for my first book, but I never heard back." He sighed, and his breath almost knocked me down. "I probably had the wrong address."

"Listen," Chelsea said. "I don't mean to be pushy or anything, but since you cancelled class today, and I don't have to work until later . . . and I have a car."

I nodded. "It's not pushy at all. I appreciate the help. But I think if you just drive me back to campus, I can take it from there." As far as I was concerned, this unorthodox situation had gone on long enough. I normally didn't even like meeting students in my office. She looked disappointed, so I added, "Maybe we can lock my stuff in your trunk, since it's so valuable." Then I made the joke, even though she wouldn't get it. "Just don't put the car in reverse."

Chelsea was nothing if not surprising. She smiled. "You mean don't get rear-ended. My grandpa told me all about Pintos. But all that stuff wasn't true, you know. I looked it up on Wikipedia."

I saw a rare opportunity to join the twenty-first century and, thoughtlessly, grabbed it. "I have a Wikipedia entry."

Chelsea drew her phone out again. Several seconds passed, during which the rush of traffic on the highway roared like the wind in an abyss. I couldn't stand the clamorous near silence, and mumbled, "It's not accurate."

"You're a poet?" A mixture of bewilderment and awe entered her face and voice.

I nodded. After all, I was nearly fifty – if I couldn't admit it by now, I didn't deserve the great gift of writing poems. For most people, the idea of a poet is unsettling – not exactly disturbing, just out of the ordinary. And when that poet is old enough to be your father, old enough to have put away childish things, a person must feel as if she's encountered a yeti. Delmore reached us just then, and recognized the situation immediately. All his cynicism and self-pity dissolved in an instant; now his tears were more universal than ever, tears of reverence, what any human on the planet in 1922 would have shed watching Greta Garbo suffer on the screen. If Delmore had been wearing a hat, he would have doffed it. He spoke calmly and clearly. "Look at the world the young live in. Look at the values they are given. We are witnesses to a different order." Then, with a low growl that I recognized from the almost indistinct middle of the night, he added, "Don't blow it." And this, too, I understood.

Very little time had elapsed before Chelsea spoke again, perhaps fifteen or twenty seconds as she read the cold facts about books published, awards won, subject matter of my poems – subject matter! – but my entire life was there. I saw a little boy with a springer spaniel on a dike looking out at a great river; I saw a young man buying foxed and yellowed books in a shop as sloppy with them as a seiner's deck is with salmon; I saw that man at his wife's side as she gave birth and at his father's side as he took his last breath. That man, that life, was as insignificant and magnificent as any other, as Keaton's, as Delmore Schwartz's, as this young woman's forming words in the cold air.

"I've never met a poet before."

I waited for Delmore to return to form, to snarl, "You still haven't." But his reverence was as genuine as his life in poetry had been. I was ashamed for doubting him, and so I quoted in a low voice some lines from his poem, "All Night, All Night": "'O your life, your lonely life / What have you ever done with it. / And done with the great gift of consciousness?'"

Delmore had had enough. He grabbed my elbow. "Stop. That's plenty." I saw the whole poem in his horrified eyes, but it was Keaton's ghost who walked up and moved his lips as I heard the single reverberating phrase, "'An endlessly help-lessly falling and appalled clown.'"

It was a moment of truth, and Chelsea's face, behind which I saw my own children's faces, their children's faces, the endless replication à la Keaton's *Playhouse*, decided me. We might indeed be helpless and in a constant fall, but to be appalled was a choice: we could choose it, or fight it, or, as in my case, and Keaton's, too, choose it and resist it with every fibre of our beings for the sake of others. Keaton was a great clown, and tragic, but never appalled. And Delmore Schwartz, like every other artist, was not appalled at the time of creation.

Let the powers of the world do what they will: this much, this joy of making, belongs to the maker.

"The great gift of what?" Chelsea asked.

"Oh. Of consciousness."

She blinked her large eyes. "Did you make that up?"

"No. A man named Delmore Schwartz wrote it. Eighty or so years ago."

A deeper growl this time. "For fuck's sake, don't tell her how old I am!"

"Delmore?" Chelsea said. "I've never heard that name before."

"His mother named him . . ."

"Oh, God, don't!"

"After a dancer in the silent movies. Frank Delmore. It's not generally a first name."

Delmore was angry now. "Enough with my mother. She's been dead a long time, longer than me. Better worry about your own."

Yes! My own! I looked wildly around and couldn't believe my luck. A telephone booth, an honest-to-goodness pay phone in a tall rectangle of glass, shone like the Holy Grail from across the parking lot. Phone booths weren't as rare as mechanical banks, but they were getting that way. As I stood there, trying to figure out how to explain to Chelsea why I needed to make a phone call but didn't need her phone, she made the situation easy for me.

"Professor? Are you feeling okay now? You're not in a hurry or anything? I was just hoping to check out this pet store." I must have looked baffled, for she went on hurriedly. "My mom just broke up with her boyfriend. I'm worried about her. I think maybe a cat, something to look after, some company."

"Oh, sure, go ahead. Take all the time you want. I'll wait out here. I need to think everything over. It's been quite a day."

"I know, right?" A dimple appeared and disappeared in one cheek, and reminded me of that old TV commercial where a finger pokes the Pillsbury Doughboy. "Here. Let me put your stuff in the trunk."

I gave her the two toys and the poster. When she had locked them securely in the Pinto, she gave me a quick little smile and made for the pet shop. Once she had vanished inside, I turned towards the phone booth. And there was Keaton, standing solemnly beside it, crushed porkpie hat in his hands. Delmore, meanwhile, had crawled – if you can say that of a bear – into the back seat of the Pinto, no doubt to sleep off his feed of fried garbage, and perhaps some mortal memories, too. I hastened to the booth, took off my glasses to read the long-distance instructions and dialled. As the phone rang in my mother's house – five times, six times – I wondered, as I always did, if she was all right. Life is fragile for everyone, but at ninety every day is a tenuous bonus. So I was relieved when, on the eighth ring, she finally answered.

The conversation proceeded normally enough for several moments – her health, her recent visits from my brothers and sister, the weather (it was sunny on the coast, still summer-warm). My mother was garrulous but large-hearted with it, and her tendency to repeat stories and information was often redeemed by a sudden, surprising memory that I'd never heard before. We'd talked a great deal over the years, especially since my father's death in 2001. So when I answered her question about what I was doing – after hesitating and deciding not to go into the whole strange business of the mechanical bank just yet – with, "Oh, I've been watching some Buster Keaton movies lately," to say that her response was shocking would be an understatement.

"Your brothers saw him, you know."

"Yes, I've heard about that."

"Of course, he was a lot older then."

Something in her tone gave me pause. "Older?"

"Sure. He was an old man when he made that railroad movie up here. But when I met him during the war, he was probably about your age. Let's see, that was 19 . . ."

"Wait a minute, Mom." I looked through the dusty glass at Keaton's ghost. The ghost, I just realized, was sometimes young, sometimes old; the bodies kept stepping out of each other. But the middle-aged Keaton, the forgotten Keaton, remained a cold corpse, forgotten even in the hereafter. "You *met* Buster Keaton?"

"Well, not exactly met. I shook his hand."

"You what!"

"Sorry, Tim, I can't hear you. The connection's bad. Or it could just be this darned hearing aid. It's not working again. I'll have to get your sister to drive me out to the hearing aid place for an adjustment. It's a good thing I don't have to pay for it. The Veterans covers most of –"

"Mom," I said firmly, and I hoped kindly. "Tell me this again. You shook Buster Keaton's hand? Where?"

The slight pause ought to have warned me.

"At the end of his arm, of course." Her laughter, which conjured up a delightful image of her face, turned into a hacking cough. After a few seconds, she recovered and apologized. "This darned hiatus hernia."

I took a deep breath and vowed not to talk to her as if she was a child. "Very good, very funny. But are you sure it was Buster Keaton's hand?"

"I might be old, but I know it wasn't his leg."

"Mom."

"I'm pretty sure that's who it was. He was selling war bonds. I remember he gave a kind of speech at the factory where I was working. Yes, Buster Keaton, that's right."

I didn't know what to say. It was certainly possible that Keaton had travelled to Toronto during the war to sell bonds; plenty of legends from the silent screen still shone with enough glamour to be good for patriotic causes, and most of them, like Keaton, were happy for the work. Well, not exactly happy in Keaton's case. His star in Hollywood had long since fizzled out and he was still drinking. He might have been in Toronto and not even cared what city he was in. I knew for a fact that the last filming he ever did took place there, when he starred in an industrial film called, of all things, *The Scribe*. But that he had touched my mother's hand! Time leapt from my corporeal frame and ran screaming silently across the four lanes of traffic. I thought of Mrs. Hatt, the old lady from my childhood who, as a little girl in London, had watched Queen Victoria go past in a horse-drawn carriage. The curious, living reach of history!

"What . . . what . . ." I stammered, "did he say to you?"

Another pause, and then, matter-of-factly, "Nothing that I recall. He seemed very shy. But it was so strange. You know, I had just met your father then, and I was already in love, so maybe I was seeing him everywhere. But I remember thinking, he could be Heck's father. I've always thought they were quite alike, your dad and Buster Keaton."

"I know. They were." I shivered the whole length of my body, a response that seemed so much more than physical. "Dad was shy, too. And wiry and muscled like Keaton."

My mother laughed. "Your brothers both said your dad, when he got old, looked just like the Buster Keaton they saw in White Rock. They said he even moved the same."

"They never told me that!"

"Well, you ought to phone *them* sometime. I'm sure they'd be happy to hear from you."

"Oh?" I was drifting back to my Edmonton reality; the train

tracks of 1964 were being ripped up by the decades. I focused on the trembling door of the pet shop as if it were a portal to the other side of silence.

I didn't quite know why the news struck me so. After all, many people were still alive who had met Buster Keaton. I knew that Gerald Potterton, the director of *The Railrodder*, was in his mid-eighties and living in Quebec, and that, even more remarkably, the wife of the mayor who had hosted Buster and Eleanor Keaton at a civic dinner in Rivers, Manitoba, was one hundred and still living there. Of course, there would even be people still alive who had met Keaton at the height of his creative power and fame in the mid-1920s, though they'd have been children at the time. But those human beings who had actually entered theatres to watch silent film when silent film was the world's most popular entertainment medium were becoming as scarce as world war veterans, phone booths and mechanical banks.

No, it wasn't my mother's having met Keaton that struck me, though it was certainly a surprise, or even that he resembled my father, which I already knew; it was that she had held Keaton's hand, that she had touched him. The hand that had soothed my brow in childhood illness, perhaps even in the autumn of 1964 when Keaton was walking the tracks of White Rock, had touched the great comedian's trembling, sweaty, alcoholic hand in 1940 something. I saw the handshake, then I saw the one hand float out of the other hand and, almost seventy years later, pick up the phone because I had made it ring from this booth in a strip mall in Edmonton, the city where Alexander Pantages had built a grand vaudeville theatre that the younger Keaton had starred in. Another few lines of American poetry came to me, these by Elizabeth Bishop: "I knew that nothing stranger / had ever happened, that nothing / stranger ever could happen." But the strangeness wasn't frightening. It was . . . I didn't know exactly, but the ghost outside the phone booth was less distant now. Absurdly, I wanted to put him on the phone. My grasp on reality, however, hadn't slipped so far.

I spoke with my mother a while longer, told her about her grandchildren's health and activities, the hockey games and play rehearsals and music lessons, and I mentioned our dog, Chinook, who, ironically, was terrified of the wind and would whimper and refuse to leave the house on stormy days. Then I said, "Yes. Okay. I love you, too," and hung up just as the pet shop door sprang open and Chelsea emerged, her head swivelling. No doubt she was wondering where I'd gone.

Startled out of my reverie, I left the booth and hurried across the parking lot.

Something – perhaps just a primitive creaturely instinct – made me pause before I had gone thirty feet. I saw the girl turn and stride to the driver's side door of her ridiculous car, the car of my youth. And it struck me all at once why I had stopped: I was testing her; no, not just her, but her whole generation, which had been raised in a culture of such wealth, celebrity obsession and materialism that it was a wonder, as much of a wonder as the survival of whales in the planet's toxic oceans, that they had any loyalty or honour at all. We had locked a thirty-thousand-dollar cast-iron bank in the Pinto's trunk, and I had walked away. My blind, antiquated, innocent faith! I had walked away to call my elderly mother from a phone booth! I might just as well have said to the Fates, "Here. Show me the way to the slaughter."

Now Chelsea had her hand on the door, and the world came crashing in. I told myself, fiercely, to move. "You will be sorry if you do not do what you should do," I heard on the french-fried air, except it wasn't Delmore speaking (he still slept in the back seat), and Keaton was nowhere to be seen (visible nowhere, present everywhere, like God). It was the voice of the mercenary usher of the practical verities, and, at long last, I heeded it. I cried out, but rather feebly, and began to run, awkwardly. Pain flashed in my torn knee ligaments and my heart jackhammered my rib cage, not from the physical exertion, but rather from the humiliation that so often attends a trusting nature in a world of self-interest and scams. Because I knew exactly why I ran. No matter what fine interpretations I put on my haste, I ran for the cash, and I ran as wildly as a contestant out of the studio audience for *The Price is Right*. The person who comes closest to the cost of his pride without going over wins . . . what? Buster's little fellow would say, the girl. Keaton himself, whose third marriage was supremely happy, might say the same. As for Delmore Schwartz, who had spent decades in futile legal dealings trying to recover some of the wealth his father had left, decades that amounted to only bitterness and failure, he went well over the cost, and the host of the show shook his hand and said with rehearsed sympathy, "Here are some lovely parting gifts: a bottle of cheap booze, some painkillers and an all-expenses paid stay in a fleabag hotel until you die."

But this was North America, 2012. Thirty, or even twenty, thousand dollars bought a lot of pride. I heard a whole lifetime of gym teachers and sports coaches shout, "Come on, come on, get the lead out!" However, just as I had begun to increase the production of lead in the pursuit of cast-iron, Chelsea ducked into the car and just as rapidly ducked back out. Perhaps Delmore had growled at her? My glasses had slid a little down the bridge of my nose and I couldn't quite make things out clearly. I came to a stop fifty feet away and tried to control my breathing. In the little storm of my teetering faith in humankind, I stood still and waited for the house front to crash perfectly over me. An inch either way . . .

"Hey, Professor!"

Chelsea's Cheshire cat grin broke off her face and came whirling like a boomerang across the yawning expanse of years that lay between us. Then the girl herself followed. As she approached, I saw the purse in her hand – it was neon green and round, and I wondered if she'd somehow stolen a traffic light in those few seconds when it wasn't yellow or red.

"I wondered where you went," she said. "I thought maybe you'd gone back to close the deal with the antiques guy."

Her face was so alive, so bright, so urgent, that I thought it had to change, just like a traffic light. I knew that kind of change took decades not seconds or minutes. The traffic gearing down around me still raced towards her, as it should. She flourished her purse. "You should see this pet shop. It's a joke. If I had enough money in here, I'd buy every one of those poor animals. Even if I just let them go, even if they just ran into traffic and got creamed, they'd be better off." Now the purse became a canteen that she was holding out to the afflicted species of our obliterating age. I almost reached out to drink from it. I hoped there was more than water inside. "I asked the dude how long he'd been pimping for the SPCA." She sniffed and tossed her head back. "He didn't like that."

Chelsea's moral outrage, her simple courage in acting on it, worsened my humiliation. I stood there, transparent to myself, like the little horse locked in the trunk. It was obvious that the girl saw nothing of my exposed faithlessness. Her whole being pulsed with some sort of bold purpose, and I waited, on the lip of a volcano burbling with ambrosia. The sleeping Delmore dreamed of flowers in meadows. The ghost of Keaton, wherever he was, squinted his twenty-nine-year-old directing eye against the lens. I saw us all, posed in a still frame, one of millions on the cutting-room floors of an obsolete world, but a world that hung on to us like sleep, heavy with sleep's blurred images and half-whispered secrets. For a few seconds, as she spoke, I saw Chelsea's mouth move and I looked all around her for the subtitle because I couldn't read her lips. Then the sound of her voice crackled through the century of decades and almost made me jump, just the way ordinary people, ordinary men and women and children, in the late nineteenth century jumped when the earliest films showed an onrushing train. How much we have learned to take in our stride! How little we translate the meaning of the train's approach!

". . . monkey. It has the saddest eyes. And I swear they follow me."

"Monkey?" I was certain I had misheard her.

She laughed. "I know, right? It's crazy. He's just a little dude, not much bigger than a cat. And he has this great personality. Come on, I'll show you."

A teenaged woman in a duffle coat and hiking boots tugged on my elbow to lead me across a strip mall parking lot to meet a monkey full of personality. It was decidedly not an ordinary day, yet the strangeness now had a natural quality. At least I could not, on the spur of the moment, think of anything more meaningful to do. But, in my middle-aged life, meaning was always companioned by anxiety. As I walked at Chelsea's side to meet the little dude whose sad eyes followed her, I felt apprehensive, not because of the strangeness, but rather because I could imagine she was my daughter about to intro-duce me to her first serious boyfriend. One of the Fates, this time in the unsmiling form of Keaton's ghost, stood at the pet shop door and mouthed, "Bleat as you enter."

I took a last look around at the parking lot, with the lemon-yellow Pinto sitting there like the caboose of some clown parade that had lost touch with the parade route, and was relieved that Delmore had not emerged from his brief hiber-nation. I couldn't imagine him lumbering into a pet shop. Then I gave my head a shake, reoriented to reality and understood that I was also the caboose of a mental clown parade, and the bright, familiar clamour of 2012 kept disappearing around the corner in front of me. I hurried through the framework of the open door to catch up.

The shop stank, of course. How could a pet shop not stink? It was every bit as small and crowded as Ollivander's antiques shop. But then, a pet shop *is* an antiques shop, for there is nothing in contemporary North America more antiquated than those other species with which we share the planet. Even cats and dogs have become relics – we have made them into nothing more than oddly shaped surrogates of our own broken and misplaced emotions. How often in cafés have I heard couples intensely discussing what I believe to be a child's behaviour, only to find out, to my dismay, that they're discussing a spaniel or – that dog who just cries out to be infantilized – a Shih Tzu. Sometimes, when out walking our golden retriever, speaking firmly to her when she pulled on the leash, I thought of the film *Planet of the Apes*; what horrible fate will befall us when the dogs take over? Leashed on *Planet of the Dogs*, perhaps it will be better if we're treated as dogs by our canine masters. To know yourself human, and yet to be kept from your humanity, would be the cruellest of fates.

I looked around at the cages and tanks. There were at least a dozen, and all were grimy. Some sort of a large lizard – perhaps a Komodo dragon – blinked up at me with its bulbous, Peter Lorre eyes. The sandpaper of its skin seemed to cast sparks against being. I could relate, too much so. I had already gathered a comic ghost, some toys, a poet-bear and a young student; I wasn't eager to add to my entourage.

The owner of the shop must have had shoulders but I couldn't see them. The huge Metallica T-shirt hung below his face the way a bedsheet hangs off a kid-ghost at Halloween. Or used to. Kids didn't go in for bedsheet ghosts anymore. Or hoboes. The sack at the end of a stick, the plastic cigar, the open road! I gave myself a mental jolt. Stay in the present, old boy, come on. I considered the owner's face. It was as old as mine, framed by long, stringy, more grey-than-black hair and poisonous. The nose was long with cavernous, permanently flared nostrils, and the skin of the broad face was pouchy. A receding hairline and small, squinting eyes completed the picture: he might have stepped straight out of the pages of *Bleak House*, if not for the heavy metal T-shirt.

When he noticed me staring at him, he said, "Hey," and the word came across the thick air of soiled cedar chips and cat pee like a soft, sinister "Boo." But I didn't jump. For some strange reason, the depressing shop comforted me. Despite the filth and gloom of the place, the presence of other species, even these poor specimens, always lifted my spirits. I remembered my Whitman:

> I think I could turn and live with animals; they are so placid
> and self-contain'd;
> I stand and look at them long and long.
> They do not sweat and whine about their condition;
> They do not lie awake in the dark and weep for their sins:
> They do not make me sick discussing their duty to God:
> Not one is dissatisfied – not one is demented with the
> mania of owning things;
> Not one kneels to another, nor to his kind that lived
> thousands of years ago;
> Not one is respectable or unhappy over the whole earth.

It's a bizarre, twenty-first-century form of comfort, but you hear it from time to time: the earth and its life existed before us, and it will survive us. Even when you don't hear someone articulate the thought, you can *feel* it.

I felt it now. The listless white mouse motionless on the tread wheel; the songbird cage as songless as the prairies; the grey Persian with dulled amber eyes; whatever flecks of colour flickered behind the aquarium glass; the sleeping Rottweiler puppies; the guinea pigs, hamsters and gerbils, of which there might have been hundreds; the old fan belt of some kind of snake; Chelsea's little monkey: somehow they all spoke forcibly of an existence so far above and beyond us that I could almost pity the shop owner more than its prisoners. Almost. For the fact remained: the owner deserved to be in a cage. Of course, he probably already was. Who could live day by day, conducting such a trade in such a place and not be imprisoned? To take in your lucre-filthied grasp the scruffs of such sadness...

Chelsea's little monkey? My double take stretched itself to a triple as I saw the spunky girl chatter to a caged primate who, to keep the Dickens theme going, played Tiny Tim to the shop's lugubrious Victorian London. His fur, mostly dark brown, was somewhere between caramel and cream around his pink-white face; he had a long tail curled like jumper cables, and more darkness to his eyes than Mary Pickford, Greta Garbo and the Gish sisters combined. He? Perhaps not. Sexing a primate wasn't something I'd googled lately. But the monkey wasn't much bigger than the Persian cat, and he/she/it was the liveliest creature in the shop by a long stretch. I stepped deeper into the stink and gloom for a closer look. The owner's eyes followed.

As I came up to the cage, I saw my own face on the monkey. But my image vanished quickly. The monkey's personality was simply too vibrant. His eyes flashed, he chattered, he scratched his chin, head, armpits; he might have been describing the private life of the shop owner in some exotic human language – Armenian or the almost-extinct Yiddish.

Chelsea, who had bent over and placed her face close to the bars, seemed to understand every word. She laughed and mimicked the sounds he made. She even took the monkey's hand in her own, a gesture that only increased the torrential flow of his speech. At one point, he turned to me, and I swear he smiled and asked after my wife and kids. He was the very embodiment, despite being two feet tall and a primate, of hail-fellow-well-met social skill. Immediately I gave him the appropriate name: Greg Arious. The second I thought of it, he chirped with delight. It was almost spooky. But since I was already spooked, and had been for weeks, what did it matter?

"Just look at him," Chelsea said, straightening up. "Isn't he great? It's like he knows me. The metal dude back there says he comes from South America. Can you imagine? South America. And now he's in Edmonton. In this shit place."

I wasn't sure whether she meant that Edmonton was a shit place or whether she simply referred to the pet shop. The former was a definite possibility. One of the main charms of Edmonton is its lack of charm, or at least the perception from outside that it is an ugly, cold, depressing, unsexy city.

"How much is he?" Chelsea waved her arm at the shop owner as if she was calling for the bill. I noticed that her mascara was streaked and her eyes were red. She must have been crying. Why? Had the sorry state of the animals affected her so deeply? Perhaps – probably – she had other things in her life to be upset about. After all, she worked several minimum wage jobs, and her mother sounded like a concern. Suddenly, I hoped that Greg Arious, whose new name sounded weirdly like that of an Olympic champion diver from the past, could communicate with her. Maybe this spunky teenager needed a friend.

Like an out-of-shape roadie, the owner dragged the heavy amp of his decades over to us. "Capu ... capu ..." he gasped, and I thought he was desperate for a caffeine fix when he finally blurted out the whole word. "Capuchin."

Of course he was looking straight at me, as if I understood. It's one curious thing about being an almost fifty-year-old man: people often grant you a degree of wisdom and authority that you don't possess, especially people close to your own age and older. With the young, there's more of a mix. Mostly they give you the authority but only sometimes the wisdom. Angus Metalhead, however, wasn't young; even his T-shirt was older than Chelsea.

"A capuchin monkey," he explained. "From the jungles of South America."

I looked at Greg again, but I couldn't picture him in a jungle, even though I could picture Buster Keaton's ghost in the post-millennial jungle. No doubt my fantastic day-dreaming couldn't include real animals. Toy horses, talking bears – yes. But real animals have a magic entirely outside of us, no matter how close we try to get to them. One of the strangest films of Keaton's triumphant era, in fact, explores this human-animal relationship. *Go West*, made in 1925, is basically a love story of the boy-meets-girl kind, except that the boy is a drifter named Friendless and the girl is a cow named Brown Eyes. Perhaps the fullest expression of a meaningful relationship in Keaton's entire oeuvre involves a man and a cow, a rather rueful commentary on his marriage. Perhaps this isn't even strange. Given what people are, or can be, given the sheer delight on Chelsea's face as she continued to engage with the capuchin monkey from the jungles of South America, perhaps we should all join a 4-H club eHarmony site.

"The only one in Edmonton. Maybe in Alberta."

I came back to the reality of the metalhead's sales pitch.

"Really tame, too. He'll just perch on your shoulder and stay there. He doesn't try to jump off or nothin'. You can take him anywhere."

"Where did you get him?" I asked, because all I could think to do was to play along until Chelsea had completed her Roddy McDowall moment.

The shop owner squinted so hard that his eyes were mere coin slots. His greasy grey-black hair swung over his face. I might have been looking through vines at our distant ancestors. "A buddy of mine had him. But he wanted somethin' easier to sneak into bars and restaurants. I think he ended up getting a ferret instead."

Because that actually sounded sensible to me, I began to worry. Now I could hear, in the near distance behind me, the lizard's eyes blinking, each click like the snapping of a photo. Keaton's cow was named Brown Eyes, but my lizard needed a less comforting moniker. Despair? Terror? Maybe just Angst would cover it.

"I paid a lot for him," the metalhead went on. "So I gotta ask a good price for him."

I had obviously missed something. "How much?"

"Two thousand."

Chelsea turned away from the cage with a whole-body sigh that I understood well, since that was how I'd been turning away from my life for months. "Come on, that can't be your best price. I'll bet you've had him a long time."

Was two thousand dollars too much for a capuchin monkey? It would certainly buy a lot of concert tickets on the Iron Maiden Reunion Tour, if indeed Iron Maiden had ever broken their union. But then, I could outfit a whole zoo with exotic monkeys if I sold my magician bank to the guy next door for twenty grand. Suddenly a bizarre image of my wife asking, "So, how was your day?" floated before me, except she was wearing a British judge's powdery wig and long robes, and what I heard was, "So, how was your life?" And on my lips was the terrible answer, "A failure. A selfish failure. I never lived up to it."

The tired machinery of the pet shop groaned and squeaked. I stood on that assembly line of denuded nature, assembling nothing, while Chelsea bartered over the price of Greg and while the ghost of Keaton – the successful, young, yet spirit-penetrating Keaton – stood beside the cage blinking his great bovine eyes. I wanted desperately to advance the plot. But, in the end, as so often happens, the plot advanced me.

"Fifteen hundred. I can't do lower than that."

"Well . . ." Chelsea looked at me, and the look was complicit. "Maybe. But I'll have to hold him first. I mean, I can't drop fifteen hundred bucks on a monkey if I haven't even held him."

I was still trying to decipher Chelsea's complicit look when the owner unlocked the cage and, to a delighted chorus of shrieks from the released primate, walked over to us with the monkey, like a pirate's parrot, on his sloped shoulder.

"He's a little ramped up," Metalhead explained. "I haven't had him out in a while."

I could feel Chelsea's spirit arch and hiss like a cornered tomcat, but she held her tongue. It was easy enough to read her thoughts, though. You asshole, you probably haven't had him out since you bought him. I was beginning to understand the full import of her complicit look, and panic, like gorge, rose in my throat. "You . . . you can't . . ." I mouthed, but, just as in the middle of the night, the words didn't emerge.

The little monkey now capered about on Chelsea's shoulder. Then he leapt across the base of her neck to her other shoulder, and back again, while she laughed and tilted her head forward and said, "That tickles."

"He likes you," Metalhead remarked, exactly as if he had said to me, "You really ought to buy this chick the monkey." But he had no idea what was going on. Too many years of too many decibels had dulled his instincts, or maybe he'd never possessed any in the first place.

Chelsea, meanwhile, seemed to know that Providence was on her side. Even before the phone rang on the owner's desk, even before he sludged away to answer it, she waited for the phone to ring and for him to sludge away. The whole scene was playing out before her, and I was gaping at it, just as the projectionist in *Sherlock Jr.* gaped at the film he wanted to enter. Except, I didn't want to enter Chelsea's little production. She was filming the world through the lens of youth; an excitement and clarity of purpose burned in her gaze. My old Bell & Howell was middle-aged and required bifocals.

"Let's go! Come on! He's not looking!" She held her arm out, like an usher at a wedding, to escort me to my place in the criminal's petty underworld. And Greg Arious – amber-eyed and afire with primitive approbation, hurling a transcending cry across the species of "Live! Live!" – danced madly along between her elbow and shoulder blade. He knew the score.

"No." My eyes darted towards the owner's desk. Metalhead appeared to be leaning, à la Jack Benny, on the empty air. Somewhere in those greasy grey strands of hair was housed a cellphone. He stood leaning on it, the dictionary definition of *oblivious*. If I hadn't been so convinced he was the sort of small businessman to keep a weapon behind the counter, I'd have felt sorry for him. Instead, I was terrified.

"Come on, Professor. Hurry!" Chelsea, big-boned, large-eyed, Pinto-driving Chelsea, advanced towards the door. Any second now, Metalhead would notice, he'd reach behind the counter, he'd see the older mastermind, the seasoned criminal who had let his apprentice accomplice leave first, he'd raise the gun and pull the trigger . . .

I scrambled out of the shop, my heart a bloodied monkey trying to beat itself to death against bars that would never open. Ahead of me, beating just as violently, swung Chelsea's green purse. I ran as if through a jungle towards the sea, the monkey's ecstatic shrieks urging me on, waves of salt pouring off the sea-green cask at Chelsea's hip. Somewhere out of the corner of my blurred vision, I saw Keaton's ghost. Though still, he seemed as rapt and excited as the monkey, no doubt because, at last, here was a slapstick scene he could appreciate: a gag with risk and action, probably a manic chase and the actors performing all their own stunts. I could hear his five senses whirring at jumped-up speed as, gasping, I clambered into the passenger seat of the car, banging my knee hard in the process. Chelsea reversed the Pinto with a squeal the instant my bum hit the vinyl. The world outside the windshield careened. Greg Arious shrieked and bounced up and down on Chelsea's right shoulder, as if trying to tear her coat sleeve off. Not surprisingly, the speed and the racket woke Delmore.

"What fresh hell is this?" he grumbled.

But I couldn't respond.

14

MY HEAD WAS turned back to the pet shop as Chelsea pulled out of the strip mall and onto the highway, alarmingly close to the front of a big rig with *Tim Hortons* and a giant brown doughnut painted on its side. The blast of the truck's horn seemed to pour straight out of the mouth of Metalhead, who by now had burst from the shop. I couldn't see a gun in his hand, but he was waving one arm. The other, still stuck to the side of his head, probably held the cellphone. Probably he had already called the police. Probably the sirens would start up any second and the ghost of Keaton would have exactly the kind of chase scene he loved. I cringed to think of the ending. Because, in *Cops*, a short that Keaton made in 1922, famous for the monumental chase scene in which Buster is pursued on foot through the city streets by an entire police force of running flatfoots, the final shot is of a tombstone. How many comic shorts from that era end with the death of the hero? Oh very funny, Buster – an innocent man hounded by the authorities and eventually executed. Ha ha ha. Existential comedy was all fine and dandy – and I had always appreciated Keaton's darkness – but that was a movie. This hurtling, monkey-motivated, lemon-yellow Pinto was no prop!

I found my voice, but I appeared to find it in the middle of a helium-filled balloon.

"Chelsea, this is crazy. You have to go back."

She turned briefly, and the expression on her face hit me like a wall of flame. She *was* the leading lady tied to the railroad tracks, except her eyes did not flash with fear; they invited the train's deadly advance. I had never seen excitement like it. Euphoria? She had crossed over to the primate side of the self; she was deep in the South American jungle, Bonnie to the monkey's Clyde.

"'Mistah Kurtz – He dead.' 'The horror! The horror!'" came a grumble from behind us.

My neck almost snapped off as I wrenched around to Delmore. The great shaggy ursine head with the penetrating, clarifying, direct-to-the-point intelligence of a brilliant poet was slashed by a hastily carved jack-o'-lantern grin. "'Take a walk on the wild side.'" He hummed. "'Doo do doo do doo do doo doo.'"

Well, I thought, of course *you* can enjoy this, your bloody hour of strutting and fretting on the goddamned stage is over. You don't have kids to raise. Hell, you never had kids. Your life was just your life. Just yours.

Somehow Delmore's sigh fell louder than the monkey's shrieks, rolling like the surf against my spirit. "Quite right. I never did."

I had expected anger, argument, some sort of intellectual

attack on the emotional irrelevance of generation. But why? I had read Delmore Schwartz's poems, and his biography and letters. I knew how deeply he had considered the conveyance of blood and cells from one human to another. I felt like a shit. But, even so, a terrified shit. Chelsea's driving, which had been reckless before, was downright suicidal now. She cut in and out of traffic as if in rhythm to the erratic tune of Greg Arious's shrieks. Jesus! Did the damned monkey ever have a contemplative moment?

The skyscraper skyline hove into view, the ordinary crags and peaks of commerce. Somewhere up in that modern sky, Charles Sleep was sending Alberta oil to the Chinese infrastructure. And that was considered sane and reasonable, the act of a responsible global worker of the new millennium. As for being an unwitting accomplice to the theft of a capuchin monkey by a teenaged cheerleader-linebacker with all the chutzpah of developing self? I didn't know what *that* was, except foolish. We had rescued a primate from a cage only to be put behind bars ourselves. Foolish? Insane.

"Why? What's insane about saving a life?"

I wasn't quite sure who spoke. Was it Delmore, suggesting that each child never born was, in fact, saved? Or Whitman again: "Has any one supposed it lucky to be born?"

Delmore was just emerging from another long, oceanic sigh. "I never had children, it's true. But I was a child myself. I was a son. That counts for something. The truth is, Tim, I've thought more about fatherhood than most men who simply perform the biological function. Experience without reflection is, in some ways, not experience at all."

"He was going to die, you know. If we had left him there. And I don't have fifteen hundred dollars to spend on a monkey."

"What?"

Chelsea's voice – calm, a little defensive – hardly registered.

I was too stunned by hearing my name spoken so tenderly in Delmore's usually oracular and sardonic tone to take anything else in.

"I'd have to work a ton of shifts to make fifteen hundred bucks."

"Being a father," I said over my shoulder, "means becoming a child again, only more so. Imagine being five, and *knowing* what lies ahead." My own idea, which I'd never really articulated before, somehow struck me as so haunting and terrible that the Pinto's wild gallop towards downtown suddenly became a pony ride at the Midwest Chautauqua. But only briefly. The exigencies of the practical almost always trump the profound insight.

"Maybe he'd have given you a layaway plan," I suggested to Chelsea, half my attention cocked for Delmore's next response.

"A what?"

Oh God, where the hell did I think I was, 1972? I hastened on. "You could have used a credit card. Everybody buys things that they can't afford sometimes. And then they pay them off. Most people don't steal."

"Then what's this little dude doing in Edmonton? He didn't get on a plane all by himself."

The girl's logic, once again, chastened me. The moral foundation of her rash act hit hard against my tired, middle-class assumptions, which were, to use the language of her age group, lame. I floundered for a response. I knew my face looked just like Keaton's at the end of *Sherlock Jr.*: perplexed, bemused, full of the wondering question, "Is this what life boils down to?" For the boy-projectionist, and for the comedian playing the part, that wonder focused on marriage and family. How does the carefree existence of youth so suddenly become the responsibility of adulthood? Keaton holds the newborn twins, and blinks. I held the inside handle of the passenger door and shut my eyes as Chelsea minnowed across the lanes.

"Not for all fathers," Delmore said with a groan. "To say that is to say that all men are the same. Which obviously isn't true. My father . . ." His words died on a choked sob.

I couldn't deal with such a massive subject now. It required far too much emotion, and I sensed a calmer opportunity would present itself. For now, I had the violence and moral confusion of the present to contend with. I mean, you could ignore a reckless driver and a shrieking, stolen monkey for only so long.

As we careened back onto Jasper Avenue, the monkey's shrieking became a continuous high howl that sounded horribly like a police siren. Then I realized that it wasn't the monkey at all. Greg Arious had fallen completely silent, as quickly as the silent movies had collapsed into sound. Even worse, he appeared to be studying me. His baseball-sized head cocked slightly to the side, his lips moving as if nervously mumbling, he perched on Chelsea's right shoulder and *stared*. It would have been disturbing, and I might have read a great deal of psychoanalysis into it, if I wasn't so stricken by the police siren, descending on us from behind like an avenging maniac. Metalhead hadn't wasted any time, and the local constabulary was obviously keen to set a new station record for response.

"Pull over," I gasped. Already I was scrambling for a reasonable explanation.

Delmore, back to his usual self, didn't help. "Tell the cops you're the monkey's uncle. That you're just taking him out on a day pass."

I ignored the remark, but I could hardly ignore the evidence. We had the goods, there was no hiding the fact. Everybody's got something to hide, I thought hysterically, especially me and my monkey. A nervous laugh slipped out. I saw Keaton's ghost blinking at me from where he stood on the sidewalk, leaning jauntily against a blood-red Canada Post box. I remembered the reason he'd once given for never visiting the elderly, moaning, forgotten silent film actors and actresses at a Woodland Hills rest home: "Some of them had never heard a Beatles record. They haven't kept up with the times." Now the Beatles themselves were old news. But, at least, unlike those silent film stars, the Beatles never had to endure the obsolescence of their art form.

"Try poetry," Delmore said. "Obsolete before you even start. Obsolete at your height, and obsolete ever after."

This was patently false. After all, I was reading his poems, I was talking to his spirit. But I couldn't engage in a debate now.

Chelsea, who remained remarkably composed, cracking her gum as she veered towards the curb, suddenly turned a gentle smile on me. I felt grandfathered by it.

"You've never had much to do with the cops, have you, Professor?"

I shook my head.

"You're lucky." There was so much painful history in her voice that, for a few seconds, I didn't even realize that the police car – lights flashing – had sped past. Once I had noticed, once I had recovered my breath, I determined to be the sensible and responsible middle-aged man that I was.

"Chelsea, you know you have to take him back. You can't keep him."

The gentleness disappeared, her jawbone tightened and I immediately regretted my common sense. After all, what good had it ever done me, except to keep me clear of the law? Yet I knew enough about power and authority to understand whom most of the laws serviced. Oil companies had all the protection in the world, whereas you'd be hard pressed to find an elephant with tusks anywhere on the planet. The process of change in a human life isn't a matter of technology; it isn't one kind of film over another. If I was going to shed my birth skin, it would have to come off painfully, with a ripping of flesh and a spray of blood.

"I'm not taking him back. I'm giving him to my mom."

"Good idea," Delmore said. "He'll treat her better than most men would."

"Your mom?" I asked. "Chelsea, a cat's one thing, or a dog, but most people don't think of a monkey as good company."

"Most people don't think of monkeys at all. That's hardly the monkeys' fault."

"She's got you there, chum." Delmore slapped the back of my seat.

"Oh go soak your shaggy head."

"What?"

My God, had I spoken that last bit aloud? I glanced at Chelsea, but she was pulling the car out onto the avenue, Greg Arious gargoyling her shoulder as always. I must have simply mumbled. To cover up, I made my plea.

"Listen. There has to be a better way to go about this. Can't we stop somewhere and talk it over? Somewhere out of sight." Driving around the downtown core in a lemon-yellow Pinto was akin to rumbling through the streets on one of the aforementioned elephants. Naked. Like Lady Godiva, except she was on a horse. Completely transparent.

"You're not without a certain capacity for wit," Delmore conceded. "But then, poets are often funny. Did you know that Eliot corresponded with Groucho Marx and S. J. Perelman? Most people figure that Eliot was stuffy and sombre." He chuckled. "Nope. Eliot was funny. One of those funny anti-Semites. By the way, you spelled *sombre* wrong. It's *somber*."

"You're in Canada," I said.

He chuckled. "I'm in death. We get to keep our own way of spelling." There followed the kind of pause that follows the first turning of the wheels of a hearse as it leaves the gravesite. "Among other things."

"Like where?" Chelsea asked.

Delmore's voice dropped so low that I could barely hear it. "We even get to keep our deaths."

But I had to give my full attention to Chelsea. I peered through the windshield and saw that we were approaching the general area of Churchill Square. Was this to be my finest hour? It didn't feel that way. But I did have an inspired idea.

"The library parkade. It's underground."

Chelsea nodded, and dropped her foot on the gas. Soon we were plunging down, out of the people-thronged streets – it must have been lunch hour – into that close-ceilinged world of oil-soaked cement and cement pillars and mostly black SUVs cattled in their stalls. Chelsea reached for the ticket, the arm of the machine lifted and the Pinto cantered into the gloom. Once we had parked, and Chelsea had shut off the engine, I almost felt that we should have immediately watered the car and wiped her flanks down. But, in truth, I was too relieved to move. My whole body released. An inaudible sigh released from every pore. For the moment, we were safe.

Safe, but confused. Or at least I was. I had no previous experience to fall back on. I fell back on my good citizenship, which, in this case, was perhaps also kindness and caring and not merely self-protection. I had heard the painful history in Chelsea's voice; I didn't want her to have any further trouble with the law. The right and wrong of the crime was immaterial for the moment, but trouble was trouble. I had grown up in British Columbia at a period of rising environmentalism; when a grandmother chained herself to a Douglas fir to save it from the loggers, the law always settled Grandma's hash eventually.

"Chelsea." I turned to face her. She was chattering to Greg, making clucking noises with her tongue, smiling for all the world as if there was no such thing as the future or the past. Her face shone with sweat, her mascara had formed little Rorschach blots on her cheeks and her red hair had come free in a few places; some strands stuck out like straw from a scarecrow's shirt. I forged on, even more convinced of the rightness of my plan. "Let's make a deal."

She stopped chattering. And the monkey – I swear – turned to gaze at me as if he were her advocate. I admired him for his pugnacious willingness to protect his protector, and the admiration completely decided me.

"I won't make you take him back, but we can't just leave things the way they are, either. It isn't practical. They'll track you down. It isn't just your car. The owner had plenty of time to study you, and he'll be able to give the police a full description." I raised my hand to ward off her protests. "And I understand that you can't, or don't want to, use a credit card to buy the monkey. So" – Delmore's hot grizzly breath burned the back of my neck; he was as interested as if I'd been T. S. Eliot pronouncing on the quality of his poems – "let me buy him for you. Let me call the owner, explain the situation calmly and then give him my credit card information. If you like, we can work out some easy terms that will give you lots of time to pay me back." I was already calculating just how I was going to budget for the purchase of a South American capuchin monkey. No doubt the credit card company would wonder if they were dealing with another case of identity theft. Books, the occasional flight to Vancouver, groceries on rare desperate occasions, some fees for children's swimming lessons and various sports and arts programs: that had been the purchasing pattern for many years. Now, all of a sudden, an exotic pet. But then, surely, the credit card company would recognize exactly what had been my consolation about identity theft ever since it first emerged as a maddening modern crime: who in their right mind would want to steal *my* identity? What self-respecting hacker would waste his time and energy on an impecunious poet who mostly couldn't even get blood from his own stones because he had long ago sold his stones to buy organic baby food or to pay the heating bill?

Chelsea broke gently into my thoughts. Were those tears sliding with Fred Astaire grace onto the mascara's black dance floor? Delmore didn't even groan at this stretch of an image; I knew that he was stunned by my offer to pay, because no one other than a serious poet who had to teach to survive could understand what fifteen hundred dollars on my credit card meant. He also understood that I had no serious intention of making the girl pay even one penny back. I had made that point for appearances only. In any case, it eventually occurred to me that fifteen hundred dollars seemed a reasonable share of the twenty thousand dollars I might just take from Ollivander for the magician bank.

"Really? You'd do that?" Chelsea asked, so softly that I barely caught the words. "That's . . . that's so cool of you."

Ah, if only my children had heard her. Was that worth fifteen hundred dollars and a monkey's freedom – to be, at fifty, called cool by a teenager? Frankly, no. Coolness had never been a part of my repertoire, not even when I was a teenager myself and briefly concerned about such things. 1980. Feathered bangs! But to help someone, to reach out, with no expectation of anything in return, as Keaton had reached out to Fatty Arbuckle after the rape trials, giving him the directing job for *Sherlock Jr.*, at least until it became painfully obvious to everyone that Fatty, his confidence shaken, no longer had the goods. Even then, Keaton had manufactured a reasonable explanation for Arbuckle's removal from the project; he told his old friend that he was wanted elsewhere, on a more important project overseen by William Randolph Hearst and all his millions, a situation that Keaton himself, with the utmost discretion, had orchestrated. What did Keaton ever gain by this friendship and loyalty? Self-respect? Peace of mind? I hoped these dividends paid off a decade later when he sat weeping on the set of all those tired MGM sound comedies in which he was miscast, or several decades later when he played unfunny bit parts to all those teenagers in the beach blanket pyjama movies. Who knows – perhaps that loyalty to Roscoe Arbuckle, more than the comic genius and the work ethic, perhaps that natural affection that led to a five-hour walk through the streets of Paris upon hearing of his mother's death, perhaps those acts saved him as much as his art did. It is certainly not true to say that impressive personal qualities are inextricably linked to artistic talent. The list of real bastards who ever put pen to paper . . .

"Why do you even write prose," Delmore grumbled, "if you can't stop digressing? There's such a thing as dramatic structure, you know." Yet I could hear him moving the solid blocks of tears from his dark eyes to his massive paws; they scraped like pyramid stones. I was almost crying myself by now.

"Well, I'm happy to do it," I said, keeping the emotion from my voice. "Think of it as a gift to your mom. She's probably about my age. I know how tough things can get."

Chelsea nodded. Greg Arious nodded. Delmore shifted some more of his Egyptian sand and, far across the slick, grey sea of cement, through the silty underwater gloom, the ghost of Keaton inspected the moving arm of the parkade's ticket machine. It seemed that death did not alter one's interests, but I wasn't sure if I was comforted by that. I made a mental note to ask Delmore about it later. For now, I had work to do.

"Could you look up the pet shop number on your – whatchamacallit – phone?" Truth be told, and as God as my witness, I didn't know whether you could call a phone with Internet access a phone. I didn't even know if all phones had Internet access. People talked about their various plans with their mobile devices, but it was all Greek to someone who still thought in terms of layaway plans, and who still used phrases such as *it was all Greek*. Understand: I make no apologies. Despite the cultural and social pressure, we don't owe our degree of currency to anyone. It's a free country. Isn't it interesting how that particular slogan never goes out of currency? Some language just always supports the troops.

Chelsea performed the petit point on the tiny digits and announced the phone number of the pet store. Then she held the phone out to me. Noticing my hesitation, she offered to dial the number. Except she didn't say *dial*. So what did she say? *Type*? But still I hesitated. The darned thing was so tiny. If I put it up to my ear, I feared that it would drop into the canal and vanish. Then I'd be hearing teenaged conversations continually, which, come to think of it, might well teach me something about life. I'd been arrogant long enough. If I couldn't quite swallow my pride, I could at least taste it. I asked Chelsea to dial the number (of course I said *dial* – I'd been raised a rotarian and a rotarian I remained), which she accomplished in about the amount of time it takes a hummingbird to complete one beat of its wings. Then I took the little phone and held it up like an explosive device to my eardrum. A few seconds later, Angus Metalhead's softly sinister voice reached out with a "Yeah?"

I took a deep breath, dragged the little phone down my jawline, and plunged in. "I was just in your store. The middle-aged man with the young red-headed woman. We –"

"You stole my fucking monkey."

Not a good start, Metalhead, I thought. Aggression doesn't encourage generosity.

"Yes, well, it would be stealing if we had no intention of paying for it. That's why I'm calling."

"I've already got the cops looking for you. That piece of shit you're driving won't be hard to find."

I'd always suspected that lovers of heavy metal music were idolaters of the bleeding obvious, and here was the proof.

"Well," I said, as calmly as possible, "you can tell them to stop looking. I'm calling to pay. I'll use my Visa. It was fifteen hundred, you said?"

During the pause that followed, Greg Arious, as if sensing the physical presence of his former captor, began to shriek like a banshee. I raised my eyes to Chelsea, suggesting that she find some way to distract her friend. And the quick-thinking girl – who might indeed prove to be a good student, if I ever found my way back to the classroom, which seemed more and more like the way Kansas seemed to Dorothy, except in reverse (and God help me, both Keaton and Arbuckle had been born in Kansas, and what exactly did *that* mean?) – dangled her go-light purse in front of Greg Arious, and he had enough sense of irony to take it as a sign to stop. Meanwhile, in the interim of shrieks, I couldn't tell whether Metalhead had spoken. So I repeated my query about the price. The response was unexpected, to say the least.

"No fuckin' way. Fifteen hundred was a deal I was giving you until I found out you were a couple of fuckin' thiefs."

Thieves, I said, but only mentally. To Metalhead, I offered reason. "We have the monkey right now. And we paid you nothing. I could just hang up." Hang up? Push the off button?

Metalhead's barrage of curses overwhelmed my pedantic interest in the effects of changing technologies on language. He certainly wasn't the brightest pixel on the screen. But he did manage to get his point across through all the expletives. Basically, no one stole from him and got away with it. If the cops didn't get us, he had friends who'd be happy to find us, and we'd better hope the cops found us first, because @?**!x!zz#@ and Z!@**!?xx, oh, and also, !!**&$!xxq@!Z.

By now, I thought the phone was indeed an explosive device, or at least an expletive device. I held it an inch from my ear until the effin ceased. Then, surprised by my own anger (normally aggression and confrontation turn me milder, as though there's a kind of emotional pendulum between people and I need to swing it back from one extreme to the other before balance can be restored), I did something I hadn't done in years, probably not since my last dust-up in a competitive soccer game. I joined the vernacular current of my times.

"Yeah? Well, why don't you go fuck yourself, you Iron Moron. We're keeping the fuckin' monkey."

At this point, I would have loved to slam the receiver down, leaving Metalhead with an extra droning tone in his clouded cerebellum. But modern technology had removed that subtle pleasure, replacing it with the silence of Internet hate. In fact, it just occurred to me most poignantly at that instant: Keaton had moved from silence to sound because of technological change, and now, over eighty years later, we had started moving back. It was in silence I held the phone out to Chelsea, whose large eyes had widened at my outburst. The little device chattered away with Metalhead's rage, and Chelsea, quite brilliantly, decided to give Greg Arious his moment in the Samsung. She put the phone up to his pink-purple lips and let him shriek. "Ha! There's fifteen hundred dollars you're not getting back, you Daft Leopard." I silently applauded.

Then I realized that I had actually spoken aloud, and that I was laughing and slapping the dashboard. For the first time in months, I was richly, deeply, wildly, fully in the moment. I hadn't considered the consequences of the phone exchange, I wasn't planning my sensible escape from Chelsea's company,

I wasn't worrying about Metalhead's posse of goons piling out of a four-by-four with tinted black windows. I was laughing, and tears rolled down my cheeks.

"That's the spirit," Delmore shouted above the din. "You won't get many chances like this, chum. Seize the day, as my buddy, Bellow, liked to quote the old Romans."

"I love it," Chelsea kept repeating, "I love it, I love it. We're keeping the fuckin' monkey. I love it!" And Greg danced on the steering wheel, holding Chelsea's hands and shrieked, not like a banshee but like a living creature who'd been saved from a life of misery. Was that also how I laughed? Was I, too, captive and miserable and suddenly, briefly free? No. Everything was much more complicated than that. I loved my wife and children, I loved too many people, and too many small things in life gave me joy for misery to be an accurate description of my state. And yet, when had I last enjoyed myself so much? More importantly, how could I keep it going?

Delmore groaned. "Too late. It's already too late. You're on the way down now."

And there was Keaton's ghost, on the hood of the car, sitting cross-legged and gazing at me with that stoic, unblinking expression of legend, as if I was part of a preview audience for the film of his eternity. I couldn't stop it from happening, I simply could not stop it. The years, the accumulation of the years, the ordinary processions of the sun: five decades could not sustain the euphoria in the way that two decades could. My laughter stopped and my worry started while Chelsea was still fist pumping and shouting, "I love it! I love it!" Delmore didn't even have to speak. I knew he'd spent his whole examined life between such extremes, the emotional highs and lows of the creator. Many people – perhaps Charles Sleep, certainly Metal-head – lived somewhere on the slopes. Was that preferable? To swallow the Aldous Huxley soma, to medicate the child's disordered attentions, to antidepress? But when the line on the heart monitor beside the hospital bed goes level, the patient is dead. Seize the day? Yes. But some days are warm flesh, some days are bone. We have to seize under all conditions. Go gentle on yourself, for the world will make no such effort.

I enjoyed the girl's happiness and the monkey's antics, even as I felt the underground go wine-dark around the little yellow car and knew that we had to move on, as the race moves, as the language moves, to stay alive.

In the eventual subsidence of noise, Chelsea announced that she was starving.

"You must be hungry, too, Professor. We really need to eat. But . . ."

I anticipated her concerns. "In for a penny, in for a pound, as my mother would say." To combat her bewilderment, I added, "I'm not going to say goodbye now. Besides, weren't you going to help me find the homeless guy? You haven't forgotten about the bank, have you?"

"Oh shit." She banged her palm against her forehead. "I did forget. Hey, if you do sell it, maybe I can borrow that fifteen hundred to get a different coat of paint for my ride."

Her ride? It took a few seconds, but I finally caught on. More than caught on, in fact. Now I really began to sober up. We were in a Keaton chase for real now, with the cops and Metalhead's friends at a considerable advantage. The underground parking lot was still the safest place to be. If it was food we needed, we needed to get out and walk. And since the day was so nice, we had to conduct our search by foot, too, if we should conduct it at all under the circumstances. Christ, let me think. There was still the little matter of my class at four. I hadn't cancelled that one yet. A sessional lecturer had to be careful not to cancel too many classes if he wanted his contract renewed. At the very least, I'd have to return to campus so I could put another message on a chalkboard that required no chalk. The desired streetcar ride seemed an impossible pleasure, but that only made it more appealing. Human nature. Try as we might, there's no escaping it. The little monkey was lucky. Or maybe he was unlucky. What on earth did I know of a monkey's life? Except that he wasn't living where he was born, which made him as North American as anyone else. It was time to go.

"How about the food court in the mall?" Chelsea suggested. "I actually work at the New York Fries there. I can get us the employee discount."

Why not? All the wild salmon in the stores came from China now, so I might as well eat fries from New York. At least New York was on this continent. Then again, the potatoes probably came from China. And they weren't wild either; they were also farmed.

"I'm glad to see you taking it so well," Delmore said. Once again, he laid a heavy paw gently on my shoulder. "Whenever I came down, I'd write a nasty letter to an old friend. Or, if I was married, I'd take it out on my wife. You're healthier than you think."

"But am I healthier *when* I think? That's the real question."

"What the hell do you expect me to say to that? Of course you are. Just stop thinking for a while and see how much you like it."

"I can't stop thinking. That's the problem."

"That's not a problem, you dope. That's your salvation. The world's filled with unthinking automatons. Farmed at the people farms. Unhappiness is independence. I might have been crazy, but I was my own crazy. I was Delmore Schwartz crazy, and I was Delmore Schwartz happy, and I was Delmore Schwartz miserable. All the way down the line, I was Delmore

Schwartz. You think I'd be here if that wasn't true? You think the old boy out there on the hood would be here? The dead don't visit the mindless, you know."

"You can see him?" For some reason, the idea almost took my breath away. "Keaton? You can see him?"

"Sure. Haven't you been paying attention? I can talk to him, too. Though I don't. He's not the chatty type. Besides, I saw all his films when I was a kid in my twenties. I prefer to let him be silent. And that's the way he prefers it. Anyway, his voice is all wrong. Real deep and rough." Delmore chuckled. "Like a bear's. Actually, to be accurate, the old boy's voice always makes me think of a tombstone being slid across another tombstone. There's more smoke in his lungs than genius in my poems, and there's plenty of genius in my poems."

A shiver ran right up my spine, which isn't a cliché, because that's exactly where shivers travel. "Could I talk to him?"

"You ain't dead, pal. That's a privilege for which you have not paid the ultimate price. And there's no credit card for that."

"But I can talk to you."

"Ah." Delmore's paw still rested on my shoulder. It felt more and more like a meteor burning into the earth of my flesh. "That's a special circumstance. Poets help poets. In fact, *only* poets help poets. It's one of the perks of the profession. Okay, it's the only perk. And since most people don't want a poet's help, and would never think of turning to a poet for help, it ain't much of a perk. You know the Jimmy Stewart movie *It's a Wonderful Life*? There's that guardian angel, Clarence, who helps George out so that he can get his wings. The angel. Are you paying attention? Well, this is the same thing, except I don't earn any wings, and I make no banal promises that life's wonderful. It isn't. So, what's in it for me? Simple, pal. You're not a half-bad poet. If I can help you through this, it might mean a few good poems for the world."

"James Agee described Keaton as a poet," I said. "Maybe I could –"

"Oh, I get it," Delmore snarled and bared his fangs. His claws bit into my skin. "I'm not good enough for you and your crisis. Keaton's the genius. I'm the cut-rate replacement. Fuck! You've read my best poems and stories, you know what they cost me, just as much as *The Navigator* and *The General* cost him. More. I had nobody's help. Anyway, if you like, I can bugger off. There's this poet in Rwanda . . ."

"No, no, no. I'm grateful you're here. I'm sorry. You're a big help." The damage control had to be quick, because Chelsea was standing outside the Pinto, with Greg Arious on her shoulder. "Please. I'd appreciate it if you stayed. You know how much I love your poems. I even wrote an essay once, saying how much I hated people describing you as a writer who never lived up to his promise."

He growled deeply, but at the moronic critics, not at me. I hurried on.

"What exactly do we promise anyway? We don't owe anyone our poems."

"Everyone," he contradicted quietly. "We owe them to everyone. But not the rankers, the schemers, the ladder-climbing academic bean-counters. They can choke on their sulphuristic jargonistic effluence." He drew in a long, raspy breath. "All right, apology accepted. To be honest, I'm almost fond of you."

"Thanks." I wasn't being sarcastic. His spirit *was* a help, and I sensed I'd need a lot more help before the day was done.

I CLIMBED OUT of the car, my damaged knee stiff, the heavy fumes of the cement circle of hell washing around me like a back eddy. "There is nothing either good or bad, but thinking makes it so," said Hamlet, which was true enough, but oh – Suicide formerly known as Prince – it's hard sometimes, especially as you get older. I walked around the unexploded trunk of the Pinto and tried to let Chelsea's smile return the euphoria. But all I could see was trouble. First of all, the monkey was going to need a diaper eventually. Second of all, and even worse, I knew without having to ask that she intended to take him into the food court. And, strangely, I knew that she knew that I knew.

"I can't leave him in the car. He'd be freaked out. Besides, in the wild, he'd be with about twenty or thirty others just like him. They're very social. At least according to the stuff I found online."

The little primate had both arms roped loosely around her neck. Somehow I couldn't bring myself to state the obvious: he'd been stolen from the jungle, put in a box and flown for hours in darkness; then bought and owned briefly by some idiot who changed his exotic pets probably more often than he changed his underwear; and finally kept in a cage in a dingy, foul pet shop in a strip mall in northern Alberta run by a fat ex-roadie for Thin Lizzy. I thought Greg Arious could probably handle an hour by himself in a locked car. On the other hand, we'd already committed theft, so the police were already looking for us. Getting kicked out of a mall's food court wouldn't make much difference.

I sighed lengthily, but only for appearances, then shrugged. "Okay. But he's not having any of my fries."

The grin on Chelsea's face widened until the dimple appeared in her cheek. "I'll keep him tucked up inside my coat. No worries."

So we ascended via the grimy, vomit-stained, urine-reeking stone stairway to the sun-splashed avenue between Churchill Square and the main branch of the public library. If not exactly a pilgrimage from hell to paradise, the change was nonetheless an improvement.

But the downtown of Edmonton had very little human touch. It was, much of the time, a sterile place, poorly planned, designed to accommodate skyscrapers and to arrange them to maximize two effects: the eradication of sunlight and the intensity of wind chill. Churchill Square itself, which had once allowed for sightlines from corner to corner, had recently been cemented and blocked up, mostly killing whatever hope of openness downtown workers might experience on their lunch hours and coffee breaks.

As for the library, I really couldn't bring myself to consider it, for its fate was the fate of all libraries in the digital revolution. The downtown branch had become a crossroads where recent immigrants, security guards, troubled youth, emergency vehicles, schizophrenics and other mentally ill outpatients, and some caring, hard-working professional librarians met to work out a bizarre transition from the book age to the computer age. Everyone and everything felt dispossessed and fragile.

We slid away from Churchill Square into the valley of the skyscrapers, Greg's baby-faced head sticking out of Chelsea's duffle coat. It was just like sliding between the panels of a black-and-white comic book. Then, bypassing a few panhandlers – and I did take a close look, thinking of the scruffy balloonatic who had sold me the toys – we stepped into the scrubbed, contemporary glare and glitz of the mall. So much light! But not sunlight. And such coolness from the air conditioning, though it wasn't warm enough outside to merit the energy expense. A faint chemical smell, mixed in with a faint leather smell, flowed through the wide corridor, as if somewhere behind the happy storefronts Alberta's cattle were being slaughtered by the latest toxic method. I could see a white-smocked Avon lady dabbing the killing perfume behind a cow's ears. And, as always happened to me when I entered a mall, I simply wanted to lie down and weep until security came to kick me in the head unless I agreed to leave this private property that masqueraded as a public market.

Chelsea, however, was completely at home, even with a monkey in her coat. We passed a Dollarama, a Second Cup, a Gap, a Sport Check, a Winners and then took the escalator into the antiseptic bowels of the place. Here, we passed a video game store, a Starbucks, another Gap. We passed some stunning women dressed to the nines who might have stepped straight off the glossy streets of Manhattan, and, as we neared the food court, we began to pass the damaged and the broken: a shaking old woman with a moustache and a shawl more frayed than together; an elderly man whose bronzed and weathered face crawled with blinks, as if he suffered from phosphorescent blindness and couldn't make it back to camp; a skinny, pockmarked girl with long greasy hair whose hands shook like half-erased parentheses around a Booster Juice Styrofoam cup; four hooded young men with cellphones who probably weren't Buddhist monks calling to make reservations at a vegan restaurant.

Finally, like a depressed bull arriving in the stadium, I looked around at the ring of franchised food joints. Each one appeared to be staffed by a bored teenager or recent immigrant, not one of whom was smiling. Their gloom lifted my spirits because, well, they should have been gloomy. Despite the light and the close proximity to consumer paradise, the mall was an unhappy place. It was like walking around inside a slow computer game, and I was about to eat something as nourishing as whatever Pac-Man used to chomp down on.

Only when Delmore exhaled noisily did I realize that he'd galumphed along beside us. He seemed particularly sullen and morose. "Why are most human beings living?" he grumbled. "Because they're alive and haven't died yet, that's all."

Given his mood, I saw no point in conversing with him. We continued on in silence.

The food court, unlike the rest of the mall, at least had a clear smell. Grease. The air was greasy. I thought if I just walked through the court a half-dozen times with my mouth open like a whale's through a cloud of plankton, I'd fill right up. Maybe that was why so many street people squatted at the sixty or eighty low brown tables. They could eat without having to buy anything.

Chelsea spoke quietly into her coat as she approached the New York Fries outlet.

"Don't worry about it," I said. "I think you could probably let him out. I'm not sure anybody would notice." The semiconscious quality of the food court was beginning to affect me. I felt like a poorly fed tropical fish in one of Metalhead's aquariums, just floating, waiting, not really hoping, my belly almost rising in the murk.

Delmore, who had been sucking on his paws for lack of any other nutrition, returned to his earlier gloomy theme. "All this talk of being born again. Ha! Being born once is no great pleasure."

Finding no sustenance in that accompanying ghost, I looked for Keaton, and found him, not surprisingly, inspecting the espresso machine at Starbucks.

"What can I get you, Professor?" Chelsea asked. "There's more than just fries here."

"That's okay. I'm not all that hungry. I'll just go over there and grab a coffee and a muffin. Then I'll find a table."

"Hey, Chels," a heavy-set, crewcutted young man with a noble Dracula nose shouted. "You got a shift today?"

"Tonight," she said.

I left before the whole subject of the primate in her coat came up. The truth was, I needed a few minutes to myself. I might even have needed a few years to myself. That is the problem. We don't get years to ourselves until we no longer want them.

I bought a tall Americano from a short Filipino and decided against a muffin. The first taste of coffee was a delight, and it helped, it really did. I felt strengthened at once as I found a table amongst the office-tower workers on their lunch hours and the street people and the shining, well-fed consumers and the lonely elderly and the Pippi Longstockings with monkeys in their coats. Chelsea still stood under the banner of the New

York Fries. I resolved to make the most of my no doubt fleeting solitude.

I checked my watch. It was almost one o'clock. I checked my pulse. It was still quick, but not alarmingly so. I checked my mood. It had sped through a few phases since the morning, and now had slid down toward where it started. Much had happened, but little had changed. I still didn't feel that I could teach a class, today or any time soon. I still didn't feel that I was a vital part of the human story. I might have been wealthier, on account of the rare mechanical bank. But I was also more vulnerable and sensitive, exposed like the transparent horse. And I had committed a crime, or at least been an unwitting accomplice who'd eventually decided to join the gang of two. Much had happened; little had changed. Was this, then, the definition of life? Or maybe I wasn't appreciating the change. This young woman, Chelsea, for example – who now walked towards me with a bag of fries in one hand and some kind of drink in the other – had she entered my life only to leave it as quickly, or had I made a new friend? The jury remained out. God! Wrong expression! I really didn't want to think about juries. Never mind the existential concerns; there were practical ones to face. We needed to discuss them.

I looked closely at my accomplice as she sat down opposite me. Her mascara had somehow been cleaned up and the red sweat-radiation had evaporated. The girl was a marvel of resourcefulness: when had she managed the cosmetic touch-up? And with a monkey in her coat? I supposed this was yet another example of the remarkable multi-tasking capabilities of the young, a product of the whirlwinds of the digital age. Every day in this millennium was a cyclonic celebration of the fast, with everyone standing perfectly positioned in the new global economy, trusting that the two-tonne house front of history would crash over us and not leave a mark. In any case,

Chelsea seemed just fine. I couldn't help but be uplifted. She was eighteen or nineteen years old and, at least for the moment, happy. If I wanted a definition of life, then why not this one? Why not this one?

She took a sip of her drink, pinched a fry in her long fingers like a cigarette and, with her other hand, held her coat together to keep Greg Arious from capering free. His tiny dirty-blond head poked out like a graduation corsage.

"Have a fry, Professor. I don't want to eat them all."

"No, thank you."

Inevitably, perhaps, an awkwardness descended over us. From the moment of our meeting, the pace of experience had accelerated, and now we were coming down off the high. Just as well, as I had no business being in her company at all. I cleared my throat.

"I was right about him." I pointed at the monkey. "You could probably bring a circus in here and no one would say a thing." But just bring in a petition to stop violence against women on the anniversary of the Montreal Massacre and see how quickly the mall security reacted. A general spiritual fatigue kept me from speaking the thought aloud, and even Delmore let it pass. He was too busy sucking on his paws and moaning something about lifting the lid on the coffin of the human character.

"Yeah. I love the food court." Chelsea's tone more or less claimed the place as her home. "I always love coming here."

"You do? Why?"

She let go of her coat and held her arms out to both sides. "Well, everyone's here. All kinds of people, I mean. You wouldn't believe who I've met here. Big business types and dudes from indie bands I like and . . ." She leaned forward, eyes even wider, and closed her coat just before Greg Arious sprang out like that creature from *Alien*. "Did you know that

Oprah's coming to Edmonton? I wouldn't be surprised if she came in here. I hope I'll be on shift then."

Yes, I had heard of Oprah. The Grand no-longer-young Oprah. You couldn't be an author and not have someone – often a family member – suggest that you should send your book to Oprah. But wasn't she the celebrity who was always dieting? Back in the nineties, at least, she was dieting. Did women on diets eat at mall food courts? I sighed lengthily but discreetly. Chelsea obviously had a good heart. She wasn't even into her twenties. Frankly, I was tired of judging everyone. Besides, the worry had begun to rise once more.

"You shouldn't drive your car for a while," I said. "The police *are* looking for it."

She nodded. "But what about finding that homeless dude? I was going to help."

Before I could respond, she answered her own question. "We'll walk. It's a nice day, and he's probably not far from here anyway. Oh? You're okay to walk, aren't you?"

I smiled. "Yes. I'm okay to walk." That was about all that I was okay to do, but I made no further comment.

"Hey! I just thought of something." Chelsea swallowed some masticated fry and sprang to her feet.

I followed her over to a table on the opposite side of the court where the shawled figure sat, hunched like a mossy stump. This whiskered, bony-jawed woman was knitting without needles or yarn. Her large, gnarled hands were mostly covered with dull-red fingerless mitts, and she rubbed them together so fiercely that the fabric might have been raw flesh. I thought of Lady Macbeth trying to remove the incarnadine spots of guilt. When Chelsea leaned down and spoke to this person (she called her Ardeth or something remotely Scandinavian), the figure looked slowly up, as if out of the depths of the girlhood she had once known.

"We're looking for a Dumpster diver who pushes a shopping cart around. He was – where was it exactly, Professor, that you met him?"

"Jasper. Jasper and 107th Street."

"Can you describe him for . . ."

Ardeth? Arleth? Abishag? I couldn't quite tell. I gave a description, emphasizing the sheer number of blue recycling bags. Even though I saw him most vividly as a Confederate soldier near the end of the Civil War – ragged, fierce and quietly desperate – I didn't think the image would clarify anything for Ardeth.

She mumbled something without lifting her head from her mitted hands.

"Harvard?" Chelsea turned to me. "Isn't that some big college?"

"Hee hee hee." I knew without looking whose delighted giggle *that* was. "Plenty of rust on the ivy. See if she knows what Yale is. Go on, ask her."

I shook my head. The American poets of the postwar generation had been obsessed with teaching at the Ivy League schools. Delmore Schwartz, who'd been both a star student and a teacher at Harvard when Jews were rather exotic and, frankly, unwelcome in that "Brahmin establishment," obviously enjoyed Chelsea's tentative definition. But I didn't have time for those long-ago politics.

"It's a prestigious American university, yes. Why?"

"Ardeth says the dude we're looking for is probably Harvard."

Again came the mumbled words spoken into the red mitts.

Chelsea said, "Oh," then turned and looked up at me. "That's just what everyone calls him because he's smart."

"Ha!" Delmore snorted.

I scowled at him, but I was mostly relieved that he had come out of his gloomy hibernation. "You should accept with grace that people still connect intelligence with Harvard. The place hasn't fallen as far as you think."

"It's only because you can't give someone a nickname like 'The New School for Social Research.'"

I didn't have the heart to tell him that the original New School for Social Research had simply become The New School, the embarrassing social research reference having been dropped by the administration some years before.

"Where do you think we could find him now?" Chelsea pressed.

Ardeth – grubby, withdrawn, wholly marginalized – reached into her shawl, which was thin as sashimi – and pulled out a cellphone. The gnarled thumbs did not move with anything like the speed Chelsea employed, but Ardeth was clearly familiar with the device. Since she didn't raise it to her grubby, quivering lips to mumble, I assumed that she was checking some sort of Google map that zeroed in on the homeless.

"She's texting," Chelsea said, as if she'd read my lame mind.

Many seconds passed. I sipped my Americano. Over at the New York Fries, Keaton's ghost fiddled with the ketchup dispenser. He removed his porkpie hat, held it under the nozzle and pushed. It was *The Butcher Boy* all over again, with ketchup instead of molasses as the foundation of the gag. But no Fatty Arbuckle or Al St. John stood on this set. Nineteen seventeen was almost a hundred years ago. And yet why shouldn't it be *The Butcher Boy* all over again? Where else should it be re-enacted but in a food court in the bowels of a mall, which is, in fact, the contemporary general store.

Ardeth studied the screen. She mumbled. Chelsea thanked her.

"She says her son saw Harvard about ten minutes ago, and he was headed this way. Sometimes he plays chess in the library."

"Harvard and the squares. Oho!" came a delighted quip.

"That's beneath you," I said to Delmore, then quickly returned my attention to Chelsea. "Well, let's go see. Maybe he's there now."

Ardeth mumbled some more. She seemed to drop the words from her lips like pomegranate seeds.

"Oh, yeah? Thanks." Chelsea turned and muttered, "I guess he's a pretty serious chess player."

Great, I thought, just great. I wasn't much of a chess player, but I knew that the opponents could sit there like – well, like chess pieces – and not move for hours. But surely even a serious chess player, if homeless, would be happy to interrupt his game for the sake of several thousand dollars.

"Do you mind if we hang here a while, Professor? I want to finish my fries. And hey, you can finish your coffee. Besides, I should get something for this little guy to eat." Chelsea smiled down into her coat as I wondered what on earth a capuchin monkey ate. Bananas seemed too obvious. Maybe he was an insect-eating monkey. Had the franchise Vietnamese places introduced the full range of the South Asian diet to the North American palate? As long as there was a ketchup dispenser to sweeten the crunchy thorax, perhaps . . .

With her left hand, Chelsea conducted an Internet search on her phone, then announced that the monkey could eat almost anything we eat, and hurried away. I found another table and sagged into the chair. My body, if not my spirit, anticipated something, and that something, I knew, wasn't going to be easy. Delmore obviously sensed it, too. He squeezed into the opposite chair – not forming a pretty picture – covered his burning black eyes with his massive paws and moaned lowly. Even Keaton's ghost had stopped horsing around with the ketchup dispenser. He sat a few tables away, suddenly middle-aged, and the ketchup trickled like blood down from his hat and stained his white-powdered cheeks. He might even have been crying blood, but he was too distant to see clearly. I felt the presence of other spirits, and they were not easy. Delmore and Keaton had tightened like violin strings. I looked around the ring of franchises, each counter manned or womaned by someone far from their native place. By the time Chelsea returned, I understood that she had more on her mind than finishing her fries.

"I'm sorry," she began, and sat heavily down. "I never . . . well . . . I haven't . . ." She shook her head and blinked rapidly. "Shit." The one whispered curse was like a novel of her emotional life, and it had been years since I'd had any time to read novels. Chelsea kept her head lowered. I waited, distracting myself with the monkey's regal gnawing of whatever he held in his . . . I wanted to say hands, but why create more humans on our already overpopulated planet?

"Don't don't don't," Delmore moaned. His black eyes roamed the artificial sky, the way they must have roamed the hallway ceiling when he lay on his back that fatal morning in 1963, in cardiac arrest, the trash from the trash bag he'd been carrying scattered around him.

Just before I could say, tensely, "Don't what?" Chelsea raised her face to me. As God – whatever god you like – was my witness, the monkey stopped eating and lifted one tiny hand and traced her jawline with it, then cupped her chin. She smiled down at him, seeming to gain some strength from the touch.

"It's just that I didn't thank you. Not properly."

"Oh." In truth, I wasn't exactly sure what I had done to merit her thanks.

"I guess I'm not used to it," she continued, losing breath with each word.

Now my confusion really set in. It must have showed, for she immediately went on.

"People your age being nice to me, I mean."

"Don't don't oh please don't."

And though I was fairly certain it was Delmore who had moaned the words, I was also not entirely certain. After all, the conversation could only get worse. What had people my age done to her? And when? Please. Don't.

"My mom hasn't had the best of luck with boyfriends."

I was breaking over the tenderness of the monkey's touch. He had placed his little hand on Chelsea's cheek and blessed her life; his palm rested warmly on the curve of the Earth as it revolved into cold space. I had to stop the direction of Chelsea's words; I could not face the boyfriends, I simply could not bear it.

"Your father," I began, and Delmore's moan rose to a howl that would, I thought in a panic, bring the security guards rushing over.

Chelsea, of course, hadn't noticed. The two words, *your father*, had hit her as they hit most human beings and always had, with the impact of Oedipus learning at last who he'd killed at the crossroads, with the impact of Hamlet listening wide-eyed to the avenging ghost of his own genesis. But the words didn't break her. Or, if they did, she somehow held the pieces together.

"He left when I was a kid." She drew in her breath, and tightened her jaw. "I hardly remember him."

"He left, he left, he left." Delmore's howling had stopped, and his moan, lower than before, resumed. Keaton, meanwhile, hadn't moved. He remained stock-still by the ketchup dispensers, gaping at us. In the odd undersea silence of the food court, I could hear a single tear land on the top of his slap shoe. It was the opposite for him from Chelsea's experience; he had walked out on his father in 1917, when Old Joe's drunkenness had made the family act an embarrassment. Maybe leaving and being left weren't quite opposite, at least not in the case of children and fathers.

Say something, I chastised myself. For once in your life, be as human as a goddamned monkey. Because it was plain from the girl's tone that she did remember her father, though I could hardly correct her. "I'm sorry to hear that." A long pause ensued. The camera panned in for a dramatic close-up. I railed against the maddening self-consciousness and stumbled ahead. "How old were you?"

Delmore stopped moaning long enough to snarl at me. "Three years, seven months and nine days. Christ! What difference does it make how old she was?"

"I think I was four. My mom doesn't like to talk about it. Except sometimes, when she's been . . . she . . ." Chelsea suddenly pulled her coat together at her neck, as if Greg Arious were the past that she didn't want to escape into the open. "And my grandpa, he used to just get angry. He never had anything good to say about my dad."

Okay, so the mother drinks, and the grandfather died. Jesus. Maybe there isn't anything good to say, I thought, trying to imagine what kind of man could walk out on his four-year-old child. But it happened all the time. And Alberta, I knew, led the country in cases of such abandonment. Never mind oil revenues building the Heritage Savings Trust Fund; the province could be filthy rich on collected child-support payments. O land of the maverick and renegade. But I was sensitive enough to understand that Chelsea wanted more than to have abuse heaped on her father. And who was I, in my current state, to provide it? I couldn't even face thirty teenagers needing their comma faults corrected – how could I possibly face one who needed her past and future resolved? Because what else could it mean to question a parent's behaviour if it didn't mean to partially answer the riddle to your own fate?

"A couple of years ago, when I got my licence," Chelsea continued, almost sheepishly, "I went looking for him. All I knew was that he was from somewhere near Brooks, down around the badlands. Well, I knew his name, too. It's on my birth certificate."

This was terrible, far too much like listening to a student explain why her essay on "A Rose for Emily" was late. I wanted to cry out to her, "But this isn't your fault! Don't apologize!" But who was I to comment? Me, who talked with my mother every other day, who had golfed almost daily with my father through his seventies and then sat by his deathbed as he died?

"My father," Delmore said quietly, "after the divorce, when he remarried, offered to buy me for seventy-five thousand dollars."

"What?" I wrenched my head around.

"Sure, he would have overpaid at that price. But this was before the crash. He had plenty of dough then." Delmore grinned weakly. "You don't know the half of it. Poets and their fathers. Poets as fathers. God, I didn't have to go through that part, at least."

"I never found him." Chelsea's eyes looked beyond me, as if in expectation of seeing her father on the escalator, descending slowly, à la Gloria Swanson in *Sunset Boulevard* in her famous DeMille close-up. "But I found the house where he grew up. It was in Patricia, which is so weird because that's my mom's name." Her voice kept dropping, each word like a tear, and soon I had to strain to catch the words. "Of course, the house was abandoned."

A sudden hope sprang up in me. "What about your siblings? Do they also try to . . ."

She blinked rapidly and started pulling at a hangnail. "I don't have any. One was enough, my mom always says." The tiny breaking of the glass around her almost drowned out the words. "But I know she's had some abortions. She thinks I don't know, but I'm not stupid."

No, you're not stupid. Before I could stop myself, the question spilled out. "Some?"

She shrugged her large shoulders, but they had no linebacker's power now. "Two or three, anyway. Usually not long after she gets a new boyfriend."

At a loss, I sought some kind of distraction. I looked around the food court to find it. But Keaton still hadn't moved. He stood there, in front of Chelsea's father's empty childhood home, waiting for the front of it to crash down over him.

But Delmore obliged, though his voice was space cold and heavy; it seemed to drag like an anchor through the greasy tide. "Consider Frost, that folksy bard. Once, in the middle of the night, he forced his wife into their daughter's bedroom, woke the girl up, drew her attention to the revolver in his hand and said 'Choose!'"

My God, I mouthed, and it could have been either to Chelsea or to the dead poet-bear whose tears gathered thick and black as oil.

"I make no judgment," Delmore continued. "Frost buried four children."

Four? The distraction was hardly a help. I returned my attention to Chelsea, who had taken her phone out and was fiddling with it. Greg Arious, strangely silent this whole conversation, kept glancing up at her. Even Keaton had finally moved half the distance closer. It was impossible not to see him slowly approaching the knocked-upon door that he opened, after not seeing his sons for nearly ten years, to find them there as young men. They had found his famous life, and it, too, was, in a sense, abandoned. But at least he had been forced away by the rage and bitterness of the boys' mother. Even so, even so, Buster . . . you should have tried harder. What film was more important?

"Genius always means failure," Delmore snorted. "The more of a shit you are, the bigger your talent. I tried – oh, how I tried. But somehow I just didn't have it in me. If you can be awful to people *and* keep your sanity, that's true genius."

I stopped listening to him. His scornful critique of society's romanticized notions of talent seemed remarkably trivial under the circumstances. Yet I had not lost sympathy for him; I knew, from reading his biography, that his childhood had been haunted by his father's constant infidelities. At one terrible point, he had even been witness, in a restaurant, to his mother confronting his father and his latest female friend. That wasn't exactly something you'd forget. No wonder there's so much pain in the story, "In Dreams Begin Responsibilities."

I turned my full attention to Chelsea, desperate to find some way to comfort her. My silence seared through my chest.

"Anyway," she said, and slipped her phone into her coat pocket. "Thanks."

"For what?" I managed to respond.

"For him." She held her hand out and the little monkey grasped her thumb and squealed. The hooded teens at a nearby table looked up cobra-like from their runic pursuits and turned in unison. Smartly, Chelsea gently closed her coat around the squeals. "For letting me keep him. It says online that capuchins can live up to forty years." She smiled down into his babyish face and mumbled, "So, thanks."

"You're welcome," I said, because I could think of nothing else to say. I'd done nothing so noble. It was only Metalhead's aggression and my own alienation from the vulgar world that had forced my hand, not compassion for this young woman's loneliness, which, in truth, I hadn't really noticed, being entirely fixated on my own psychic state.

Nothing, in short, had changed, yet something had been

clarified between us. We both sensed it. Somehow the awful artificial light of the food court – the manufactured glare that needed a Vermeer to redeem it – seemed a kilowatt or two gentler. We sat calmly in it, not quite looking at each other, not quite looking away, either. It seemed a small kindness to be nice to her. But I suddenly realized that being drawn into another person's world was much stranger than stealing a monkey or finding a thirty-thousand-dollar mechanical toy, stranger than any poem or film.

"We should go find this Harvard dude," Chelsea said at last.

Delmore, quick as ever, took his chance. "But Tim's not smart enough to go to Harvard, kid."

"Very amusing, very droll." But I was grateful for the change in tone. It had been a draining few minutes, the kind that requires a shower for the psyche. I checked my watch. My afternoon class was still a few hours away, the room waiting there like a doctor's office in the middle of the night, waiting for the succession of widened eyes and the man with the chart. "I have the results of your test back," he says. "I'm afraid the news is not good." I knew I couldn't face the job, but I did have to return to campus and announce the cancellation. The chances of encountering another Chelsea were about as high as stealing another capuchin monkey, a thought that, on the surface, should have comforted me: I didn't exactly relish any further adventure. Yet, the thought did not comfort. In fact, as I rose from the mass-produced table in the mass-designed food court, the thought began to ache. And because I lacked the courage or the energy to analyze the ache, I had to ignore it, just as I ignored the ache in my knee. Delmore's prolonged sigh of brotherhood and his heavy paw on my shoulder certainly didn't help: I knew exactly how he'd define the ache. But I wasn't an egomaniacal middle-aged poet from the 1950s constantly needing my fragile ego massaged; I was . . . what was I? Afraid, lonely, heartsick at the tears in things, at what the Japanese call the slender sadness, all the loss and fulfill-ment of life hanging there in the dawn sky's sliver of moon. O what did Whitman mean when he wrote, "Has any one supposed it lucky to be born? / I hasten to inform him or her it is just as lucky to die, and I know it."

THE LINES stayed on my lips as I took my place beside Chelsea on the escalator and rose slowly towards the common level of the day. And they stayed on my lips as the artificial light of the mall gave way to the lambent late summer sunlight that softened the edges of the skyscrapers and the sidewalks, but not the faces of the strangers whose luck was no business of mine. I could note the differences in each face, the unique composition of bones and features, but they were all the same, all human and bound for loss. Why weren't the faces rent by screams? Why did the earth not open and swallow us all and be done with it?

As the bloody hand of the intersection light changed to the little white man and I obeyed, the sweat beaded on my brow and my step leadened. I dropped slightly behind Chelsea as my mind raced ahead. This day will end, and you will return to what is meant to distract you but can only destroy you: the getting and the spending, the interminably quick subtraction of time, the grief in the last look of your grieving children, the knowledge that can't be put off but is put off, grandly, in the building of a vaudeville theatre, and tragically, in the abuse of a child and in the boardrooms of violence. Where were all these strangers going? The theatre's gone, I wanted to shout. The Three Keatons are gone, and everyone they know. There! There! Can't you see Buster's ghost?

For it stood, unsmiling as ever, just ahead of me, holding open one of the library's glass doors. Bone-white face, space-black eyes, the high cheekbones of a proud and defeated race. And though it looked at every passing face, as I looked at every passing face, I knew why the ghost was really there. Behind me, Delmore sighed – in expectation, I realized – for he was a man – he had been a man – whom art had kept alive until his heart burst. And movies, almost as much as literature, had been blood to him.

When I passed Keaton's ghost, and caught up with Chelsea inside, I said to her, "They play chess upstairs. I'll be along in a moment. I have to use the washroom."

"No!" Delmore said ferociously. "Stay with her."

"Why? What are you –"

"For once in your goddamned life, stop asking questions."

His look froze me. It was brutal in its insistence, and for a moment I was stymied.

"There." He pointed.

Across the open space of the library's main level (whole shelves of books had recently been removed to improve the sightlines between the security guards and the troubled youth who congregated at the computers), I saw Keaton's ghost. He stood by a computer terminal, his face oddly lit by the images on the screen.

I struggled to explain the situation to Chelsea.

"You know that poster I bought? Of Buster Keaton? I'd like to show you one of his films. Well, part of one, anyway."

She shrugged, smiled, said, "cool." And waited.

"Lay on, Macduff," Delmore said gruffly.

Now Keaton seemed like an usher, his whole being the flashlight that directed us to our seats. Even Greg Arious understood that entertainment was in store; he chattered and chirped so loudly that the troubled teens had to turn up the volume of their "Fuck yous" to be audible. A tall, gaunt security guard – fresh off the killing fields of the Sudan – looked on through eyes that were like bullet holes filled with blood. Sensibly, he didn't move. He didn't appear to notice either the cursing or the monkey's excitement; perhaps he didn't notice anything. Did that make him better off in this second decade of the twenty-first century? What melting ice caps? What mass conformity? What exploited peasant class? What shrinking rainforest? What dulled emotion?

The questions dissolved as soon as I reached the screen. Across it rolled Keaton's great gift to us all.

"This is *Sherlock Jr.*," I whispered to Chelsea. "It was made in 1924. Those two men are trying to kill Buster with an exploding billiard ball."

And so it was, all over again. The villainous butler, having left the table for Buster – as the famous detective, Sherlock Jr. – to run, bolts from the room in anticipation of the killing blast. When it fails to arrive, he creeps back to the doorway to watch. Buster sinks shot after shot without striking the tampered ball. Finally, there is no choice; the ball is the next to be struck. Nothing. Silence in the silence of the silent movie. Our faces – mine, Chelsea's, Delmore's, even the pale-pink little mask of Greg Arious – had inched closer to the images on the screen, closer to each other. Our grin became one grin. Keaton's ghost, too, shared in it, though there was no change in his expression. After all, comedy is serious business. If a preview for a movie mattered in 1924, how much more did a post-view matter in 2012? Keaton had suffered enough to know the answer; he knew the value of his art to the human condition, even if most humans didn't know. I marvelled yet again at his youthful grace and skill. The scene at the pool table, for example. There's no fakery in it. Keaton himself made all the shots in the order they needed to be made so that the gag would work. It required hundreds of takes; it had to be perfect. He failed and failed again. You couldn't shortcut a gag any more than you could turn your back on an old friend and colleague whose career had been destroyed by scandal.

"He's really good-looking," Chelsea said, as the camera moved in for a close-up. "He must have been a big star."

"One of the biggest," I said. The pride I felt couldn't be sustained. The crying man on the MGM set, the straitjacketed alcoholic, the absent father, the bit player in the beach blanket movies, the cancerous old man who didn't know he had cancer: I kept seeing these figures step out of the sleeping figure of the good-looking boy-projectionist.

Delmore knew what I saw, and he didn't like it. At least, he didn't like my failure to be completely immersed in the film. "Give the old boy a break, won't you? Everybody suffers, everybody fails. But hardly anybody leaves anything behind that can make a girl and a monkey happy almost a hundred years later."

He was right, of course. Intellectually, I agreed. But on every other level I simply couldn't see the blood in the security guard's eyes drain away because of some flickering images salvaged off some fragile nitrate film stock. Yet, what kind of person couldn't delight in Buster's sinking of the final shot, his clean escape (he had replaced the exploding ball), his outwitting of the villains and his eventual winning of the girl? But wait, the winning of the girl: wasn't it ambiguous, even troubled? After the madcap chase scene with the legendary risky stunts, after the restoration of justice, *Sherlock Jr.* ends with Buster puzzled by a future involving a wife and two babies (a future that paralleled his difficult present at the time). That enigmatic face, I knew, would become tortured and tear-stained a decade later. A kind of time-lapse photography of human suffering played before my eyes, and my grin dissolved.

"We should go," I said.

Chelsea's puzzled face turned to me. "Professor . . ." She hesitated. "I walked over here with you, and the movie was already on the screen."

"Uh-oh," Delmore said. "Time for a *deus ex machina*. I'll see what I can do."

I couldn't very well tell her that the ghost of Buster Keaton, who had been travelling with me most of the day, had set everything up. I couldn't say, "Well, Keaton was always fascinated with technologies. If he hadn't been a comedian, he would have liked to have been a mechanical engineer. He used to chide Chaplin because Chaplin hated TV and wouldn't let his kids watch it. If you're not careful, Keaton's ghost will steal your cellphone and take it apart to see how it works, like he did with the first movie camera he ever saw."

But I didn't have to speak. I didn't know what Delmore had done, but suddenly a fight broke out amongst the teens, the security guard woke from his horrified catatonia and ambled towards them, and I took the opportunity to say, "Come on, let's go upstairs. If the police show up, I don't want them to find you and your little buddy."

So we moved on, walking up the broken escalator, with Delmore breathing raspingly behind and Keaton's ghost, of course, already at the top, bent over, inspecting the unmoving corrugated iron steps. I knew the main branch of the library well, and so, once we'd passed Keaton, I didn't hesitate.

To the immediate right of the reference librarian counter were two dozen computer terminals, in pairs and back to back, with various patrons huddled before them. Ten feet beyond the computers, several figures sat hunched at tables over chessboards. Not everyone and everything had been digitized. The scene warmed me, the way a cabin's orange light shines at night through the dark woods to warm an exhausted traveller. Slowly, I led our advance upon the contemplative human past.

17

I SCANNED THE chess players' faces for Harvard, the balloonatic toy merchant, but couldn't spot him at first. The players composed rather a motley crew (Metalhead the monkey abuser should have been there): an elderly Asian man with a face like a melted wax blossom, a high-cheek-boned Slav with pre-Communist-era Coke-bottle glasses, a fat young man in a short-sleeved White Stripes T-shirt that revealed his marbled ham-hock arms, and a petite red-haired woman in a pale-green pantsuit who must have been my age but who gazed down at the board with all the giddiness of Anne of Green Gables after tippling Madeira. The intensity coming off these faces was different than the intensity coming off the faces of the patrons at the computer terminals; the former were more committed somehow, relying on the prospect of a remote and satisfying future, whereas the latter were hardly adjustable in their torpid ecstasy, changing little with each mouse-click. The chess players might have been staring directly into their own fates, but without panic or even unease, with, rather, a kind of inspiring yet terrifying philosophical calm. Taken together, the computer users and the chess players smashed the glowing window of my dream cabin in the woods. And one player, notably more intense and still, clenched his long, narrow hands so tightly that it seemed blood must run through his fingers. Watching him over the chessboard was like watching someone flay the skin off his face with thought.

At first I didn't connect him to the homeless street merchant floating along Jasper Avenue on his blue recycling bag balloon ship. Perhaps it was the fluorescent lighting of the library, the institutional near silence of murmurs and coughs and unidentifiable electronic hums and beeps, or the lack of motion – something came between me and my memory of the man. As I studied him – the bloodshot eyes in the sparse, nicotine-yellowed beard made him look like a Custer who had survived Little Bighorn and gone to seed on narcotics – I wanted that something to be a brick wall. But this was Harvard. And by now the day had its own strange momentum. I couldn't fail my entrance exam.

As I stepped towards the chess table, however, Delmore grabbed my shoulder. I turned to see his eyes widened to dinner plates and more human than ever over the great bear's snout. It was as if the young man who had written the poem was fighting with terrible desperation to return to the world through the legacy of what he'd created.

"Don't," he said, and pulled so hard on my shoulder that I staggered back a step.

"Are you okay, Professor?" Chelsea squinted at my obvious confusion. She waited, two feet off to one side and slightly behind, her coat zipped almost to her chin.

"Yes. I'm fine." I was still looking at Delmore. His whole great bearish bulk was trembling like a blancmange.

"It's death," he said hoarsely. "It's death. I can smell it."

His claws sank into my skin. His voice rose. "Stop and turn around. Go back. Now."

Grimacing, I pulled away from his thick paw. It fell off into the dry air like a block of ice. Chelsea waited, her expression still quizzical, verging on concerned. All at once, I felt foolish. After all, she was young; all her ghosts were still living, and her absent father, a phantom, was nevertheless real. How could I explain to her the presence of the spirits that took fifty years to conjure? More than embarrassed, I was unwilling to add to her troubles. Let her save her concern for herself, her mother, even the little primate her courage and optimism had rescued from a dreary existence.

Delmore, still on his hind legs, backed away slowly. "It is here. It is close. Oh God." His human eyes locked on the chess players, and he began to whimper. "Child, come away, come away."

I couldn't tell whom he was addressing. Chelsea, perhaps? I certainly wasn't a child; that other self grew dimmer with each passing year.

"It's all right," I said, impatient with his melodrama. Delmore Schwartz, as is clear from his biography, relished the making of mountains out of molehills, especially as he aged. I turned back to the chess games.

There stood Keaton, just behind Harvard's hunched form, as if to study the next move in the game. Except Keaton wasn't looking down at the board; he was staring at me, his white mask almost giving way to an identifiable expression. I couldn't quite read it. The stare went on and on; it stayed on my face, yet seemed to pass through me and travel the seven hundred miles to the edge of the salty sea where I'd been born, where he'd once ridden a motorized railway handcart.

Confused, I finally decided that the ghost's presence at the chessboards was a form of encouragement, and approached the homeless man who'd sold me the rare mechanical bank.

Delmore cried out, "I can't . . . I can't help with this . . ."

I didn't turn back to him. I'd never been a risk-taker, but now the die was cast. In truth, I saw no risk.

"Sorry to bother you." I stood over the chessboard, smiling down at the two players. Harvard's opponent, the young man with the fleshy arms, looked up with a scowl, then immediately dropped his eyes. Harvard didn't even move. "We met earlier today," I went on, "out on Jasper. I bought those toys from you, remember?" Still no reaction. Yet the air thickened around the silence. I became aware of the pounding of my heart.

"Tim," Delmore pleaded softly, "come away."

The use of my Christian name changed everything. It was as if my mother had called me, as if her voice had travelled out of my childhood to give me an important piece of advice. But the die had been cast. Nothing could be changed.

"One of the toys," I said, my mouth and throat dry, "was a cast-iron bank. It turns out that . . ." A deep growl came from nearby, and at first I assumed that Delmore had taken a more aggressive approach to lead me away. "It turns out," I continued, "that the bank is worth quite a lot of money."

Harvard's hands tightened even more. I thought the bones in them might snap. Too late, I realized that the growl – which was now repeated – had come from him. Too late, Chelsea shouted, "Professor! I forgot. You shouldn't bug him when he's playing . . ."

But I had already placed my hand gently on Harvard's shoulder, the way Delmore so often placed his paw on mine. The touch set off an explosion.

Chelsea screamed. "Professor! Watch it!"

Her cry reached me at the same time as Harvard's skull. He

drove his head straight into my chest and knocked me to the floor, scattering knights and pawns around us like acorns shaken off a tree. Before I recovered from the shock, I felt a hard kick to my ribs. Chelsea screamed a curse. I widened my eyes against the pain to see her launch herself at my attacker, her face contorted, both arms flailing. Greg Arious shrieked, again and again, in an ever-increasing crescendo, as Chelsea struck repeatedly at the head and torso of the snarling figure now sprung back from my prone form. I struggled to get up, my breath short, the pain flaring along my side. Other voices – shouts – flooded over me as I stood. "Call security!" "What the fuck, man!" "Help her!"

Oh, I tried. I tried harder than I'd ever tried anything in my life. But it was like attempting to hold back tears with reason. Before I could reach the fight, I heard the cry, "He's got a knife!," and it was the same as hearing, "You're too late! You're too late forever!" But I kept moving forward, my thighs, my chest, in heavy swamp water. I might even have cried her name. The way my mother had cried mine, from the very depths of our beginnings together.

Harvard's knife slashed the air seconds before my arm reached out. But it wasn't the knife that did the damage. Chelsea's assault upon my attacker had somehow released Greg Arious, too, and, instinctively, he had taken up Chelsea's cause, with a ferocity surprising in such a small, cheerful creature. His shrieking attained its highest pitch yet; his fangs flashed a sharp and terrifying whiteness in his babyish face as he leaped on to Harvard's head. From there, the little monkey raked its claws over the grizzled cheeks of the man, who whirled and shouted and waved the knife dangerously around his own face, trying to stab at whatever drug-induced nightmare he must have thought had followed him into the day-world. Meanwhile, Chelsea, who had sensibly backed off at the cry of "He's got a knife," perched at the edge of the whirling figures, her whole being coiled and tensed like a cougar's above its passing prey. How much I pushed against the dark waters to reach her! Yet I hardly moved. I saw the monkey's fangs, heard Harvard's shouts of pain and rage. The knife dropped from his hand with a thunk. He yanked the monkey off his skull like a great scab, gave a wild, gargled cry, and hurled his body sideways at a broken run, like an Olympian about to toss a hammer into the sky. There was a sharp crack as the monkey's head struck the side of the chess table, and the shrieking ceased. Two, perhaps three, seconds of silence followed, sliding across us in the same awful way that death slid across the monkey's twitching little body. Then Chelsea cried out, lunged forward and dropped to her knees.

"No! Oh no no no no . . ." Her pain and moaning were so much worse than Delmore's, for she was young and alive, and I had not dreamed her. So why couldn't I move? It all happened in an eyeblink, yet I saw everything unfold with such clarity that I might have been sitting in a darkened theatre gazing at a screen. Even then, the plush curtains finally close and the lights come up. I knelt beside her. She had lifted the monkey's fluttering ancient eyes close to her own and was whispering, "Please please don't go please." Tears and sweat blurred her freshly repaired mascara into a primitive mask, and when the broken creature's eyes stopped fluttering and its body gave a last spasmodic twitch, the mask hardened. She looked at me, and it was obvious that she did not see me, nor did she hear me, my weak, horrified, repeated, "Chelsea, I'm so sorry." She placed the little corpse into my hands as she rose, her cry one long ferocious vulgarity, her linebacker's shoulders launched in the direction of the bleeding, bewildered form of the man who had just wakened from his own violence.

"You fuckin' douche bag, you shithole, you fuckin' . . ."

Chelsea drove herself at Harvard, but, even in bewilderment, his strength did not abate. He received her violence and threw it to one side. Chelsea landed on her knees in a brief, graceless slide. Now, at last, I moved. If he was going to attack anyone, it wasn't going to be her. My chivalry served no purpose. From far off, the wail of a siren drifted out of the city and up the broken escalator and over the stricken faces of the two dozen library workers and patrons scattered around us like the knights and pawns I stepped on as I moved, the monkey a limp, still warm offering in my shaking hands.

The siren woke something in Harvard. It gave him back whatever grip on reality he had, for he shook his bleeding head at the sound and, at a half-run, headed for the escalator, passing the security guard who had just arrived at the top, his hand twitching on the holster at his hip, his eyes full moons of blood.

Chelsea scrambled up and, still shouting, followed.

I called after her. "Chelsea! Stop!" Pain pierced my side, and it hurt with each gasp, but I kept going. For I did not doubt that Harvard would crack her skull as easily as he'd cracked the little monkey's. My haste, however, proved unnecessary. The man had all the speed of mania to propel him – mania in fear of persecution – and not even a woman's grief and vengeance could outpace that. By the time Chelsea reached the main floor, Harvard had banged through one of the swinging glass doors, knocking some books out of a woman's hands as he whirled out into the warm air like a great, nectar-drunk drone driven from the hive.

Outside, I finally caught up to Chelsea as she stood on the curb of an intersection, looking wildly around in all directions, her mask liquid again, her shoulders trembling, her chest heaving.

"You fucker, I'll kill you you . . . you . . . you . . ." But all the strength had gone out of her curses now; they were turned inward, driven down into the place of doubt and pain where her father kept closing the door of her childhood and walking casually away. Soon the peal of the siren was so loud that it drowned out even her harsh, broken breathing. The pain on her face was louder than the siren and it turned full force on me now. It did not even light on the death in my hands. It settled on me and stayed there. Pain and confusion and sorrow, and the terrible unspoken question that age is supposed to answer. Words would not come to me as the traffic revved by and the passing eyes of the world stared at the bizarre end to our bizarre chase scene. But words – the tools of my working life – were useless now, and I knew it.

I placed Greg Arious gently on the filthy sidewalk and stood like a child lost in a crowded market. Chelsea turned into me, sobbing, her head on my chest, and it was all I could do to fight the pain and weakness in my body and remain upright. But I managed. As I held her, and soothingly said the words that language must contain to orient us to the earth – her name, my regrets, my reassurances – it's all right, Chelsea, it's all right, it'll be fine, I'm so sorry – everything that must be said to resurrect sanity on the borders of madness – I didn't hold her as a professor or as a father or even as a middle-aged adult. I held her as one suffering human holds another, without a past or a future, with only a chasmic, unforgiving present. Her tears dripped like solder through my shirt and seared the skin. I'm sorry. I'm so sorry.

The siren screamed louder. Over Chelsea's head I saw the flashing red lights. Something of the little monkey's fierce loyalty rose up from the pavement and coursed through my blood. Sensing her shock subside to exhaustion, the rage and pain to the beginning of the long dull ache of grief, I whispered, "Come on, we have to go."

I bent over and discreetly gathered up the corpse and held

it pressed to one side under my arm. With my free hand on Chelsea's upper back, I guided her out of the muted, broken sunlight through a doorway to the parking lot's stairs. The heavy door closed, and we descended into the gloom and undersea silence, the hollow echoes of the arcade investing the place with a mysterious, fogbound quality. Even in a heavy fog, the Pinto would have appeared. It was bright as a block of sunlight, though cold as we climbed inside. Chelsea didn't seem to notice that I had gently taken the keys from her purse to unlock the car, ushered her into the passenger seat and then occupied the driver's seat myself. I sat there, a little lost, the dead monkey on my lap. It had been years since I'd driven a car. There'd been no need. And now the need was greater than I could ever have imagined, even though I had no idea where I would be driving and for what exact purpose. Seconds ticked heavily by. Chelsea began to wipe her tears.

"Let me take him," a gruff voice said from the back seat.

I turned, and there was Delmore, his great, shaggy face heavy as granite and his eyes swimming with human pain. I had forgotten all about him, and about Keaton's ghost.

"Where did you go?" I asked as I gently placed the corpse into his thick paws.

"Death does have dominion over the dead." The human sigh out of the bear's throat seemed even more vulnerable than a normal sigh. "But you're not dead. I'm glad of that. And the girl's not dead. For a moment there, I was . . . well, I almost tore the eyeballs out of my head with fear." He glanced to the side, then delicately handed the body of Greg Arious back to me. "You have more work to do. Harder work."

I returned my attention to Chelsea, whose question Delmore had clearly anticipated.

"Where is he?" she asked in a small voice, a child's voice.

"Here," I said. "He's right here." I placed the dead monkey

in her lap and watched her large hands run tremblingly over his crumpled, pale face. By the time she spoke again, a tear or two had dropped from her chin onto the fur, as in a fairy tale, but there would be no magical resurrection. I could almost hear the little girl she'd once been wishing fiercely for it; her quivering lips would have planted that transformative kiss if there'd been any hope. I couldn't measure what hope she might have felt, though the battle – between the only child of a tragic, single mother and the young woman whose favourite literary genre was fantasy – heated the cool interior of the Pinto with a friction that lifted the hairs on my forearms.

"It's all my fuckin' fault," she said, her head bowed. "I'm so fuckin' stupid. I should have warned you."

"No." My response came quickly and firmly; I could not bear her taking this death upon herself as she had probably taken her father's departure for the past fifteen years. "No. It isn't your fault. There's nothing you could have done. Someone like that . . . mentally ill . . . maybe schizophrenic . . ."

Chelsea's face turned to me; it was a moon plunged under dirty water. The black-smeared white of it seemed about to slip off like the powder of the silent film comedians. "She told me. Fuck. She told me."

"Who told you? What?"

"At the food court." Chelsea's eyes fluttered slowly, the lids like iron. "She told me . . . told me never to bug him when he's playing chess. Fuck . . . fuck." She smashed the hard bottom of one palm into her forehead and dragged the hand down over her smeared face.

I knew what she meant now: the old woman with the Scandinavian name – Ardeth or Agneth – who had told us where to find Harvard.

"I never warned you. She said he hates to be interrupted when he's playing chess. Fuck. Stupid stupid stupid . . ."

"Chelsea." My own battle now – between firmness and tenderness – played out in my voice. "I wouldn't have thought that meant he'd attack me. You can't expect that kind of violence. Not from anyone." Especially not from a chess player named after an Ivy League college, I thought, but didn't speak. Who could predict the swiftness from concentration to violence? It wasn't a chess move; it was the move of a digital age, except the blood and the grief weren't virtual. When a computer game ends, when you reach the final level or fail to reach it, the world – the dull, old, ordinary dial-up of the senses – is exactly the world you left behind. This game was different. I felt the change not only in my psyche, but in my primitive practical brain. After all, I had to act. I couldn't think clearly through the aftermath of all that had happened with the speed of a shrike's killing descent.

Where would we go now? The police were in the library, and the numerous witnesses to the murder – for murder it undoubtedly was – would be telling them about us, what we looked like, that we had run outside. Presumably a search of the area would be made. And though the theft of Greg Arious seemed a petty crime in light of his violent death, I still didn't relish having to explain it; I especially didn't relish putting Chelsea's guilt and pain into the purview of the official janitors of human messes. Discreetly, but with shaking hands, I inserted the key and started the engine. I knew as I backed out of the stall only that I had to get the Pinto's vivid yellow coat out of the downtown. Once I'd done so, I could turn my full attention to Chelsea.

The task of driving away wasn't so simple. The car bucked and reared as I inexpertly applied the gas and brakes, and I was the recipient of two horn blasts and at least one middle finger salute as I plunged down the steep hill beside the Hotel Macdonald, the grand granite railroad hotel where Keaton and

Chaplin and other vaudeville stars had once stayed. But the sun, golden and soft over the valley of the North Saskatchewan River, raised my spirits. I drove across the Low Level Bridge, sibling to the High Level a few miles to the west, and poured on the speed as I approached my home territory of Mill Creek, with its comfortably renovated old homes and stately Dutch elms and cozy little cafés and bakeries. Chelsea, meanwhile, kept stroking the fur of the dead creature on her lap, kept dropping tears in a doomed effort to alter reality. I could sense a resolve starting to form in her, deep below the shock, and I had to fend it off. Given what I knew of her – a surprising amount in such a short time – I knew what she would want to do. If I could distract her long enough, perhaps the desire for revenge would abate. The trouble was, how could I distract her?

Food and drink, first. I was desperate for a coffee myself, though I was in no shape to sit in a café, and neither was Chelsea – and she wasn't about to relinquish the little corpse. My mind raced. The girl did have a mother, after all. Maybe I could drive Chelsea home and let whatever maternal skill that woman possessed take over. Then there was my wife, too, as resourceful a person in an emotional emergency as you could want. Oh, but the explanations required – the idea wearied me to the point of collapse. From what I had gathered about Chelsea's mother, she'd likely be drunk and depressed and in need of care herself. What to do? What to do? I had no experience to fall back on. I had fathered three children and raised them to the ages of fourteen, twelve and ten; I should have had some useful resources. It seemed that I'd lived half a century without awareness, numb to my own capacity for human response. For a long moment in the middle of a modern urban centre, I'd dissolved all ego and definition and held the ancient, essential anonymity in my arms. As powerful as that was, it couldn't go on. The deepest moments happen, and soon after you're driving around your neighbourhood in a yellow Pinto with a crying student and a dead monkey and thirty thousand and five dollars worth of mechanical bank and transparent horse in the trunk.

"Haven't you forgotten something?" Delmore grunted.

I was so relieved to be reminded of his presence that I almost drove up onto the curb. Recovering, I immediately sought his advice.

"I was never much good in a crisis," he said. "And you know how I fared with women." He sighed, but inside the sound was the obvious desire to be faring with crises and women all over again. "I can't even really feel the sun, you know. And the trash I eat, I can't taste. Being dead is a lot like what you'd expect. We're right to dread it." I could see exactly one half-foot rectangle of black eye and brown fur and snout in the rear-view mirror, but I heard Delmore's whole life in his voice. "You don't know how lucky you are. Whatever you decide to do, it'll be according to your nature. And I wouldn't be here, frankly, if you were an asshole."

The comment was of some comfort, though what I really wanted was concrete, practical advice.

"You wouldn't listen to me in the library, so why should I waste my breath now?"

I could hardly argue with this point. I hadn't listened, and my failure was tragic.

"I'm sorry," I said. Too late, I realized I'd spoken aloud. Then I realized that Delmore had no doubt intended me to do so.

Chelsea's watery gaze blinked at me briefly as I took my eyes off the road. "Why? You haven't done anything. None of this is your fault. I drove you to the antiques store, I stole him . . ." Her voice broke again. "It was me who didn't warn you."

How could I even begin to explain to this woman just beginning adulthood what my day had started out like? I could hardly even explain it to myself. The cold, creeping dread of fifty that puts ashes on your tongue and in your hands – how much it needed life, the surprise and promise of it, to usher in the gratitude and humility that could be the only jewels of age, if there were any jewels. The search, at least, must be made. Chelsea's guilt and pain against what I woke to each morning . . . how could I warn her? I couldn't, no more than I could warn my own children, or should. Such life was in the living. And the death of such life, too. I assumed the authority that was mine, all that I had earned through the accumulation of the decades.

"Listen, now. What's happened is over. It wasn't your fault. You're a good person, Chelsea. You care. You need to learn how important that is. Not everyone cares the way you do." I reached my hand out and lightly touched the monkey's broken skull. "Imagine if you hadn't come into his life. Think of what you gave him. Gave him back." I could hardly keep going; the tears came heavily in the back of my eyes. "He died for you because of it. And that's a good thing. He was full of life when he did it. You gave him back everything that he was. He wouldn't have had it without you." I might have been speaking for myself; I didn't know whether she could understand. She was so young, and the grief was dew-fresh. I wasn't arrogant enough – not now – to believe my words could lift a lifetime of self-blame. But I had to speak them, just as I'd had to hold her; there wasn't anything else to do. "You can't blame yourself for everything that happens."

I had been driving with minimal attention, keeping to the streets and avenues I knew, obeying the lights. When I finally focused, I could hardly believe my eyes. The Pinto had come to a stop on Whyte Avenue, in the heart of Old Strathcona, the character district of the city, which had, a century before, in fact been a separate city entirely from Edmonton. A rail crossing bar with flashing red lights had descended, stopping traffic in both directions as a bright red diesel engine dragged the nineteenth century across the rapid speed and vision of the twenty-first. The train was barely moving – the tracks extended only a block north of the avenue – and the switching happened infrequently, even less often than a decade before. But Keaton's ghost took full advantage of the opportunity. Just as in *Sherlock Jr.*, he sprinted along the top of the boxcars, one hand clutching his porkpie hat to his head, his tiny figure moving with remarkable grace as he leaped and kept on going, the past that pursued him, or the mid-life that he hadn't even smashed into yet, far behind and losing ground fast. The same force that had been in the monkey's caring touch on Chelsea's face and in his shriek as he threw himself into her defence radiated from Keaton's young body, as if the powder on his face had formed a kind of phosphorescence around him.

What could I do? What could anyone do? He was out there trying, out there transcending those tears he had shed on the MGM sets, just as Delmore's poems and stories were out there trying, trying for whoever could hear them. Maybe most people never would, even the caring, loving people who would respond in kind, even this young woman beside me, who might never watch another Keaton film or read a Delmore Schwartz poem in her life, whatever her life might become. She had already invoked the spirit of their art, and what was their art for if it wasn't for the permanent honouring of what already resided in her being, and in mine? Keaton ran and jumped and always escaped, even as he rode the railway hand-cart into the salt depths with the chasmic miles behind him; even as his suffering, mortal self proclaimed, "It's all too late" to the world that bestowed attention and adulation on him in the year before he died. And as his old age passed my infancy once more, the wake of salt settling on my lips to be tasted now, in another place, with wholly another need and existence in my heart, something stood up inside me and raced along the boxcars, too. As the flashing bar slowly began to lift, nothing was decided. The nothing in which we all have to endure.

I didn't need to hear Delmore's weary sigh, if weary it was. I didn't need the translation of a dead poet's philosophy to tell me about the thinness of the ice. Art, too, was human and fallible. Its consolations depended on many factors – mostly the horrible weight of time and the randomness of experience – and, as a result, it often failed. Even so, it had to be created even to have a chance at success. Keaton had to run, he had to ride blindfolded on a motorcycle to escape the villains, before he cracked his neck on the tracks and woke a decade later to the concussive effects of the world's vast indifference. The film had to play, and the millions, in darkness and tension and hope, had to stay in their seats until all the seats were tipped up again and made into tombstones. Here lies the fate of the world. And the young bow their heads before it.

I drove across the tracks, and they were not only in Edmonton, Alberta, in 2012. To my left, the nineteenth century groaned as it moved back, a snake gorged on blood and dust and soot returning to its burrow. But the tracks – of Hollywood in 1924, White Rock in 1964, Edmonton in 1916, Toronto in that last year of the earth's innocence of the atomic bomb – extended into the sky, their deep black silvering as they reached, becoming the frames of a silent film in which the unborn actors would perform everything again. The consolation of art – because it is real – is cold and it hurts, and it drives us back to the essential hungers and the little decencies of life.

When the Pinto reached 109th Street, I turned and drove north towards the river. Halfway there, I quickly angle-parked outside the Upper Crust restaurant. Beside me, Chelsea had gone unnervingly still. Only her hands moved, stroking the dead monkey's fur. Her stillness seemed almost religious, and I was loath to disturb it. But I didn't want to leave her by herself, not without some explanation. She was in no state to sit in a restaurant, nor was I, frankly, so my options were simple enough. Very quietly, I said I was getting some food and would be back soon. I asked if she'd like a coffee, and she responded with an almost imperceptible nod.

Outside, I stretched painfully, my side and chest aching, my knee stiff and numb. Sweat soaked my shirt at the back and under the arms. Oh, but the air and the light – together they satisfied one of the essential hungers. I thought then of Greg Arious, of just how much escaping that dark, stale pet shop must have meant to him. Regretfully, I wished we had never wasted a moment in that food court, in all the false light and greasy air. If I'd known the little monkey's fate, I'd have set him free in the river valley to fend off the bewildered coyotes.

I spent ten minutes – no more – in the restaurant. But when I emerged, the Pinto was gone. It was as if a yellow slab had been removed from the Pyramid of Cheops.

"I'll Cheops you in the neck, you idiot." Delmore, more bearish than ever, his bulk down on all fours, glared up at me from where the car had been. "You're not the sharpest image in the anthology, are you?"

"How . . . what?"

"You left the keys in the ignition, chum. She didn't wait more than ten seconds. I had to scramble like hell to get out."

Now it was my turn to glare. "What did you get out for? Why didn't you stop her?"

"If you haven't figured this out by now, let me be clear. I'm dead. I'm a projection. Do you think anybody else in this burg is stumbling around talking to a Jewish bear? I can't get in the way. Not of the big stuff. A minor diversion here or there, maybe . . . You think I wouldn't have kept the monkey alive for her if I could have? The little lady's a peach. First-class spunk. And you're a grade A ass. A real *mentsch*, sure, but not too bright."

I gazed to the north. The great black span of the High Level Bridge wasn't visible, yet I could imagine the Pinto racing illegally across, going the wrong way, like a bold character on some tricky level of a video game. But this was no game. I knew what Chelsea intended, and all the blood in my body froze. Nothing reached my brain. I couldn't think.

Delmore snarled and reared up on his hind legs. Halfway there, he half-transformed – again. His figure slackened, though it remained bulky, and I could see the human intelligence in the ursine features. If the change kept on, he'd be as white-faced as Keaton's ghost, standing there in a stained brown suit and worn loafers, middle-aged and failing. He was all power and control when he spoke. "Get a cab, will ya? Be resourceful. She's going after the crazy guy. Do I have to paint you a picture?"

A cab. Of course. But I didn't have a phone. Wildly, hopelessly, I looked around for a booth.

Delmore surged forward and gave me a shove. "That's a main road, isn't it? I know this ain't Manhattan, but I'm sure you can hail a cab. Or at least a goddamned sled with dogs. Hurry up. I'm right behind you."

It didn't take long. A few minutes later, I was sitting in the passenger seat of a yellow cab, telling the smooth, jet-black-haired young driver to head downtown, fast.

"What address, please, sir?"

"What? Oh. Uh, just downtown."

Once he'd cut a sharp right before the bridge and started down a steep hill to the valley floor, I began to collect my bearings.

"Good thing she drove off on us," Delmore grunted. "You're

a terrible driver. You'd have got us all killed. The two of you would have been enjoying my company. Permanently."

"Oh, lay off, will you. I feel bad enough as it is."

To my surprise, Delmore didn't bother to respond.

At this point, the driver's neck appeared to flush with concern. I could hardly blame him. He kept glancing at me without turning his head, until I felt that I was pulling his eyeballs on strings. I tried to explain.

"I'm looking for someone in another car. It's very important. The car's easy to spot. It's a Pinto. Bright yellow."

"A Pinto?" Now he did turn, as lost as if I had said a DeSoto.

Briefly, hastily, poorly, I tried to describe the car. "Very vivid yellow," I ended. "You can't miss it. Brighter than your cab. Like the sun."

We were ascending the hill on the other side of the river now, a half-mile from Jasper Avenue. Tall apartment buildings closed around us; the daylight dimmed. The driver's aquiline nose twitched. I knew he was trying to assess the danger I posed, but I couldn't reassure him, because I didn't know what danger lay ahead. Besides, I was too busy scanning the streets at each intersection, desperate to see a flash of yellow, the coffee cooling and unsipped in my hands.

"Just head east along Jasper," I urged. "Then turn north on 100th towards Churchill Square."

I noticed little over the next several minutes, except how dismally lacking in colour the traffic was. Grey, grey, black, grey, dark green, dark blue, grey, black. That such a prismatic world should be so drab in its routine motion!

Perhaps the police would find her first. Or even Metalhead and his motley crue out to avenge the theft. Anyone. Anyone else. Please. Please. I must have begun to murmur aloud, for the driver's glances became even more frequent and he ran his tongue over his lips. Outside, along the crowded Jasper sidewalk, Keaton's ghost kept pace, walking fast, then sprinting, then disappearing and reappearing at the next intersection. My heart beat faster, counting the seconds the way the meter did, adding them up inexorably towards some fare I doubted I'd ever be able to pay.

After ten minutes of cruising – something I hadn't done since I was a teenager – and once we'd come to a stop at yet another red light, the driver cleared his throat and, with remarkable discretion, asked, "Sir, are you certain you wish to continue looking?"

My head-turn must have been rapid, or my eyes wild, for he quickly added, "It is fine if you wish it. But the fare . . ."

Christ! The fact that I had to pay for this ride had completely slipped my mind, just as had my thirst and hunger. The two coffees cooled in my hands like Olympic torches after all the medals had been given out; I still hadn't even taken a sip of mine. The brown paper bag on my lap, containing two sandwiches and two muffins, sickened me when I looked down on it and noticed its resemblance to the monkey's corpse. All of a sudden, everything crashed in on me, the whole perplexing weight of the long, unpredictable day. I had to lower my coffee-cup-filled hands to my thighs out of weakness.

Calmly and discreetly, the driver pulled over to the curb and waited. He stopped the meter. "Can you perhaps look some other time?"

I didn't even know what money I had in my wallet. Perhaps I'd have to use a credit card. The same credit card I'd been willing to use to buy a charming monkey that wound up getting killed by some homeless guy who'd sold me a grotesquely valuable mechanical bank. Only then did I remember the Pinto's locked treasure. Thirty thousand dollars. Gone. I hadn't even given it a thought. Stupid, stupid.

"Be kind," Delmore whispered. "You're a mentsch,

remember. It's not the worst fate. Your friend, there, he never thought much about money either."

I stared through the windshield to see Keaton squatting before a newspaper box, trying to open it without putting in a coin. And succeeding, too, as I had done a hundred times as a boy, in the Vancouver rain, waiting at bus stops. So long ago now. I never took the papers. Theft wasn't the point. It was finding a challenge for the moment's boredom; it was putting the mind keenly to the abyss. Keaton's ghost didn't take a paper either. Why should he? The headlines and the stories weren't really any different than they'd been on his last visit to Edmonton in 1916 – money, death, death, money. Suddenly I could see Chelsea slumped against an alley wall, a knife thrust under her ribs.

"Drive on," I said hoarsely. "Please. Once more around."

The driver's last bit of fear evaporated. He smiled sadly, and did not start the meter. I might have rejoiced at the simple human gesture, under different circumstances. But imagination had made me desperate once again. I saw the little girl behind Chelsea's eyes as she stood before an abandoned house in a small town with her mother's name and tried to call up her father's image. My skin prickled. I mouthed her name, and I refused to see the passing city as a grave over which my whole life cried. I looked harder at the world than I'd ever looked. The cab slid along the streets like a tear that would not be broken.

The moments passed in a curious silence. My desperation was great, my heart pounded heavily, my imagination raced with scenes of violence that I arrived just seconds too late to prevent; yet the interior of the cab remained hushed. I allowed the driver to complete one more circuit – past the library and Churchill Square, down 102nd Avenue west towards the MacEwan campus, then back around to the east along Jasper. No yellow Pinto appeared – no Pinto of any colour. No Gremlin, no Pacer, no little seventies vehicle born out of the energy crisis before the current energy crisis. There wasn't even a single yellow vehicle on the streets other than the cab we circled the downtown in. Keaton, however, kept the faith. The old comedian who'd once bragged that he worked more than Doris Day now raced the late-summer afternoon, sweat pouring down his immobile face and smearing the white powder, his baggy trousers seeming baggier with each block. Had we kept on, I believe he'd have been ground into the dust from which we all come.

The driver never showed any impatience or concern. Somehow satisfied that I was not a lunatic, he drove with tremendous care; I noticed that he even slowed at intersections to afford me a more incisive look down the crossroads. And the meter remained off.

I took a trembling sip of lukewarm coffee to recharge my voice. Then I asked him to stop the car.

He pulled deftly to the curb, not far from where I'd first encountered the homeless killer, and blinked his long-lashed brown eyes at me.

"I am sorry that we could not find this Pinto," he said.

I nodded and forced a slight smile. "We tried. Thanks for your help." My voice had little strength in it now, but I made a conscious effort to rally. "What do I owe you?" Behind the question was the knowledge that I couldn't pay, not with something as cold as money, for the instinctive discretion he had shown.

"You will forgive me, sir." The coffee-brown of his eyes reached me with more warmth than the lukewarm coffee against my palms. "I am young, but I have done this job for some time, many years, here and other places. I have met many people."

My eyes lowered to the brown paper bag on my lap. Strangely, I could smell Chelsea's perfume faintly on the air, hear the rhythmic snapping of her gum. I half-expected the paper bag to transform back into the fierce monkey that would return her safely to the world. I wished it, just as intensely as she'd once wished for a letter from a wizarding school to lift her out of her fatherless life and her mother's dreary and heartbreaking routine of heartbreak. The magic of the world is rarely dispensed predictably or in large amounts, and I knew that I'd already had my letter. The day had come stamped, and if the ripping open of it meant more death and loss in the end, it did not quite dispel the magic. After all, what is more magical than change?

"Black magic though it is," sighed Delmore. This time he laid his heavy paw with a sparrow-lightness on my shoulder. "It's almost over."

"Over?" I turned, and the driver took my motion as encouragement to continue.

"Many, many people. And I must tell you, sir, this search that you're making – it is for love that you do this. I can tell."

No tears came, but that welling-up feeling intensified behind my eyes, and for a myriad of reasons. Delmore's last words had turned my body ice cold.

"This is why," the driver went on, "I cannot charge you the fare. It would not be right. In the eyes of my god."

Keaton's ghost stood directly in front of the cab, not moving, not blinking, his face wrinkled and woe-papery, like my father's. I looked again. I couldn't be sure it wasn't my father standing there, gazing at me with all the sorrow he did not speak in life. My father, who I loved more than any man, and whose absence hurt me just as the absence of Chelsea's father hurt her. Different situations. But as the poet says of pain, we call it many things, but it is pain.

"Thank you," I said quietly as I put one coffee on the dashboard and opened the door.

"Sir?"

I waited.

"I drive all over. Many hours. Night and day. If I see this yellow Pinto, I can text you and let you know."

"No cellphone," I said. "No car either. I wouldn't be able to act on the information. But thank you." Retrieving the other coffee, I stepped out of the cab.

The warmth of the day surprised me. I had almost forgotten that it was summer, that the people walking along the sidewalks wore short sleeves and light jackets, that the sunlight on their faces was the same sunlight that gave every tall sunflower its final few hours of reaching. However, I couldn't sustain the warmth. I began to tremble, chilled right through to the bone as my sweat dried. Once I'd found a garbage can and rid myself of one of the coffees – I kept the paper bag of food, just in case my luck changed and I suddenly came upon Chelsea – I focused on Delmore. What did he mean by "It's almost over"? In a panic, I whirled around. Where was he? Did he even follow me out of the cab? And Keaton . . . I had lost sight of him, too.

My side and chest ached more than ever. My hands shook. For a long moment, I could not see to see. I felt the bodies of people flow past me; I felt their eyes on my face; but there was only wariness and indifferent curiosity, not concern. I tried to conjure up an image of the Pinto, to believe in and commit to some sixth sense that would lead me to a happy resolution. It was the kind of absorbed longing that I hadn't experienced since childhood, and it was strange, like flensing all the dead cells that had coalesced around the heart.

At last, I opened my eyes slowly, and the colours of life flooded in. Keaton reappeared. However, he remained firmly black and white, as did the creature with him, whose presence horrified and appalled.

Calmly squatting on the stone-faced comedian's right shoulder, no more than ten feet away along the sidewalk, was a monkey with a quizzical, baby-faced look. I knew the expression. I had known it in life, less than an hour before. Inquisitive, searing, almost human, the eyes fluttered and took me in. A chilling breeze blew along the avenue, but it didn't stir anything to motion. It was the draft from the door closing between one world and another. I tried not to believe what I was seeing. After all, Keaton had worked with a trained monkey before, in *The Cameraman*. There was no reason to identify this little primate as Chelsea's murdered pet.

There was every reason. And all of them tore at my nerve endings. My jaw unhinged. I looked at Keaton's unblinking face, the monkey's blinking face and sought some difference in the emotion they levelled on me. But there was no difference. The look was pitying. And the pity had in it the coldness of art, the coldness of the ocean's sculpting of driftwood, the wind's long commitment to the fluting of stone. But what was being created?

I felt Delmore's breath before I heard or saw him; a warmth touched my neck and was all the warmer for the contrast it made with the pitying looks of Keaton and Greg Arious. I turned weak in the limbs. The remaining coffee cup slipped from my hand and landed with a splat on the pavement.

"Steady, now," Delmore said. "Almost there."

His great bear's face was less furred than before, the snout not as long, the eyes more human than ever. And – thank God for small mercies – the tears in them were warm with sorrow and understanding. Still, I couldn't fend off the chill. I stood in winter while summer strolled all around me. I waited for the terrible words that Delmore had uttered in the library: "It's death. It's death. I can smell it." And every cell of me cried out in protest. Not now. It's too soon. My children. The coffee pooled like blood around my shoes. My breath came fast and heavy. From a long way off, the sound of a siren slowly, steadily increased.

I clutched at Delmore's huge sinew-thick shoulder. I could feel the bone and the tremble deep inside it. "If she's killed," I gasped, "I'll see her. Won't I? I'm going to see her."

The fur had almost gone from the face; it was down to heavy shadow. Fleshy jowls sagged beneath the black eyes, which grew larger, deeper, more piercing. "Look at your watch. There's time. You can just make it."

"Time?" I glanced at my wrist. Three forty-five. "Time for what?"

"You need to go. There's nothing more I can do."

"What are you talking about?" I looked back to Keaton and Greg Arious, but they had vanished. When I returned my attention to Delmore, he was also gone. Not for long, however. I saw him at the intersection fifty feet away. He waited, down on all fours, the grizzled brown of his massive bulk no longer thick. I walked towards him, my shadow long among the swirl of leaves on the cracked sidewalk. When I got to within ten feet, he vanished again, only to reappear to the north, about a block away. Desperate, my side throbbing, my face warm and prickly but my body still frozen, I followed. My shadow lengthened with each step, the first snowflakes sticking, making my progress visible behind me, though I did not turn for fear of losing sight of Delmore. Like a sunspot, he appeared and disappeared, leading me slowly, inevitably, towards the grey factory towers of the university campus. Each time he vanished, I was afraid he'd be gone for good. Or, worse, that I'd see Chelsea with him, that she'd have joined the dead troupe of vaudevillians along with Keaton and Greg Arious.

By the time I reached campus, sweating and breathless, hardly able to lift my head to the faint constellations high over the towers, I forced myself into the nearest building. Throngs of young faces drifted past, laughing, intense, unseeing. Blossoms in winter. I gazed wildly into every passing female student's face with a mixture of fear and hope. If Chelsea were here, did it mean she was alive or dead? How could I negotiate the slippery interstice between the worlds of this hard age I had come to?

The young women did not return my searching gaze. A man of fifty, I was as invisible to them as Delmore. And yet, given the provincial statistics – no, the statistics of the race – I could have been at least one girl's delinquent father, returned at last to help with tuition, returned like a blunt needle along the selvedge of her frayed past, perhaps only to complicate and further tear the pattern.

The wintry sun still trickled through the falling snow. Blinking the flakes off my lashes, I followed the weak light along a narrowing corridor. My shadow reached the length of it. The students vanished. Ahead of me, at the open door to a classroom, Delmore waited. He was no longer a bear, but a fifty-five-year-old, puff-faced manic-depressive in a stained and baggy brown suit. Both his parents were long dead. He had divorced three wives. His fame was old news. Beside him, incongruous as a wooden-box beehive, sat a full trash can, spilling trash like guts from beneath its crammed-on lid. The truth rushed in with the ferocity of a steam engine, and I stood shivering on the tracks.

He smiled apologetically. "I told you this wasn't a Jimmy Stewart movie. It always happens this way."

Terrified, I said, "You're going to die, aren't you?"

He shrugged, and his once-young, Apollo-like face regained a little of its vigour. "Sure. But it won't kill me."

When I didn't laugh, he sighed, and with more tenderness than I deserved, explained. "It's the price of admission. But don't feel bad for me. When it happens now, I don't lie unclaimed in a morgue for three days. Think of it. Every time

I die, a poet is right there, dropping tears on my cold face. And those tears are the tickets to the next show." He nodded at the open doorway. "You never can tell, you might have to perform for one of the kids in there someday."

By now, I was shaking so hard that I didn't feel I could hold myself up. I understood that what was about to happen would happen regardless of my presence. I needed to be strong, though I sensed that more than the death of Delmore Schwartz was in the air.

"Besides," he said, "in death my death is never exactly the same." His breathing came harder. "It changes with the circum . . . circum . . ." He reached his doughy, long-fingered hand out snail-slow to the handle of the trash can. With a great effort, he hoisted the can up in front of him and staggered forward, as he had done that last day in the Bronx in 1963, with no one looking on. His face stiffened, the eyes flared and rolled, and the trash can dropped to the ground, the lid rolling away, the garbage spilling out like the contents of some rotted horn of plenty. Everything happened slowly and in complete silence. I waited several seconds before approaching Delmore's collapsed human form. Then I knelt beside it and gave the only benediction I could to that torn moon of a face, all that I was meant to give.

At last, when I rose, and saw my own body there beside the poet's corpse, I backed away from it, bemusedly almost, the way the boy-projectionist steps away from his sleeping self to become a new man in a new reality, that was only and always an unreality, as life is an unreality, rolling away in the magical dark with all of us chasing, performing our own dangerous stunts. The corporeal form of all the time I had lived, the green time – vaudeville, youth, the first excited productions of the blood – lay without comfort or mourners. Nor did I seek to comfort or mourn. The death Delmore had referred to at the end was never meant to be his. Or Keaton's. They had had their deaths.

Even so, after a brief time, when both bodies had vanished, I didn't feel a resolution so much as a kind of chapter break in an ancient holy book, the monk nodding off in candlelight. Exhausted, in pain and bewildered with newness, I decided I could not face the young. Not now. At least not for long.

I stepped into the classroom and two dozen pairs of eyes looked up from their phones and laptops. I had no strength to lecture, but I wanted to say, "Never mind the comma splices. Listen to me. Don't buy the lies you'll be sold. It isn't easy, and it was never meant to be. It's hard and it's dark and it's cold. But not unredeemed by beauty. Never unredeemed." Two dozen pairs of eyes looked up, like the eyes of old French women clacking knitting needles at the guillotine. But the execution had already occurred. Time in its black cloak was cleaning the blade. The eyes were blank in the rolled head. The young simply couldn't live in the age of my suffering, and it wasn't their fault; it was, in fact, their salvation. I couldn't face their ordinary and bracing reality. I cancelled the class, claiming illness.

Now there was only one thing left to do. Outside again, in the late summer sun, I felt lighter but not much warmer. After all, life – for poets and everyone else – must be lived to the end. Delmore Schwartz, despite whatever deep knowledge his suffering had given him, had had to leave his cheap room in a fleabag hotel to take out the trash. I was lucky. Even blessed. For no such banal continuation lay ahead of me. Not yet. For most of my life, I had been a son with a son's approach to the world. Then I had been a father to my own children. Now I had come to the border of a strange, new land, and, with the grizzle on my cheeks heavier, I had to find my way home.

Chelsea wasn't dead. The fact washed over me like an ocean breeze as I began walking away from campus to the southwest, into the almost-continual siren cry of urban life that heralded some new crisis. She wasn't dead, but she suffered. Greatly. My invigorated blood, I knew, had a purpose that could not exclude or forget her.

But all days must end, and I was, despite the change, in grief. The heavy bear no longer walked with me, and I missed him already, so much so that I scanned the streets as I advanced, not only for him, but for our silent companion.

Keaton did not disappoint. About a block before my destination, he appeared on the sidewalk a few yards ahead, and I fell into step behind him. Chelsea's little monkey remained on his shoulder, looking back at me with glee, chattering though no sound could be heard. Our pace was much slower, but I suddenly realized that Keaton's ghost and I were re-enacting the trailing scene from *Sherlock Jr.* Keaton didn't look back and my concentration increased with every step. It had occurred to me, when I first caught sight of him, that I might have to witness his physical death as I had witnessed Delmore's. The thought was disturbing. According to his biographers, Keaton's death was a particularly restless one. In pain and confusion, he had risen from his bed and walked in endless circles, as if trying to restart the creative energy deep inside him. The vital, athletic vaudevillian did not relinquish this world of gags without a fight. Keaton had referred to Arbuckle's rape scandal as "The Day the Laughter Stopped," but this was the real lowering of the curtain.

That death happened in 1965, however. The year after he'd crossed Canada on a motorized railway handcart and come within a mile of my sleeping infant self. How strange that, over fifty years later, I'd be trailing him into the darkening west, the world silent all around us, black and white, and the waiting streetcar older than the demolished Pantages Theatre he'd once performed in.

Keaton climbed on and, from the doorway, turned. Except it wasn't Keaton at all. I wondered, then, if it had ever been him. The resemblance was, as my mother said, striking. On my lips I formed the word that Oedipus formed, and Hamlet, that Chelsea formed out of tears and longing and the warm clay of first things.

I might have said Delmore or Buster. I might have spoken my own name.

I found a spot on a wicker seat right behind the conductor. The streetcar, almost empty, rattled into motion. The silent camera whirred. Offstage, the great sun applied its red powder for the final performance. All around my life and its ghosts, the clamorous age raged on, "the scrimmage of appetite everywhere," as Delmore once wrote. The current rushed that I would soon rejoin, jumping in like Keaton at the end of *Our Hospitality*, all urgency and drama, to effect the rescue of others, which was the only rescue of the self. Sitting calmly as the streetcar crept out onto one of the highest streetcar crossings in the world, the river nearly two hundred feet below, I stepped out of the straitjacket of lived time, freed to the rest of my redeemable life.

— Epilogue —

I NEVER SAW Chelsea again. She didn't attend my class that term, nor did she return to work at the New York Fries in the food court near Churchill Square. Despite my disappointment, I understood. She had revealed too much, and the pattern of self-protection she'd had to create from childhood was not completed. Even so, I searched for her with great effort, and not without a selfish motive. After all, she had the valuable mechanical bank, and I simply could not be cavalier about so many thousands of dollars. When I phoned the owner of the antiques shop that next morning to find out if Chelsea had returned to make the sale, he was dismayed.

"You do not have the bank?"

I admitted that I did not.

The silence was long and I couldn't interpret it. But there was some amusement in the elderly voice when it resumed. "And the monkey? Do you still have that?"

I considered telling the whole truth, but the idea of making the effort fatigued me. So I just said no.

"Ah, well. You certainly ruffled the feathers of my unesteemed colleague next door. I must admit that I've been enjoying his discomfort."

The owner, with some passion, urged me to call him if the bank ever returned to me, and then our conversation was over.

My other investigations proved equally fruitless. Chelsea had vanished without a trace. I was sorry, in part because of the money, but more so because I felt that I could be a friend to her, even in some small way – not as a replacement father (I was never so foolish or vain to believe that), but just as a fellow human being who had shared an uncommon and memorable experience. Besides, the knowledge of her pain and loss continued to hurt me. Even as the weeks went by, I felt the grief of her absence, though it dulled, as all grief does. At least I had the unusual pleasure of keeping my eye out for a lemon-yellow Pinto every time I left my house, just like in *American Graffiti*, when Richard Dreyfuss keeps looking for Suzanne Somers behind the wheel of that white Thunderbird. It was a small pleasure, but remarkably regenerative. I consoled myself by thinking of that elusive seventies car as Chelsea's partial payment for the mechanical bank.

About six weeks later, when the summer had also vanished into the first snowstorms of the long northern winter and I was deep into correcting run-on sentences and vague pronoun use, I checked my mailbox in the English department. What I found there surprised me at first, but then, when I thought of the tall, angular Pippi Longstocking girl with the quick laughter, I wasn't surprised at all. I took the grimy transparent horse into my trembling left hand as I held open the scrawled letter in my right:

Hey Professor,

I guess you're wondering why I ditched you like that. It was just something I had to do. I was pretty tore up about the monkey and I wanted to get that guy back. (I never did. I wanted to but I couldn't.) Anyway sorry. I'll bet you've been pissed about the bank. I don't blame you. I would too. So here's some cash. Not half but almost. I figured you would of gave that homeless dude half anyways. I sold it to a dealer on eBay for about what we were told it was worth. Drove it down to the States in person. My mom got some of the money for rent and stuff and I needed some. I hope this is OK. I dropped out of school but maybe I'll come back. If I do I'll for sure take your course. Your a great prof.

Chelsea

The handwriting was atrocious, and it took me a while to make out the words. The shaking of my hand didn't help. But the money – five thousand dollars in thousand-dollar bills – was clear enough, as clear as money always is. For a long time afterward, I pictured Chelsea entering the English department, the transparent horse tucked into her duffle coat the way the little monkey had been, but even that image grew dim by Christmas. Life had to move on, and it did. I used the extra money to give my family a slightly more bountiful holiday, and then I put the rest securely into RESPs.

Now I teach my classes and accompany my children to their sports games and music recitals and carry out the responsibilities that must be carried out. And every now and again, when there's a calm hour in the maelstrom, I watch *The Railrodder* or *Sherlock Jr.*, and smile with the knowledge that the film goes on beyond the salt edge of the sea, where the magic happens in darkness, and the subtitle of a young woman's promise, "But maybe I'll come back," is the same promise that looks out from the eyes of the always astonished and astonishing world.

Acknowledgements

The author is grateful to the Edmonton Arts Council, the Alberta Foundation for the Arts and the Access Copyright Foundation for their support. He also wishes to express his gratitude to Paul Vermeersch, Ashley Hisson and Noelle Allen for their editorial insights.

Bibliography

Atlas, James. *Delmore Schwartz: The Life of An American Poet.* New York: Farrar, Straus & Giroux, 1977.

Blesh, Rudi. *Keaton.* New York: MacMillan, 1966.

Frost, Robert. *A Further Range.* New York: Henry Holt, 1936.

Horton, Andrew, ed. *Buster Keaton's* Sherlock Jr. Cambridge Film Handbook. Cambridge: Cambridge University Press, 1997.

Keaton, Buster, and Charles Samuels. *My Wonderful World of Slapstick.* London: George Allen & Unwin, 1967. First published 1960 by Doubleday.

Kerr, Walter. *The Silent Clowns.* New York: Alfred A. Knopf, 1975.

Knopf, Robert. *The Theater and Cinema of Buster Keaton.* Princeton, NJ: Princeton University Press, 1999.

Orrell, John. *Fallen Empires: The Lost Theatres of Edmonton, 1881-1914.* Edmonton, AB: NeWest Press, 1981.

Schwartz, Delmore. *Portrait of Delmore: Journals and Notes of Delmore Schwartz: 1939-1959.* Edited by Elizabeth Pollet, New York: Farrar, Straus & Giroux, 1986

———. *Summer Knowledge: New and Selected Poems, 1938-1958.* New York: Doubleday, 1959.

———. *The World is a Wedding.* Norfolk, CT: New Directions, 1948.

Apart from appearing as a main character in novels that he has written, Tim Bowling also works in many other genres of literature. His nineteen books have been shortlisted for major national prizes in fiction (the Rogers Writers' Trust Fiction Prize, for his most recent novel, *The Tinsmith*, in 2012), nonfiction (the Hilary Weston Writers' Trust Prize) and poetry (the Governor General's Award and Canadian Authors Association Award), and in 2008 the John Simon Guggenheim Memorial Foundation awarded Bowling a fellowship recognizing his entire body of work. His writing has also been nominated twelve times for the Alberta Literary Awards and nine times for the City of Edmonton Book Prize.